# NEW AUGSBURG

## BOOK I

# CHRISTA PETZOLD

Library of Congress Control Number: 2023913854

ISBN: 979-8-9888190-0-4 (paperback), 979-8-9888190-1-1 (ebook)

Printed in the United States of America

Original artwork and map by Elaine M. Pszczolkowski

Quoted hymns are in the Public Domain

www.christapetzold.com

# PRAISE FOR NEW AUGSBURG

In Christa Petzold's newest book, a novel set almost 100 years into the future, the fears many Christians hold in 2023 have come true. With new laws and policy threatening the Christian worldview, a few hundred Lutherans have withdrawn from the world to a safe-haven in Wisconsin. *New Augsburg* is named for the setting—a town preserved in a kind of bubble while the streams of time rush around it. The people of New Augsburg are committed to keeping their town's bubble from popping. However, no bubble lasts forever—whether that pointed attack or pressure comes from without or within.

*New Augsburg* invites the reader to a place of delight and relaxation—a slower pace of life, an intent focus on the Word and the Church's teachings of it. In the midst of this lovely picture, however, Christa weaves a thread of tension that goes beyond the fear of the idyllic breakdown of New Augsburg, but the question of how are Christians to live in the world while remaining people of the Word.

> —**Sarah Baughman**, author of *A Flame in the Dark:*
> *A Novel about Luther's Reformation*

It was a delight to journey to New Augsburg, a town a century in the future with the feel of a century in the past. Through this unique setting and a cast of well-developed characters wrestling with hard choices and heartbreaking losses, Christa Petzold showcases God's unchanging nature and that His truth and His Church will always prevail, no matter what evil is happening in the world. I loved the gentle love story between two characters who were looking to serve the Lord and find their place in His kingdom. Petzold's strong theological background, already familiar to readers of her nonfiction, shines authentically in this debut novel, enhancing the story naturally and adding depth to characters you will long remember.

> —**Jennifer Q. Hunt**, author of the Sorrow & Song Trilogy
> and the Wisteria House Trilogy

*New Augsburg* is a page-turner! Set in the future, Petzold takes us to an idyllic Christian town, where a local press still operates outside of hostile government control. Lydia's circumstances—the loss of her parents and her brother's unwillingness to take over the family business—lead her to pursue a relationship that might solve all her problems. Or will this perceived solution only lead to new difficulties? You won't be disappointed by all the twists and turns along the way.

> —**Candice Yamnitz**, author of *Unbetrothed*

# PRAISE FOR NEW AUGSBURG

Christa Petzold enchants readers with her captivating tale set in "New Augsburg." With well-developed characters, readers form deep connections and empathize with their faith struggles. Petzold beautifully illustrates God's grace and peace through the messy yet precious gift of the Church. As secrets are gradually revealed, intrigue and suspense heighten. Each chapter leaves readers yearning for more about these beloved characters. The book's satisfying conclusion provides a sense of anticipation for the future.

—**Michelle Diercks**, host of the Peace in His Presence Podcast, author of *Promised Rest*

Christa Petzold has created a seemingly idyllic place in New Augsburg. A place filled with loving townspeople struggling against a confusing and foreboding future world. The novel's sincere characters drew me in immediately and with each page turn, I wanted to know more about them. In particular, I wanted to see how Lydia's life would turn out when we find out that not everything in New Augsburg is perfect. A gentle book with just enough suspense to keep you reading. The story of flawed characters attempting to live a life of faith is the story of all our lives.

—**Sharla Fritz**, Christian speaker and author of *Measured by Grace: How God Defines Success* and *God's Relentless Love: A Study of Hosea*

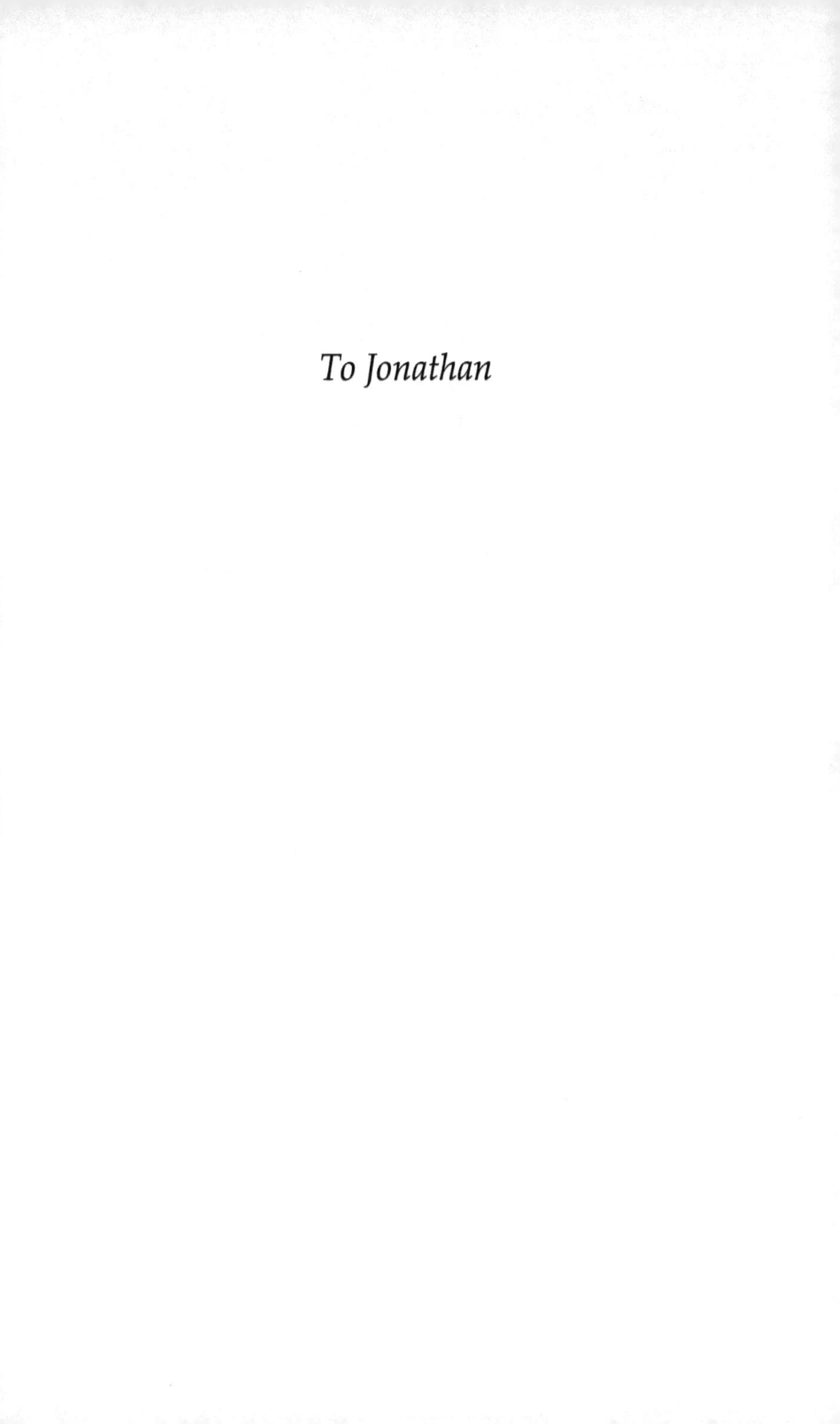

*To Jonathan*

*"The grass withers,*
*and the flower falls,*
*but the Word of the Lord*
*remains forever."*

1 Peter 1:24-25

# NEW AUGSBURG

BOOK I

CHRISTA PETZOLD

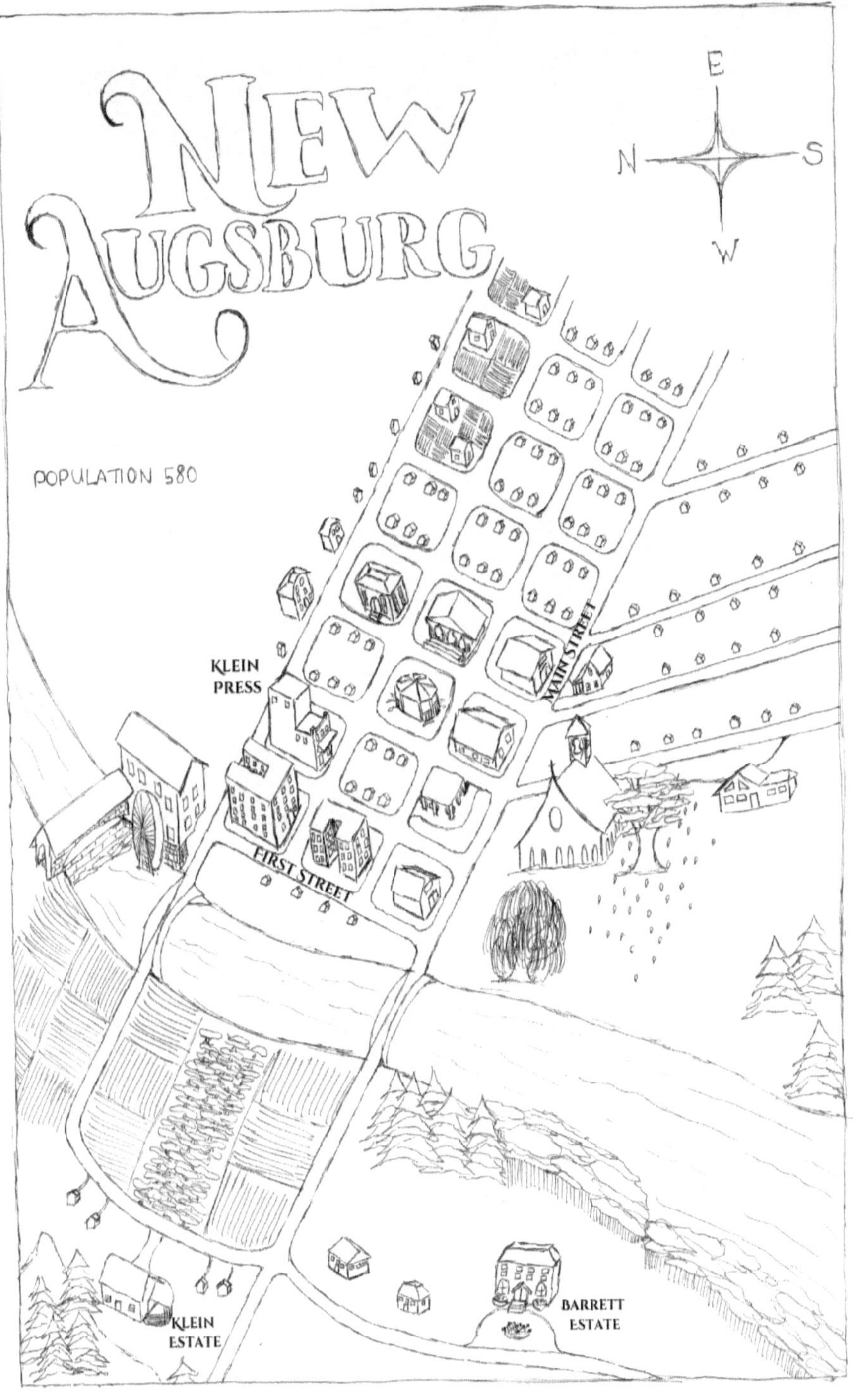

NEW AUGSBURG
POPULATION 580
E
N S
W
KLEIN PRESS
MAIN STREET
FIRST STREET
KLEIN ESTATE
BARRETT ESTATE

# CHAPTER ONE

*October 30, 2117*

*New Augsburg, Wisconsin*

Lydia started back to consciousness at the sound of her front door opening and slamming shut. The thumps of a suitcase hitting the floor, followed by those of a man's footsteps, informed her that the vigil was over. The clock above the window read 11:00 p.m. Several hours later than she had expected him, her brother was finally home.

"I know, I know . . . I'm sorry . . ." Micah said as he shuffled through the narrow hall towards the kitchen where she sat.

She studied him for a moment, still waking up from her unintended repose. How much of her thought process could he guess? She wanted to jump up from the table and throw herself into his arms, but something held her back.

He stood there, taller than she remembered, his broad shoulders filling more of the door frame than they used to. He averted his eyes from hers, surveying the kitchen they'd grown up in as if seeing it for the first time. His stature may have been that of a grown man, but his hand ran through his sandy-colored hair in a self-conscious motion that Lydia knew well.

"I've missed you," she said.

"I'm sorry," he repeated, still looking anywhere but at her face.

"I haven't seen you since . . ."

"Mom's funeral. I know." He finally looked at her.

Their eyes locked for several moments—his daring her to produce the guilt trip they both knew he deserved, hers pleading for things to feel normal again between them.

After a moment that threatened to stretch into eternity, something in their sibling bond cracked the ice. As if on cue, they both smiled. Lydia leaped up from the table, giving him a hasty hug as she shoved him into the chair beside hers, then crossed the kitchen to retrieve the apple pie and instant tea kettle that had been standing at attention waiting for this moment for the past several hours.

"I know it's late, but I'm sure you're still up for some pie. How was your trip? And would you like peppermint or orange spice tea?"

*October 31, 2117*

Lydia pulled her wool coat around her as she exited the church and turned down the road toward the river. The late fall wind was brisk, the air far too cool for comfort. The triumphant chorus of "A Mighty Fortress" still rang in her ears as she fumbled for her gloves and tried to calm her racing thoughts. She was expected in the community park, but she needed a few minutes to collect herself before braving the social demands of the occasion.

The residents of New Augsburg always celebrated Reformation Day with a potluck and dancing, but this year the planned festivities were especially elaborate in honor of the Reformation's 600th anniversary. In her role as manager of New Augsburg's press, she had overseen the printing of a special, commemorative edition of the Book of Concord. A copy would be given to each family represented. In fact, the news that new copies of the Lutheran Confessions would be available had prompted many individuals to travel to New Augsburg in the hope of receiving one. Lydia had eagerly anticipated this day for over a year. But as often happens, reality was not living up to her expectations.

The late-night reunion of the Klein siblings had left her with a significant sleep deficit. And when she had greeted her prodigal brother again over breakfast, she had not anticipated the charged, throw-down exchange that followed, consuming her entire morning. The lack of sleep, combined with the morning's emotional exertion, had left her exhausted. Slipping away from the crowd exiting the church, she found her way to her favorite spot: an old stone bench overlooking the river, hidden from view of the road by a mature weeping willow tree. While most of the trees were almost bare, her willow's leaves were always among the last to fall. Today, they enveloped her in a golden canopy that rustled in the wind.

*I will only sit here for five minutes*, she told herself. *I know Danielle needs me in the press booth.*

As she sat lost in thought, watching the ripples of the water as it flowed over the rocks, Lydia did not hear the sound of a couple approaching until they stood just on the other side of the tree, partially screened from her view.

"This town is every bit as quaint and charming as I had imagined. Are you sure you don't want to move here, dear?" spoke the woman.

"It's pretty isolated." Lydia supposed that the man who answered was the woman's husband from their manner of addressing each other. "It'd be a big change from Milwaukee."

"True, but change can be good," the wife continued. "It would be refreshing to live among like-minded people, not feeling guilty all the time, like I'm living a lie."

"Are we starting that again?" the man asked in a tired voice. "I do my best. I think God understands. You know full well that if I'd refused to sign the pledge, I would have lost our business license. We have too much debt to close the bakery now. If we chose this moment to take a stand, we'd be sunk financially. I doubt we'd even have the money to move to someplace like this."

"Well, I know I don't have peace about it," the woman said in a dejected manner. "And I don't suppose we could convince the kids to pack up and come with us now. Perhaps it's too late. We should have had this conversation when they were younger and at home. I always hoped that things would get better, but every year I find myself turning into more of a cynic." She paused before adding, "This is a pretty view though."

There was a quiet moment where Lydia hardly breathed. Clearly, they had not seen her. It wouldn't be the worst thing in the world if she was spotted, but it would certainly be a moment that she would classify as awkward. As one who always did her best to avoid embarrassing encounters with strangers, she now sat motionless, hoping they'd walk away soon.

As the couple began to move farther down the road along the stretch of river that wound through town, Lydia exhaled. She sometimes forgot how sheltered her life here in New Augsburg was. These annual gatherings that drew fellow faithful from multiple states away were her primary reminder that life went on outside of this town and that she knew very little of it. Maybe Micah was somewhat justified in his angst. Gathering herself, she rose and headed back up the hill, past the church, and toward the community park. She could hear the sound of the band from blocks away, and the tantalizing aroma of bratwurst wafted toward her as she approached. No matter the current state of the world, this day was a reminder that the Word of the Lord endures forever, and Lydia meant to shake off her malaise and join in the fun.

The usually peaceful Founders' Park buzzed with activity. In front of the community center, a large food tent had been erected. The Travis family, owners of Main Street Café, the only restaurant in town, were busy serving bratwurst, sauerkraut, a spiced apple dish, and their signature coffee oatmeal stout. Directly opposite the food tent stood a large pavilion with tables and chairs, and beyond that was a dance floor where the band played at a volume Lydia considered much too loud. She walked past the crowd gathered around the refreshments and approached the press booth. From behind the stacks of Bibles, hymnals, and devotional resources displayed on the table, an accusing voice called out, "Where have you been?"

"I'm sorry, Dani. I took a little detour."

"Well, I've already had folks trying to buy things, and I didn't quite know the procedure, so I asked them to come back later." Danielle looked relieved as Lydia entered the booth and purposefully reached for the clipboard she was holding.

"We should have gone over it on Friday to be prepared. That was my fault. And I should have come straight over, or even left during the dismissal hymn. Have I missed many customers?"

"I'm sure they'll all be back." No longer alone in the booth, Danielle instantly relaxed. The two young women pulled out the cash box, readied the clipboard, and began arranging the prized items of the day for display: dozens and dozens of newly printed copies of the Book of Concord. "I thought perhaps Micah would be here to help," Danielle observed as they served their first customer.

"I don't know where he is. He sat by me in church but was gone before I made it out of the sanctuary."

"Is everything alright between you two? Does this have anything to do with your post-church detour?" Danielle inquired.

"I don't know." Lydia's voice was tired. Danielle was her oldest friend. They had grown up together, and their relationship was close enough that almost no question would be off limits between the two of them. "He got in late last night, which was fine, but this morning at breakfast, things got a bit intense. We were debating for hours."

"Debating or arguing?" Danielle asked playfully. Having grown up with the Klein siblings, she had witnessed their verbal skirmishes often enough to know that the line between a spirited debate and a tense argument was often a fine one.

Lydia smiled. "I'm not sure. I don't know if he's coming back after college. I can't tell if he's truly disillusioned with our life here or if it's all about Callie. I should have just asked him, but I think I got lost in the weeds of the philosophical side of our conversation and neglected the interpersonal factors."

Danielle's eyes danced with amusement. "You neglected the interpersonal factors?"

Lydia laughed. "I know, I know. . . As always, I'm trying to solve people like equations. But honestly, I don't know where he could have taken himself."

They did not have time to discuss Micah further, for as people finished eating, their booth became busy. A steady stream of customers kept them completely occupied. Within two hours, they had sold all but a handful of the books on display.

The festival started to die down. The music played softly, the crowd thinned, and some folks were swing dancing while others sat around and talked. As they began packing up the booth, Lydia observed Pastor Pedersen approaching.

Pastor Pedersen had been the sole pastor at New Augsburg Lutheran Church for Lydia's entire life. He was warm and friendly, and there was a firmness and stability in his countenance that made Lydia feel simultaneously safe and intimidated. Although never openly expressed, Lydia assumed that the entire town must have been expecting his retirement for the past twenty years. As he walked slowly and purposefully towards them, the girls exchanged a concerned look.

"This must be about the town council meeting," Danielle whispered.

"I suppose so," Lydia replied. "I almost managed to forget about that." She sighed and then composed herself to greet their guest. "Good afternoon, Pastor. Happy Reformation Day!"

"Happy Reformation Day, ladies," responded Pastor Pedersen. "Indeed, the Word of the Lord endures forever." Lydia and Danielle merely smiled and nodded, so he went on, "I came over to let you know, Miss Klein, that the town council has decided to convene tomorrow evening at six to go over the financial situation regarding the press and to discuss plans for succession regarding its management." He looked at Lydia with sympathy. "You know, people always assume the pastor is in the loop, but nobody has told me. . . . Do you know how your mother left things in her will?"

"Yes," Lydia said. She thought her voice sounded hoarse as she spoke. "The family estate is left jointly to Micah and me, but the management of the press is designated to Micah, pending council approval."

"Ahh," Pastor Pedersen said softly. "I saw Micah in church today. Is he here?"

Lydia looked about nervously. "I know he plans to stay for a few days, but I'm not sure where he is just now."

"Well then, I hope you will pass along the information about the meeting to him and that he will attend." Pastor looked back and forth between the two girls, no doubt noting Danielle's concerned expression and Lydia's unease. "I know this must be difficult for you and Micah, my dear. We all miss your parents very much. It's not fair for you two young people to have to make decisions that will impact your lives so significantly so soon after your mother's death. I want you to know that you are both in my prayers and if you ever need anything, don't hesitate to ask."

"Thank you, sir," Lydia replied, avoiding eye contact. "Micah and I will be at the council meeting tomorrow night."

"Wonderful. I will see you there. And thank you both for your service here today and for all that you do at the press. Getting these books into the hands of the faithful is a noble vocation. People today need to know the truth of God's Word, perhaps now more than ever." He gave them a benevolent smile, turned, and walked away.

Lydia exhaled deeply as she resumed boxing up the materials. She could feel Danielle watching her. Resolving not to let her emotions take over, Lydia made it another ten seconds into her task before the nervous rambling thoughts started spilling out. "I'm going to kill Micah. Where is he? I sure hope he comes to that meeting tomorrow and doesn't make me out to be a liar to Pastor Pedersen."

"If you thought he wasn't going to come, why did you promise he'd be there?" Danielle asked. It was a fair question.

"Oh, I don't know! I should have hedged, but I suppose I was just embarrassed that I didn't know my own brother's plans or whereabouts. He's been off at college for three years, and I've been here alone doing all the day-to-day work of running the press while he takes all these classes and reads and studies all day." Lydia stopped, hearing the jealousy in her words. "I wasn't alone. I know I had Mother."

Danielle had stopped working and now leaned on the box she'd been packing, giving Lydia her undivided attention as she vented.

Lydia's voice was quieter as she continued, "It's been five months since she passed away, and this is the first time Micah has been back since the funeral. But he's nowhere to be found. I know he's read the will, but we haven't talked about it once, and now it looks like we'll have to have that conversation in front of the town council." She rolled her eyes and grinned, attempting to play off her frustration with sarcasm.

Danielle laughed. She had accepted long ago that humor was how Lydia let off the pressure when the emotions built up too high. "Well, perhaps we should hunt him down and insist he have that chat before the meeting tomorrow night." They each picked up a box and started down the road toward the press office. It was only a two-block walk to put their supplies away.

"Want to come back to the house with me tonight?" Lydia asked. "We have ice cream, and hopefully Micah will be there waiting."

Danielle looked apologetic. "Normally I would, but I'm planning to meet up with John after this." John worked at the press, running the printing process and managing the warehouse. He and Danielle had been courting for over a year now, and everyone sensed their engagement was imminent.

"Of course," Lydia replied. "Thank you so much for helping me out today. I couldn't have done it without you."

"Always, Lyd. Let me know if you need anything tomorrow, before or after the meeting. And if I see that brother of yours, I'll send him your way." They dropped off their boxes in the press' front office before parting ways. Danielle continued back up the street into town, and Lydia turned toward the river.

# CHAPTER TWO

Lydia did not see Micah that night. He wasn't home when she arrived, and after a few hours of reading and watching the door, Lydia chose to go to bed. In the morning, she was almost surprised to find him in the kitchen making coffee, eggs, and toast.

He looked up and smiled as she came into the room, either oblivious to or choosing to ignore the confused expression on her face. "Hey, Sis. Is Monday still our day for farm shift?"

"Yep," Lydia replied. "I'm supposed to help out in the apple orchard, but I'm sure you'd be more valued in the fields." She hesitated before adding, "So you are planning on sticking around?"

Micah's smile faded. "I heard about the town council

meeting tonight. Sounds like I am supposed to stay at least until then."

"Who told you? I didn't see you at the festival yesterday."

"Mr. Barrett stopped me after church and informed me of my duty." He rolled his eyes.

Lydia nodded. The Barrett family owned the power plant and had a de facto seat on the town council as a result. There were five families who had made the greatest financial investment in founding New Augsburg, and each held a seat that was always occupied by the family patriarch. To prevent an imbalanced oligarchy from running the town, the other five seats were elected at large every three years.

Micah did not volunteer any further information about his intentions, and the siblings ate in silence for a few minutes. The familiar anxious tightness came to rest in Lydia's stomach. She wished that Micah would take charge of the conversation for once, but it appeared that she would have to carry the weight of all their difficult exchanges.

"So, are you going to take Daddy's seat on the council and his role at the press?" Micah stared into his plate and said nothing. After a brief attempt at waiting for him to respond, Lydia continued, trying unsuccessfully to keep the frustration out of her voice: "I think I deserve a straight answer. It's been five months since Mother died, and we haven't had any conversations about what we're going to do next. Now, we're about to be asked these questions point blank at the meeting tonight, and I don't have any idea what you're going to say."

Micah maintained his stoicism and refused to look up.

"Micah, please. Let's figure this out. We can come up with a plan together. I've been working so hard to keep the press going, and I can keep doing what I'm doing. I just need to know if you're in this with me. Honestly, I'm not sure what the options are if you're not." When his silence persisted, she invoked the one name sure to force a response. "What does Callie think about it?"

That did it. Micah jumped up and started rinsing dishes with intensity. "Callie! I can't ask Callie to move here with me. I can't live without her, and I won't ask her to do this." He gestured with feeling as he spoke.

Lydia winced as the dishes clattered under the effect of Micah's frustration. "Why not, Micah?" she asked, attempting to remain calm. "Why won't you ask her to 'do this' as you put it?"

"She's not like the girls here, Lyd. She's not like you. She has a plan—a whole career. She's been working toward it her entire life. She's invested so much money and time in it, and she loves it. You should see her in action. She was made for that life. She wants to make a big difference in the world. I can't ask her to give all that up and play house with me while I run the family printing business."

Lydia tried to resist the bait but failed. "Do you think I don't have a plan? Do you think what I do isn't a career? Do you think I wasn't made for my life? What are you saying, Micah? What are you going to be forcing me to give up when you follow her to Washington so you can 'play house' with her, as you put it?" It was a tactical error, making it about herself instead of Micah's dilemma. But he didn't give her a chance to take it back.

Micah walked swiftly out of the kitchen and slammed the back door.

Leaping to her feet to follow him induced a sharp pang in her gut—a side effect of conflict that she'd experienced as long as she could remember—and she decided against it. Instead, she finished cleaning the kitchen and gathered her things for the day. Her first stop would be the press office to make sure everything was running smoothly before heading to the apple orchard for her shift at the farm. Perhaps Micah would seek her out there, and they would be able to finish their conversation, but Lydia began to despair of them presenting a united front at the council meeting. Her brother was not ready to take their father's place, but he also did not seem at peace with relinquishing it. She regretted the way she had lashed out, but he was the one who needed to make a decision, and she would just have to wait for him to make it. Too bad she had never been good at waiting.

The orchard buzzed that morning with the excitement of the final week of harvest. The sounds of laughter and feminine chatter filled the air as women and girls of all ages worked their way through the rows of trees in twos and threes. All the remaining apples were to be picked and gathered into bushels.

Lydia found herself stationed at one of the long wooden tables outside the cider mill, sorting out the seconds to be pressed into cider. Compared to the relative quiet that her work at the press entailed, she usually enjoyed the camaraderie and fellowship of a morning such as this one. Today, however, her thoughts were with Micah and her parents. She responded when spoken to, but the memories would not leave her alone, and after enough one or two-word responses, the other women chatted on without her.

One particular day kept replaying in her mind. It was her fourteenth birthday, and her parents had given her a miniature antique printing press with washable ink and removable type. She still remembered the exact look of joy and pride on her father's face as he watched her open it. They had set it up together in her bedroom and printed out the first batch of flyers for distribution. She'd chosen to make invitations for a birthday party for Micah as her inaugural project. Their birthdays were just three days apart, and that year throwing an impromptu surprise party had seemed the natural response to her receipt of a printing press. Micah had received his sixteenth birthday party with grace, but looking back on that day now, Lydia knew he would have preferred a day of camping with a few friends. That was the last year their father had been there for their birthdays.

"Lydia!"

She snapped out of her reverie and looked up to see Danielle walking quickly across the field, a heavy wicker basket on her arm.

"I thought today would be a good one for a picnic," her friend called out as she approached. Danielle worked with her mother as a seamstress. They had a shop on Third Street and lived above it, so for Danielle to put the effort into packing up a lunch and adding a half-mile walk to her Monday was a kind gesture. "I know today is a big day for you, and I thought you could use the company."

With gratitude, Lydia followed Danielle away from the others and helped her spread the picnic blanket at the base of a large oak tree. As they ate, Lydia brought Danielle up to speed on her conversation with Micah that morning. "I messed it up," she concluded. "I snapped at him just as he was opening up and starting to share his real feelings."

"Maybe, Lyd, but he does owe you an explanation. You two are family, and you need him. He should be able to be present for your feelings without running away like that."

"I suppose so, but I ran away emotionally, even if he was the one who literally walked out."

Danielle acknowledged this with a shrug. "Here he comes now," she said. "Who is that with him?"

The men had started to trickle in from the field for lunchtime. Micah was with them and appeared to be engaged in good-natured banter with another young man who was tall and well-built, with sandy brown hair and bright blue denim overalls that looked strikingly untouched by fieldwork. "I think that's Zach Barrett," Lydia said as they approached.

"Oh?" Danielle raised her eyebrows. Lydia smiled and rolled her eyes. Zach had a habit of asking her out once every few months. Lydia had never accepted his invitations, but she'd lost count of how many times he'd reissued them. It had always struck her as a running joke. Zach was a year older than Micah, in addition to being arguably the most handsome and popular young man in town. She'd never taken his professed interest seriously.

The men spotted Danielle and Lydia and broke away from the rest of the group to approach them.

"You two look cozy," Micah said with a smile. "This must be the small-town charm I keep coming back for."

Danielle returned the smile, but Lydia didn't know where to look. Her brother always could brush an argument under the rug before she had time to process what had happened.

"Join us!" Danielle offered. "I packed more than enough. I knew I couldn't come down to the farm during harvest without running into extra friends." The two men sat down and were elbows deep in the picnic basket before she had finished speaking.

After a few minutes of comfortable, friendly conversation, Zach startled Lydia by stating matter-of-factly, "Micah told me you two have a big meeting tonight. So, the moment has finally come for the future of the press to be determined."

Lydia almost dropped her iced tea. She stared down

at her lap for a moment, feeling her cheeks turning red. Rallying quickly, she looked up and met Zach's eyes. "That's right. It's all up to Micah. Tonight's the night." Micah tried to look nonchalant, but Lydia detected a hint of discomfort as he shifted positions and reached for a second piece of cold chicken.

Zach, apparently unaware of the tension he had surfaced, went on, "Micah says that you're the one who really runs the press. And it seems he has big plans out east with this Callie person." He gave Micah a good-natured shove. "So, it sounds like you're the one driving. Are you going to make a move for a council seat?"

"Of course not. You know women don't sit on the town council. That seat is Micah's. And so is the press, technically. I can run it for him, but it belongs to him, and he can't escape it that easily." She tried to keep her tone light and playful, flashing a smile at Zach and hoping it masked her discomfort.

Zach returned her smile gallantly. "Well, if the way you run the press is any indication of your general abilities, I'd be happy to let you run my whole life for me." He winked at her, and she blushed and looked away.

Micah laughed and teasingly lunged for Zach. "On that note, I'd better get you away from my sister and back out in the field. Thanks again for lunch, Danielle. Lydia, I'll be home for dinner, and we can prep for the meeting then."

As Micah and Zach joined the group of men heading back out for the afternoon's work, Lydia could feel her friend's eyes on her. She finished her iced tea and began re-packing the picnic basket.

"Why can't women sit on the council, though?" Danielle's question sounded rhetorical, so Lydia waited a moment. "I mean, from everything I've read, it's okay for women to hold leadership positions as long as they don't involve spiritual leadership. I'm pretty sure Paul's words to women are about the pastoral office and have nothing to do with the town council."

"Perhaps you're right. New Augsburg is weird, but that's the point." Lydia responded thoughtfully. "Our founders set it up this way because they wanted to try something radically different from what the rest of the world was doing. Maybe they were wrong, or maybe they were right. I wasn't alive back then, so I won't pass judgment. Honestly, it's never bothered me."

"Until now?" Danielle's tone suggested that it was starting to bother *her* on her friend's behalf.

Lydia shrugged. "If we lived in a town where women could sit on the council, that would be one thing. But I'm not going to be the town's first feminist. I can't ask people to change everything just for the sake of my peculiar circumstances."

"Lydia, Lydia," Danielle smiled and shook her head. "You've never been one to stir the pot."

"I think you stir it enough for the both of us." Lydia playfully elbowed her friend as Danielle closed the basket, and they rose to their feet.

Danielle dusted the grass from her gray denim flared jeans and adjusted her pink ruffled top as she prepared to walk home. "Honestly though, Lydia, you don't have to stay here. You could move out east to D.C. with Micah if you wanted."

Lydia raised her hand to her eyes, shielding them from the sun's bright rays, and stared out over the orchard, down the hill toward the lane that led to her home—the only one she'd ever known, where generations of her family had lived. "I can't leave New Augsburg," she said quietly. "It's all I have left of them."

Danielle nodded. They both knew whom she meant. "Well, let me know how it goes tonight, and if a pot needs to be stirred, just point me in the right direction."

# CHAPTER THREE

The Klein siblings walked the twenty-minute route from their home to the community center in silence. They had finally managed to finish an exchange about the future of the press, and although Lydia was still unsatisfied, she felt able to face the occasion with at least minimal composure.

As they entered the hall, the clamor of the crowd and the number of people to maneuver around took her by surprise. The nine members of the town council were taking their seats at the U-shaped table in the center of the room, and a significant number of other citizens occupied chairs set up along the wall. Pastor Pedersen was there, and Lydia noted that the bishop was with him—an unusual occurrence. Pastor nodded to them warmly as he showed the bishop to a seat at the rectangular table opposite the council and positioned himself at his elbow.

As they stood in the doorway, Lydia wished she had attended one of these meetings before. It would certainly be helpful to know what to expect or even where she ought to sit. Before she had time to second-guess herself, she saw Zach moving towards them purposefully.

"This way. I've saved us seats," he said with a smile and a wave.

"I didn't realize you'd be here," she said as they followed him across the room to the same table where the bishop and Pastor Pedersen were sitting.

"I come to all of these," Zach replied. He leaned down and whispered conspiratorially, "Someone's got to know what the old folks are up to around here."

Lydia took note (not for the first time) of their disparate heights. He towered a full foot over her as he pulled out her chair. Micah and Lydia took the seats he indicated, and Zach helped himself to a seat directly behind them.

The meeting was promptly called to order, and Pastor Pedersen opened in prayer. Without further preamble, Mr. Barrett stood and launched into the business of the day.

"We are gathered tonight to discuss the matter of the future of the press. As we all know, our town was designed by our admirable founders to be self-sufficient—to need little in terms of outside resources or support. We are, however, not a community of hermits, cut off from our sense of calling in the world. The singular way we have chosen to focus our resources for the benefit of our brothers and sisters throughout the world is through the operation of our esteemed printing house. By continuing to print the great works of our faith tradition, we have been able to lend a service to the Church that is not without great value."

He continued in this manner for a good deal longer than Lydia felt was necessary. As he spoke of the founders' vision, the theology of vocation, and the deplorable state of society as a whole, her mind began to wander. She felt something poking her from behind, and as she reached her hand behind her back to smooth her dress, another hand grasped her own and smoothly placed a piece of paper in her palm.

Zach! She looked down at the small card now clasped in her lap. What was this, high school? She didn't want to risk reading the note in the meeting but struggled to resist her curiosity. Holding it under the table, she ventured a quick peek.

> *Dinner tomorrow?*
> *You look lovely tonight, by the way. ~ Z.B.*

She turned her head ever so slightly, and Zach winked at her. *He overuses that move,* she thought to herself. Too late, she realized she had no idea what Mr. Barrett had been saying.

"Miss Klein?" he said. "Would you please report on the current financial position of the press?"

"I'm sorry, yes." Lydia stammered, attempting to sweep away her momentary confusion. She stood, took a file folder out of her bag, and began to pass out her financial report. She observed nervously that the note had fallen to the floor as she had risen from her seat. Hopefully, nobody would notice. "Our financial situation is holding steady since last quarter. We are still not profitable but are breaking even. There is not as much cushion as I would like but no cause for immediate concern." The council members looked over the reports as Lydia reclaimed her seat.

"Thank you for your dedication, Miss Klein. The council has asked permission to review the legal matters after your mother's death. With Micah's permission, we have obtained a copy of your mother's will and your father's legal directives signed before his . . . departure. We are satisfied that they intended to leave the management of the press to their son. Micah, we recognize that you and your mother have been joint owners of the press since you were sixteen. Will you now be accepting the full management and ownership of the press?"

Micah stood slowly. Lydia thought he looked remarkably calm, given the circumstances. "I thank you all for calling this council meeting on a night when I am in town. I know it is inconvenient for many of you, especially on All Saints' Day. While I realize that my father's legacy is one that it would be a great honor to carry on, I cannot at this time accept ownership or management of the press. I am in my last year of university studies and have plans to live and work elsewhere after graduating." The room was uncomfortably quiet. He paused as if not knowing how to conclude. Finally, he managed, "Thank you again for your time and for everything you do for this town," and took his seat.

There was a moment of awkward silence. Mr. Barrett looked at his notepad before turning to the gentleman on his right and asking, "Okay, Tom, you're the procedure and bylaws guru. Where does this leave us?"

Tom McKenzie stood slowly and looked at the Klein siblings seriously from over his glasses. The McKenzie family owned more than seventy percent of the land New Augsburg occupied. Silas McKenzie had been the most prolific writer, as well as the lawyer among the founders. Their family inheritance was not only literally the town but also, by custom, the legacy of maintaining the order and vision of the founding families. "Micah and Lydia," he began. "We are all deeply grieved at the loss of your parents at such young ages. Your father's dedication to the press and this town is a great legacy for your family, and we know you must both be very proud of him. Micah, you are the rightful owner of the press now. According to our governing code, the press (like the mill, the power plant, and the farm) passes within the family to the eldest son. If you will not maintain residency in New Augsburg and manage the press, it will likely have to be sold to another resident of New Augsburg to continue in operation. It cannot legally be purchased by a nonresident (nor would we ever permit that to happen). Lydia, while fully capable and trustworthy as an acting manager, is obviously ineligible to own the press or hold the corresponding seat on this council."

Lydia felt her stomach twist into knots. She wanted to speak but couldn't bring herself to do so. All of her energy was focused on appearing calm, professional, and collected.

Micah spoke, "My sister has been managing the day-to-day operation of the press for years. Perhaps there is someone who would be willing to own it and hold the council seat while she continues to run things?"

"I do not believe there is anyone in town who currently possesses the capital necessary to purchase the press from you, Son." Mr. Barrett looked apologetic. "I seriously wish that you desired to stay among us and do your duty, Micah. I'm sure it's what your parents would want."

Lydia could practically feel the color rising in her brother's cheeks, even without looking at him. Without thinking, she spoke out: "Micah has a keen sense of duty, Mr. Barrett, I assure you. We could not possibly have known that he would be in this position three years ago when he started university. In that time, he has developed a relationship with a young woman, and now his sense of duty branches in two directions. I'm sure this decision is not easy for him." Micah shifted uncomfortably in the seat next to her. Apparently, having his honor defended by his sister was no more comfortable than the attack on it had been.

"Be that as it may," Mr. Barrett went on, "it puts our community in a difficult position. There are challenges besides simply finding a suitable buyer for the press. A sale and purchase agreement triggers taxes and government paperwork, which could lead to unwelcome oversight of our operations. You both know this. This is not a problem we will be able to solve tonight, I fear. Micah, the council requests that you retain ownership and management of the press for the next year while we consider how to plan for succession. Lydia can continue to run things for you while you are away.

"After a year's time, if you cannot come home and take your place in this community, you will need to sell the press. I realize that you very likely would need the proceeds to establish yourself in the world, as it is your inheritance, but the council will not approve the sale to a nonresident, and you may have to sell it at a loss if the capital cannot be raised. Meeting adjourned. See you all at church."

Rising to her feet, Lydia busied herself gathering her papers into her handbag. She did her best to ignore the hushed, curious, gossipy murmuring that surrounded her. She tried to avoid eye contact with anyone as she followed Micah out of the town hall.

Even from behind, she sensed the angry energy that her brother was exuding. Anticipating his desire for space, she allowed the distance between them to grow. Zach, who had followed them out unnoticed, almost tripped over her as she slowed her steps.

"You dropped this," he said softly, placing the note he had written in her hand for a second time that evening.

"Oh, sorry, I . . ." Lydia stammered. She had briefly forgotten about the note and Zach's offer.

"Don't worry about it," he replied gently. "That was a rough meeting. Possibly not the best place for me to choose to ask you out."

Attempting a smile, Lydia looked from Zach to the people walking toward the church. "I'm going to the service now," she said, knowing it delayed giving an answer to his proposition. "It's All Saints' Day."

"Right, your mother . . ." Zach looked almost uncomfortable—an unusual occurrence for him as far as she had ever observed. He hesitated, then said, "Can I walk with you? I'll go too."

Responding with a nod, they continued toward Main Street in silence. As they ascended the church steps to the sound of the prelude, Lydia noticed Micah crossing the river, heading home. She filed into her regular pew.

Zach stopped beside her and whispered, "Don't worry about my question tonight. I'll stop by the press tomorrow afternoon. You can give me your answer then." He crossed the aisle and took the seat beside his father two rows farther up.

Lydia chose to remain in her seat as her fellow parishioners exited. She needed a moment of silence to let her emotions breathe. Closing her eyes, she imagined her mother sitting in the pew beside her, as she had done every week of Lydia's life until just a few months ago. She had always loved the All Saints' Day service, but this year was different. The organist was playing an arrangement of "For All the Saints" as a postlude, and tears filled her eyes as the music washed over her, bringing the familiar words to mind. This had been her mother's favorite hymn.

> *O blest communion, fellowship divine!*
> *We feebly struggle, they in glory shine;*

She was certainly feeling the struggle as she wiped away her tears with the edge of her sleeve. She wished Micah had come; she hated to feel so alone.

The music stopped. When she opened her eyes, Pastor Pedersen was standing a few feet away, his hands folded in front of him, quietly watching her. One quick glance around the sanctuary informed her that she was the last person there.

"Oh! Sorry to keep you waiting," she said as she hastily moved to get up.

"No, dear, take your time," Pastor Pedersen said gently. "Your mother sure loved that hymn. She never neglected to tell me it was her favorite any time we sang it."

Lydia smiled, resisting the catch in her throat and standing to go. "Thank you, Pastor," she managed.

"Of course, dear. Thank you for being here tonight." Pastor Pedersen looked thoughtful. "I wanted to let you know that Bishop Hart was here for the meeting because the press is very important to our synod. As you know, we would be unable to print much of what our church body publishes through traditional print houses, at least not without the red mark. This work that we do here in New Augsburg is of immense value to the Church as a whole."

Lydia nodded. She knew all of this, but Pastor often took time to warm up to his main point.

"I don't want you to feel like you are alone, Lydia," he continued. "We are all invested in your press, and we will do what we can to help. Churchwide resources are stretched thin right now, but God has it all under His control, and this is not just your burden, my dear."

"Thank you," Lydia replied. "I wish I could get through to Micah, though. We used to speak so openly with each other, but lately I feel like he's completely . . . inaccessible."

"Grief is a strange thing, Lydia," Pastor Pedersen said softly. "Micah lost his mother, too, and he's probably struggling more than he lets on. He will be okay. Give him time and space. But not too much space."

Lydia forced a smile. She liked her pastor very much. He could not fix the heaviness in her heart, but he so often showed up when she needed a dose of God's truth. They spoke together for a few more moments, sharing memories of her mother and reflections on the service before she said goodnight and started for home.

# CHAPTER FOUR

The church, surrounded by the cemetery, was situated on the east side of the river that cut through town. Woods stretched from the southern end of the cemetery and ran south along the riverbank. The bulk of New Augsburg was on this same side of the river, with numbered streets running parallel to it and increasing from First Street to Eighth Street as they moved east. Two bridges spanned the river to the west side of the community, one by the church and one on the north side of town by the mill. Along the west side of the riverbank ran the community farm. Beyond the farmland, there were several larger homes on more significant acreages. The founding families had purchased the property in the 2020s when it was an all-but-deserted ghost town. It had formerly been a small community built around a forestry operation, but the original company, which had been the only significant employer, had gone out of business in the late 1990s.

The founders were independently wealthy families who had worked together to develop a vision for a new kind of community built around their shared faith and values. They had planned carefully, strategically purchasing the land and assets necessary to run their town almost completely autonomously. Lydia's great, great-grandparents had been founders. A few short years after establishing Klein Press their foresight was validated when the federal government mandated that all books and published works be scrutinized for "harmful content." Books deemed repressive or hateful were either heavily abridged or forced to appear with a warning label that came to be known as the *red mark*.

The Klein estate, although not one of the largest, was on the west side of the river and was large enough to feel quite lonely with Micah away at school. As Lydia approached, she could see the light was on in the kitchen.

Micah looked up as she entered. He sat at the kitchen table, his head in his hands, an empty ice cream carton pushed to the side inches from his elbow. Lydia took a seat in the opposite chair and waited for him to speak. After several minutes of silence, Micah finally laughed and conceded, "Fine! I'll talk first." She smiled and continued to wait.

"I'm sorry, Lyd. I know this isn't fair to you. I know you want me to stay here and run the press with you. I know you're probably frustrated with me for being unwilling to commit to a life here." He paused, then added, "And I'm sorry I didn't come to church with you tonight. It would probably have been good for me to be there."

Lydia nodded without saying anything. She didn't want Micah to be wracked with guilt. All she wanted was for him to be at peace. She still didn't understand why he couldn't be at peace here in New Augsburg, but she was hoping that if she was quiet long enough, he would manage to tell her. It was hard for her to hold her thoughts in, but experience had taught her that doing so was the only way to get a glimpse into Micah's inner world.

But something in Micah snapped. His fist fell to the table with a thud, and Lydia could see the pain in his eyes as he continued. "Honestly, though, this place makes me crazy! I mean, it's so coercive! So manipulative! It's practically a cult. What was that at the meeting today? The guilt trip? The threats?"

His chair scraped against the floor as he pushed away from the table and rose to his feet, pacing the eat-in kitchen that stretched across the back of their home. "I don't understand why me wanting to live in a different city and do something else for a living has to mean I lose my inheritance. It just doesn't feel right. Dad gave everything to this town, to this *vision*." The last word came out dripping with bitterness. "Where did it get him? We don't even know." He stopped walking, staring out the window into the night, waiting for Lydia's response.

Lydia's thoughts had begun to race as he spoke, and her resolution to stay calm was fading quickly. "Were we even in the same meeting? Threats? Guilt trips? That's not what I heard! The council members did nothing but state the facts. And calmly and compassionately, given the circumstances!"

"The circumstances?" Micah turned to face her, yelling now. "I want to have my own life, and apparently, I can't without ruining everyone else's. Those are the circumstances! What's compassionate about that?"

"Micah! Don't you believe in what this town stands for? Don't you see all the sacrifices and the intentionality that generations before us have put into this place? You've been out there, Micah! You've lived in the world, and you still don't see the beauty of this? The importance of it?"

"That's just it! I have lived in the world. There's plenty of beauty out there too. You have no idea, Lydia! You've never known anything else." His words were no longer angry, and as she looked at him, she saw her own loneliness reflected in his eyes.

"You're right. I don't know anything else. You've taken the opportunities that I chose not to take." She didn't remind him that the reason she had not also gone to college was because of their mother's illness. They both knew it to be true, but it would be cruel to say so. "Now you're planning to leave me here, alone. If I'm going to live in this town without my family, don't also try to talk me out of my good opinion of my home."

His shoulders relaxed, and looking deflated, he dropped back into his chair at the table.

"And it's not a cult, Micah. In a cult, you can't leave. Every year, people move into and out of this town, and you know full well that at least half of our generation will settle down elsewhere."

"But it feels that way to me, Lyd. Because *I* can't leave. Because I'm the 'heir to the Klein estate, son of a founding family.' " He rolled his eyes as he said it, voice dripping with what Lydia knew to be defensive sarcasm.

"Fair enough," she said softly.

He was shutting down on her, putting on that look of false calm that she knew from experience signaled the end of their argument. "I know you believe in all of it." His voice was quiet now. "I'm sorry to disappoint you. I want to believe in it. I do believe in our parents, in their good intentions, and in you and my friends here. But I just don't want to accept that the world is hopeless. I don't think that there is only one right way to be faithful. Isolating ourselves, trusting no one . . . is that really what being the Church is about?"

Lydia wasn't sure how to respond. "And there's Callie."

He smiled at this reminder. "Yes, there's Callie."

Feeling that what was most needed in the moment was some resolution and hope for the future, Lydia transitioned the conversation to a lighthearted one about Callie and her many virtues. She expressed how much she wished to meet her, and Micah agreed that it was time. He had the idea of inviting her to come home with him for Thanksgiving, and Lydia voiced warm enthusiasm for the plan. They were about to retire for the evening when Lydia remembered Zach's invitation and showed her brother the note.

Micah looked up from the note, a teasing twinkle in his eye. "Well? Are you going to go out with him?"

"I don't know. Should I?"

"I guess that depends on whether or not you like him," he said with amusement.

Lydia rolled her eyes. "I don't know, Micah. Shouldn't I like him? I've known him my whole life, and obviously, he's a nice guy from a respectable family. He's close enough to my age, and he lives here. He also seems to want to spend time with me. What's not to like?"

Micah laughed. "There should be more to it than that, don't you think? Like a 'spark' or something?" The siblings shared a smile at this inside joke.

Their parents had always made fun of the traditional romantic tropes. Their marriage had been an arranged one, and they had been blissfully happy, as far as their children could tell, but there had been no "falling in love" courtship story, and as Lydia reflected on it, she felt that she had no example to follow for how to go about finding a spouse. Now, with both parents gone, an arranged marriage seemed out of the question. If she was to marry, she would have to arrange it herself.

"You know," Micah said thoughtfully, "maybe you should marry Zach. It would solve all your problems.

He could own and manage the press. The council would probably let me give it to you if it became his upon marriage, and the whole issue of sale and government oversight would be sidestepped quite nicely."

Lydia looked up with surprise. The thought had not occurred to her, but now that it was put into her head, she couldn't imagine why it hadn't. Clearly, what she needed was what a Jane Austen character would have called *an eligible match*. And as much as she had never thought about Zach in that way, *eligible* would certainly be the right word to describe him.

Micah looked as if he could read her thoughts. "Perhaps there is a 'spark' after all," he teased.

# CHAPTER FIVE

Thoughts of Zach's invitation distracted Lydia for the entirety of the following morning. She said goodbye to Micah at breakfast before he left for the airport in his rental car. Then she headed to the press office, where she and John checked over the layout samples for the latest book in their classics line. The majority of their work consisted of printing books for underground Christian publishers who would send them completed files for production. But before her passing, Lydia and her mother had started a new passion project—reprinting classic books that were in the public domain but no longer available through mainline publishers. This collection of classics involved much more work, as Lydia and her team had to find authoritative versions of the text and edit, lay out, and proof them before printing.

Lydia was still working out the details of distribution. Word of mouth had secured some modest orders, but she longed to see these works in the hands of the greater public once again. It was a delicate dance. If they printed too many and distributed too widely, it could attract unwanted attention.

The second half of her morning was spent giving a tour of their operation to Bishop Hart before he left town. Throughout the morning, Lydia struggled to think of anything but Zach and her conversation with Micah the night before.

Zachary Barrett was twenty-six: four years older than Lydia. He had been one year ahead of Micah in school, but she had spent little to no time with him in intimate settings, despite growing up in the same small town and having known who he was for as long as she could remember. He had first started asking her out years ago when he would come home from university on breaks. At the time, she had considered him too old for her and had not taken his suggestions as anything other than teasing playfulness. Thinking back now, she wondered if he had been serious the whole time. Now that they were both in their twenties, he certainly was not too old for her, and unlike Micah, he seemed eager to settle down and establish himself as an adult in their hometown.

Zach was undeniably handsome—possibly one of the best-looking young men in town. Tall, broad-shouldered, with piercing, steel-grey eyes and perfectly styled light brown hair, he could always be seen sauntering through town with a confidence Lydia had often admired from a distance. She wondered why she had never thought about him before. Perhaps her preoccupation with her mother's illness could be held responsible for her completely missing the charms of a young man who was so obviously interested in her. Despite these reflections, she was aware that she did not know Zach well enough to have a good idea of his character or how well their personalities might mesh. But was not such discovery the point of a courtship?

When Zach entered her office promptly after lunch as promised, she had all but resolved to accept his invitation. She told herself that her feelings toward him were no more than curiosity and nervousness, yet her stomach still did a somersault as he walked in. He sauntered through the door with a confident smile and got right to the point.

"So?" he asked. "Will you go out with me?"

The date took place the following midday. The emotional turbulence of the past few days had left Lydia desperate for a quiet evening at home. Zach was happy to accommodate, and the proposed dinner was amended into a lunch date for Wednesday. Her first dating experience would naturally require a thorough debrief with her best friend, so Lydia planned to take the whole afternoon off.

After parting ways with Zach outside Main Street Café, she headed straight for Danielle's house.

Lydia found Danielle and her mother in their sewing room in the back of the shop. Mrs. Thomas was laying out patterns and cutting at the work counter while Danielle sat by a window sorting through boxes of fabric. The fabric was recycled and purchased in bulk. The Thomas family had developed a distinctive style over the years. They would upcycle old, donated garments and linens, bought at a fraction of what new fabric would cost, sort them into patterns and fabric styles that would work well together, sew the remnants into larger pieces, and then make clothing with traditional patterns and silhouettes. Of course, citizens of New Augsburg could travel twenty miles to the nearest shopping center and buy clothes there, but the consensus was that the popular fashions of the day did not exemplify their values. Most of the women in town wore clothes made either by Mrs. Thomas herself or inspired by her fashion ideas.

Lydia had worn her favorite outfit for today's occasion, which consisted of a simple, cream-colored, boat-neck top with three-quarter-length sleeves and a tea-length full skirt made of at least twelve different floral print vertical panels. The colors were perfectly selected to blend together, and the skirt flared and swirled so beautifully when she moved that Lydia always felt like dancing when she wore it.

An extra chair stood waiting beside Danielle, who looked up eagerly as her friend walked in. "So?" she asked.

"Tell me everything!"

Lydia sat and reached for a pile of fabric. She knew what to look for: Many afternoons had been spent this way over the years of their friendship. As they sorted, she went over the details of the date. Zach had arrived with an extravagant and expensive-looking bouquet of flowers. She had awkwardly excused herself momentarily to put them in water; then, they had walked together down to the café. The conversation had flowed smoothly enough. His amusing university stories had entertained her. He'd asked about her favorite books and pastimes and shared his dreams of travel and adventure. This had taken her slightly by surprise; she had always assumed that the young people who had the opportunity to study at a university would have fulfilled their dreams of travel. But Zach seemed to crave more than a four-year residence in a different state at a small, conservative liberal arts college. He talked of seeing Europe, China, the Holy Land, and more.

"I found his enthusiasm and curiosity contagious," Lydia admitted. "I was almost ashamed that I had never thought seriously about seeing the world. He asked me where I would go if I had the chance to go anywhere, and I didn't know what to say. I think I said Rome or maybe Egypt. It does sound amazing to see all the places we have read about in our studies." She paused a moment before continuing. "I think I've just always pictured my life here. My dreams are simpler. Getting married, raising children, being a part of this town. I've always been content with this. Does that make me boring?"

Danielle shook her head. "You are adventurous, Lydia. You explore the world through books and ideas, and you want to share that world with others through your work at the press. I've never seen you as a person who lacked enthusiasm for your life."

Lydia looked down modestly, but her friend's words were soothing. It felt good to be known.

Danielle continued, "Did it sound like Zach didn't want those things too? Marriage and a family here in this town?"

"I didn't ask him directly. Do you think I should have?"

"Well, I suppose that's what a second date is for. Is there going to be a second date, Lyd?"

"He didn't say anything about a second date. Was I supposed to do that?" Lydia looked alarmed. "Did I mess it up somehow?"

"No," Danielle reassured with a chuckle. "I think it's his job as the man to follow up if he's interested."

"I don't know. He's expressed a lot of interest up to this point. Maybe I should have asked him. I obviously don't know what I'm doing!" The anxiety in Lydia's voice was increasing.

"You should relax, Lyd. If it's meant to be, it will be." The girls sorted in silence for a few minutes as Lydia worked on relaxing. But Danielle couldn't resist, finally dropping her fabric and asking the one question on both of their minds. "But do you *like* him?"

As Lydia walked home that evening (Mrs. Thomas had invited her to stay for dinner, and she had done so, grateful for the company), she thought over Danielle's question again. She had said yes. She thought she did like Zach. It had been a pleasant date. He was funny and interesting, and his interest in her was flattering. Although his direct manner made her uncomfortable at times, there was something empowering about being sought after. She did wonder if her growing enthusiasm for this new relationship might have more to do with the situation at the press and her own loneliness. What if she only liked him because he liked her? Even if that were true, was there anything wrong with that? What did it mean to "like someone" in the context of a budding relationship? She felt that she knew from her parents' examples what it looked like to love someone unconditionally and build a life with them, but how was that supposed to look and feel in the early stages?

As her thoughts swirled, she chastised herself for her typical overthinking tendencies. In novels, the heroines always know if they're in love or not. *Surely,* Lydia told herself, *I will just know.* Then a second later, *but how will I know that I know? Maybe I should call Micah and interrogate him about what being in love feels like, just so I have at least one good data point.* She almost laughed out loud as she pictured how that conversation would go. *No, he would hate that.* She resolved to take Danielle's advice: relax, wait, and see. But despite the strength of her resolutions, she spent the entire night replaying the date in her mind and trying to parse out what her own feelings on it had been.

It was a welcome relief when she opened her front door the next morning and found a single pink rose on her doorstep. Attached was a note that read:

*I had a wonderful time yesterday.*
*Dinner tomorrow? ~ Z. B.*

# CHAPTER SIX

The next few weeks were full of new experiences for Lydia. She and Zach spent a few hours together almost every day. They went for walks along the river, met at the library coffee shop, attended the weekly Friday night movie at the community center, and ate at the café two more times. Always the perfect gentleman, Zach said the right things, was polite to everyone they encountered, and exuded confidence and self-assurance. Lydia found his attention flattering and his conversation entertaining. Their dates provided a welcome distraction after the heaviness of the past year, but Lydia's feelings toward him did not become clearer. Zach often asked her views and opinions in conversation, and he would listen attentively, but Lydia found herself doubting whether he was truly interested in her responses. His energy level was significantly higher than hers. His conversation was simultaneously exhilarating and exhausting. She missed her quiet evenings at home. And yet, no one had ever expressed so much eagerness for her company. Her confidence and self-esteem grew with each passing day.

The Saturday before Thanksgiving, Zach called at her house, inviting her to walk to the coffee shop. She kept him waiting as she searched through the closet for her winter coat—the November wind had greeted her when she answered the door, reminding her it was time to make the transition. She hadn't reached this far back into the coat closet since last winter. Her hand froze on the sleeve of her mother's coat, still hanging where she had left it. Waves of emotion caught in her throat, but with Zach watching from the doorway, she simply put on the coat and followed him onto the porch, noting its perfect fit. She and her mother were exactly the same height and build. *Had been.*

Gingerly, she slid her hands into the pockets, stopping when she felt her mother's gloves, each still folded tidily in half. Pulling them out, she put them on, remembering how she'd helped her mother with the same task mere months ago, the last time they had walked outside together.

Lost in thought, she did not notice Zach talking to her until she realized, too late, that he had stopped. He was looking at her inquisitively. "I'm sorry, what?" she asked, embarrassed.

"The dance," he repeated. "Will you go with me?"

Lydia's brain worked to play catch up. Of course, he was referring to the Thanksgiving dance. Always held the Friday after Thanksgiving, the dance marked the beginning of the town's holiday festivities. She had pictured going to the dance with him from the morning of their first official date. To this point, their meetings had been casual and friendly. Inevitably, some of the townsfolk must have noticed, but they were not an official couple yet. Lydia knew the act of going to the Thanksgiving dance together would constitute a public declaration of their courtship. She wondered if things were moving too fast. Yet, refusing his invitation risked bringing it all to a grinding halt. They walked for a minute in silence while Lydia wrestled with her thoughts.

Zach grew uncomfortable with her hesitation and spoke again, "Do you feel it's too soon? Are you concerned about what people may think if we go together?" Without waiting for an answer, he stopped walking and reached for her arm. "Lydia, I feel like this is going really well. I like you, and I think our roles in New Augsburg complement each other in an obvious way."

She looked up at him sharply. Was he thinking of the press? They had not spoken about it since the town council meeting, although it had been on her mind constantly. Of course, she had wondered if he'd thought through what their relationship might mean for the town. It seemed that he had.

He continued, "I think we should make this an official relationship. I'm in if you are."

She searched for a reply, startled to realize that, for the first time in their acquaintance, Zach almost appeared unsure. He licked his lips, thrust both hands into his pocket, and watched her nervously in anticipation. Lydia was gratified to know that she had the power to inspire some nerves in him—his impenetrable self-assuredness often struck her as intimidating. She smiled at him, attempting to set him at ease as her mind worked to compose a response.

"Zach, that is very flattering. I've enjoyed our time together too." His shoulders relaxed a bit as he waited for her to go on. "I would be happy to accompany you to the Thanksgiving dance."

Zach smiled, his self-assured swagger restored by her acceptance. "And may I introduce you there as my girlfriend?"

Lydia blushed. Thankfully, they had arrived at the library. She managed to sidestep his question by flashing him a smile and skipping quickly ahead of him into the coffee shop. She rubbed her arms with her hands, hoping that he would interpret her non reply as an eagerness to get in from the cold and not as evasiveness.

The library coffee shop was one of Lydia's favorite places. She considered Maybelle Whittier—the town librarian—a personal friend and a grandmother figure. Maybelle radiated warmth and hospitality—one could hardly enter her library without receiving a beverage, a conversation, and a personalized book recommendation. Lydia made it a point to spend at least one afternoon each week in the library and always spent an hour or two of that time in conversation with her friend. Maybelle's knowledge of the classics was an asset to Lydia in her work at the press, and her life experiences and empathy made her a valuable mentor. Lydia trusted Maybelle's discretion to not prematurely kickstart the town rumor mill, making the coffee shop the perfect spot for her and Zach to get to know each other.

On this occasion, they entered to find a young woman close to Lydia's own age behind the counter with Maybelle. She wore a barista's apron, and held a notepad and pencil, which she nibbled in concentration as Maybelle showed her how to use the espresso machine.

"Excellent! Customers to help you practice!" Maybelle exclaimed as they walked through the door. "Lydia and Zach, this is Elizabeth. Her family just moved to town. They bought the old farm lot between Seventh and Eighth."

"Ah, yes! The Schaeffer family, right?" Zach smiled and extended his hand in introduction. "I had heard that you were coming! I hope you had plenty of help moving in?"

"Yes, so many neighbors showed up to help. I'm sure I'll never remember all of their names!" Elizabeth smiled brightly at them, and Lydia was struck by both her obvious confidence and her beauty. She was several inches taller than Lydia, with dark brown hair coiled into a bun. She wore a green silk top and black skintight leggings. Lydia hadn't seen any local young women wear anything so formfitting in New Augsburg, but Elizabeth was new to town, and she reminded herself not to pass judgment. She glanced in Zach's direction, wondering if he had observed her *worldly* attire. If he noticed, his demeanor gave no indication.

Elizabeth took their coffee orders and started to work on the lattés. As Lydia watched her scoop the freshly ground espresso, she wondered how she had missed the fact that a new family was moving to town. Granted, she had been quite self-involved the past few weeks.

"Moving must be so much work." Lydia attempted a segue. "Can I bring your family a meal tomorrow, perhaps?"

"Why, that's very kind!" Elizabeth replied, not taking her eyes off the milk she was steaming. "But we are a big family and bringing us a meal might be a bit much!"

"Oh, please don't worry about it! How many siblings do you have?"

"I'm number four out of eight. But my oldest three siblings are grown and out of the house, so I get to play at being the oldest now."

Lydia assured her that bringing a meal for a family of seven would be her pleasure and no trouble at all, and she and Zach took their coffees and retired to a table in a semi-private corner between a bookcase and a window.

Although the conversation at the coffee counter had lasted a solid ten minutes, Zach had not forgotten where their prior exchange had left off. As soon as they were seated, he leaned forward, whispering, "So? Will you be my girlfriend?" His eagerness was almost comical. It reminded her of a puppy, but behind the playful impatience simmered an intensity that she could not quite comprehend.

After a moment of thought, she took a deep breath and countered with a smile and a question: "Would you elaborate on what you meant earlier when you said that you thought our roles in New Augsburg complemented each other?"

He sat back in his seat, sipping his coffee without breaking eye contact. "I think you know what I meant, Lydia. Do you want me to go over it all for you?" His tone was lighthearted, almost teasing. She couldn't tell if he was annoyed with her or not.

"You know what?" she said, trying to match his casual tone with her own. "That's a great idea. Would you do me the honor of laying it all out for me?"

Irritation showed on his face for the briefest of seconds before his nonchalant demeanor returned. Leaning forward across the table so their hands almost touched, he replied, "Anything for you, of course." He paused for a moment before pulling back and going on. "I'm sure the thought has crossed your mind that you and I both hold significant roles in this community. I will own and manage the power plant and sit on the town council upon my father's retirement, and you and Micah own the press. As you desire to keep the press and Micah seems to have his heart set elsewhere, our alliance" —he hesitated— "relationship could be mutually beneficial. If Micah signed ownership of the press over to you, we could manage it together."

Zach's face betrayed a hint of color, but Lydia thought he was maintaining his cool rather well for having issued such a forward statement. Of course, what he had proposed was nothing short of what she had been contemplating herself, but to have it stated so explicitly between the two of them—and before they had even solidified their relationship status—seemed a bit shocking. She had hoped hearing what he had to say would give her time to think of a response, but she found herself just as lost for words after this declaration.

Feeling that she was not clever enough to be demure, Lydia opted for total openness. "I admit, I've had the same thoughts. Clearly, we both see the advantage of such an arrangement to *me*, but I have to ask, what is in it for you?"

Zach smiled. "Aside from the love of the most beautiful and intelligent woman in all of Wisconsin?"

Lydia forced a laugh. "Yes, aside from that." Surely, he didn't think he could sidestep her question with such blatant flattery.

"I suppose I want to be the means of securing such a valuable asset to New Augsburg. We both know the press is the heart of the town. And to be quite honest, the power plant is continuing to cost more in upkeep. The town's infrastructure will need updating in the next decade or two, and cash flow is an issue. I think the press has the potential to be more profitable, and by joining the two assets together, we may be able to find some creative solutions to future challenges."

"My, my," Lydia teased. "You go from complimenting my beauty and intelligence to discussing infrastructure and cash flow with shocking rapidity!"

Zach laughed. "Well, you asked!"

While she was not sure what she felt for Zach, Lydia appreciated his humor and his straightforwardness. She hated having to guess what people were thinking, and clearly, Zach was willing to divulge. Some kind of answer regarding their relationship was now necessary, but still, she felt a reluctance to go all in.

Zach sensed her hesitation. "Lydia," he said in a more serious tone, "I don't want to pressure you. It is enough for now that we will go to the dance together. Why don't you take the week to think it over and let me know at the dance?"

Lydia was grateful for the gesture but impulsively decided to save herself from an agonizing week of deliberation. Without giving herself time to be nervous or change her mind, she blurted out, "No, Zach, I'm sure. I'll be your girlfriend. Let's go for it!"

David Schaeffer turned on his headlights as the sun sank farther behind the evergreen tree line. After twelve hours of driving, he was impatient to stretch his legs. His car's navigation informed him he had only minutes left before reaching his parents' new farmhouse, but so far, no town had appeared. All he had seen for miles was evergreen forest, opening up rarely to reveal a farm or small town. The last city that boasted a grocery store was a solid twenty-minute drive behind him by now.

He rounded a bend, and from between the trunks of the pine trees, he could see the silver gleam of a river. A large, imposing home emerged on his right, between him and the water, then came another, significantly more modest home, then one more, before his vehicle directed him to turn right and take a bridge across the river. This was it: the renowned New Augsburg. He passed a traditional church building on his right, strikingly larger than one would expect to find in a town this size, and continued down the road for seven blocks, past several businesses and a good number of homes. There were only a few cars out on the roads. It seemed a quiet, sleepy little town for 5:00 p.m.—a time of day he was accustomed to associating with rush hour. One turn and two minutes later, he was driving down a long, curving driveway and parking in front of a picturesque house, bright white with navy blue shutters and a door to match, complete with the wraparound porch his mother had always fantasized about.

Before the car was off, the front door burst open, and his two youngest sisters, Allison and Marta, came tearing down the stairs toward him. He opened the door, leaped out of the car, and gave them hugs that swept them up into the air, spinning them each around in turn before setting them down. His sister Elizabeth was standing on the porch now, smiling and waving, and before he had time to retrieve his suitcases from the back seat, she was at his side, leaning over his shoulder to grab one of them, asking him a steady stream of questions about his impression of their new home.

"How was your drive? What do you think so far? It's quaint, right? Wait until you see the library! It's not big or anything, but it's like something out of an old movie. So cozy! I got a job as a barista there. How many days will you be staying?"

"I'll drive back on Sunday after church," he managed to squeeze in as they crossed the threshold before he was pounded on the back by his two younger brothers and warmly greeted by an equally lengthy barrage of questions from his mother. He laughed good-naturedly at his family, all noisily greeting him in an entryway that was hardly big enough to hold them all. "I see you brought the Schaeffer chaos with you from Philly. With all the familiar noise and commotion, I'm not sure I'll have time to notice that we've moved!"

The laughter and teasing continued as he was whisked down the long hallway into the large, brightly lit kitchen. David shook his head in quiet amazement as he settled into his seat at the farmhouse table, surrounded by his large family. He never truly noticed how lonely it was to live alone until he was home. He sent up a silent prayer that God would bless him with a family so large and joy-filled of his own one day before digging into the satisfying meal prepared by his mother and sisters.

# CHAPTER SEVEN

Tuesday evening the week of Thanksgiving, Lydia walked home from the Thomas' dress shop, the box containing her gown for the Thanksgiving dance in her arms. After Zach had asked her to the dance, Lydia had taken her old blue dancing dress to Mrs. Thomas to see if it could be made over new; she'd hoped for something more elegant and mature. She and Danielle had sat, eagerly discussing all the particulars of Zach and Lydia's budding relationship, dissecting the thoughts and motivations of both the interested parties at great length, all while Mrs. Thomas went through her stash of lace and silk, thoughtfully holding up new trimmings and embellishments, taking measurements, and muttering to herself under her breath.

When Lydia had tried the dress on that morning, she had

barely recognized it. The base was still blue, but a full layer of cream-colored lace had been added over the floor-length skirt. The neckline had been changed from a high, square one befitting a teenager to a slightly more open, off-the-shoulder line. The bodice now boasted delicate rouching, and the entire effect took Lydia's breath away. Certain that such a lovely gown would attract attention, she almost felt nervous when she pictured herself wearing it on Friday.

Micah and Callie were expected to arrive the next evening, and the Kleins were hosting Danielle, John, and Mrs. Thomas for Thanksgiving dinner in addition to Zach. As she passed the press office on her way to the bridge, her mind preoccupied with menus and cooking schedules, she thought she heard footsteps on the stone steps leading up to the office behind her. Turning around revealed a young man knocking and peering through the window. Lydia started back toward him, shifting the large box that completely occupied both her hands as she did so.

"Excuse me," she called. "No one is in. The office is closed until Monday for Thanksgiving."

He turned, and she realized, to her surprise, that she had never seen him before—a rare occurrence in New Augsburg. "I manage the press," she continued. "May I help you with something?"

"Oh, sorry," the stranger said in momentary confusion, abandoning his position at the door and coming back down the stairs. He was dressed in blue jeans and a knee-length trench coat, a red plaid scarf was wrapped around his neck, but his head and ears were uncovered, their redness revealing the cold of the evening. He was not dressed for the northern climate. "I did have some questions about personal reprints of classical theology works, but I hate to bother you if the office is closed." He seemed to do a double take as she approached.

"I'm Lydia," she offered. "Do you think you could come back Monday morning?"

"Actually, I'll be gone by then," he said. "I'm just in town visiting my family for the holiday; then I return to grad school."

Lydia nodded. "Well, would you like to come inside now? Or, if you have a list of what you want, I can look into it on Monday and reach out to you."

He was staring at her intently and did not reply immediately. She shifted her box uncomfortably, unsure what to do in response to his steady gaze. She tried something else: "You said your family lives here, but I don't think we've met before."

The stranger started and looked a bit embarrassed. "Right, I'm sorry. Yes, they just moved here, but this is my first visit to town. I'm David Schaeffer. My family now owns the farm up by Seventh Street." He extended his hand instinctively, but his eyes landed on Lydia's box, and he pulled back, compensating for the awkwardness with a smile.

"Ah, yes! I've met your sister, Elizabeth, at the library coffee shop, and I brought your family dinner on Sunday,"

Lydia replied. "Where do you attend school?"

"I'm a seminary student," David said, followed by a look of concern. "I don't want to keep you here in the cold. I can return with a note listing what I'm looking for and my contact info and leave it in the mailbox."

Lydia agreed that this would work and promised to respond to him as soon as possible within the next week. They shared the usual polite exchanges before parting ways. She walked toward the river, struck by the realization that this David she had just met was quite handsome. She didn't think he was objectively more attractive than most other men, but there was something in his expression that made her not want to look away. In their brief exchange, she had struggled to know what to say next, yet the content of their interaction had been straightforward and ordinary. And there had been that moment when he held her gaze and appeared to have lost his own train of thought. . . . She laughed to herself, facetiously thinking: *Perhaps that is the "spark" Micah speaks of.*

As she went about her day, making cooking checklists and schedules, ordering groceries, and cleaning her guest room, she found herself thinking more often about this David than about Zach. The realization annoyed her, and she redirected her thoughts to the somewhat stressful reality that she was going to meet Micah's girlfriend on the same occasion that he would observe her and Zach as a couple for the first time. She distracted herself from replaying her brief interaction with David Schaeffer by mentally rehearsing worst-case scenarios for Thanksgiving dinner and making lists of conversation topics that should be safe for general consumption.

David watched Lydia go, balancing her oversized box in both arms and stepping around patches of ice and snow as she worked her way down the hill toward the river. He admired the fur-lined boots she wore that came up almost to her knees where they met her thick, full-length coat. Rubbing his hands together and blowing on them, he wondered how quickly rush shipping could secure him a comparable set of winterwear up here in the Northwoods. He would have to ask Elizabeth.

Several seconds passed before he realized he was still standing outside Klein Press, watching Miss Klein walk away. No longer merely admiring her winterwear, he now caught himself staring at the way her reddish-blonde hair emerged from under her grey, hand-knit wool headband cascading down her back in perfect waves, and bouncing ever so slightly as she walked. He shook his head as if to shake out the image of her face with those piercing blue eyes and cheeks pink from the cold. He had not expected the manager of Klein Press to be so. . . *distracting*.

He stuffed his cold hands into his pockets and cut diagonally through the park on his way to the grammar school. Mother had asked him to walk his sisters home from their Latin class, which let out in a few minutes.

The school building struck him at once as rather odd. It had four Grecian columns with the words "Verbum Domini Manet in Aeternum" inscribed above them. The architecture was simple but classical, and it would not have appeared odd but for the fact that not a single other building in the town was constructed in the same style.

Passing under the columns, David opened the door and entered. He found himself in a large, open foyer. Pillars lined the walls, and Luther's rose was engraved in the center of the stone floor. While the design of the space was rather grand, the scale was not overwhelming, and around the room's perimeter tables, chairs, small couches, and cushions were clustered sporadically. There were about a dozen children of various ages spread throughout the room reading and working on homework, and two women who appeared to be the mothers of some of the children present looked up as he entered and smiled at him curiously.

Approaching the nearer woman, David inquired, "I'm picking my sisters up from Latin class?"

"Oh, you must be the seminarian! David, isn't it? Allison and Marta talk about their family so much. For being the new kids in town, they don't seem shy at all, do they?"

"No, shy is a word I've never heard used to describe them." David smiled and followed her as she motioned him to the end of the room.

"I'm Mara, by the way," she offered as she gestured toward the closed door between two of the pillars. David could see and faintly hear through the glass panel a semicircle of six students performing declensions and conjugations while a teenage girl who could not have been more than sixteen stood in the center of the room leading the recitation.

"They'll be done any minute," Mara explained in a quiet voice so as not to disturb a young couple working on physics problems at a table just a few feet from them.

"Would you mind?" David began with hesitation, but curiosity got the best of him. "I'm new here. How does this school work? Do all the kids in town attend here?"

"This doesn't seem like enough, right?" The mother had anticipated his question, and he nodded. "We emphasize classical education in New Augsburg, but our highest value is on parental choice. This building is more like a hub or resource center. There are multiple curriculum options for each age range, and parents can either check them out for a year and use them at home, or they can network together and hold classes here throughout the week. Most students are doing some kind of hybrid between homeschooling and taking courses. Our pastor is kind enough to teach theology classes here in the evenings twice a week—one for the pre-confirmation kids and one for the older students. Parents and any residents are welcome to join. And if, at any time, the school doesn't have a resource that a family is looking for to teach a subject, we usually try to get a copy of it."

David nodded, studying the space anew, noticing the floor-to-ceiling bookshelves that lined the wall opposite the entrance, generously stocked with reference works, classic literature, and theology texts.

Mara observed his gaze and pointed to another side door opposite the Latin classroom. "We have our complete curriculum library in there. These are just the most commonly accessed books. And then, of course, there's the regular library, which is also well maintained."

Just then, the door opened, and Allison and Marta rushed upon them along with the other students. David had the pleasure of listening to them jubilantly talking over each other nonstop for the duration of the four-block walk home.

# CHAPTER EIGHT

Despite Lydia's nerves, dinner with Micah and Callie on Wednesday night was a smooth and pleasant affair. She prepared lasagna, garlic bread, and salad, and Callie contributed a bottle of her favorite Pinot Noir. As they chatted comfortably over the savory meal, Lydia discovered to her delight and relief, that she liked her brother's girlfriend.

First impressions revealed that Callie was her opposite in every way. Bubbly and upbeat, Callie's easygoing extraversion made this meal the most enjoyable one Lydia had shared with her brother in years. Her dark, chocolate hair hung in long waves down her back, contrasting sharply with Micah and Lydia's honey-blond genetics. Everything about her screamed outsider, from her turquoise flared dress pants to her factory-knit magenta cabled sweater, yet she never seemed uncomfortable, and Lydia could not help but be at ease in her presence. Although it was her first time in their home, somehow, it seemed as if she had always been there. She jumped in to help without any awkwardness or asking what she should do and provided a constant flow of conversation. Within an hour or two, Lydia felt as if they were old friends.

Callie's family lived in Ohio. Her parents had both been teachers in a Christian elementary school until the state outlawed private education ten years ago. Her parents took early retirement packages while Callie was still in high school, but both spent the next two years working warehouse jobs and saving every penny for her to be able to attend college. As their only child, her parents had devoted themselves to paying tuition at the same private university that Micah attended. Micah's major was business administration and marketing, while Callie was studying the history of political science and constitutional law. She dreamed of running for office and fighting for the religious liberties of families like her own. Lydia noticed that while Micah usually avoided talk of politics and controversial subjects, when Callie spoke with passion, his eyes shone with pride. He joined in rarely but nodded enthusiastically at all her assertions.

After the dinner dishes had been addressed and the pies for the next day had been put in the oven, Lydia and Micah took Callie on a short tour of the west side of town.

They strolled along the road tracing the perimeter of the community farm, pointing out the press and mill on the north side of the town before turning back and walking to the southern end of the farm until the church and Main Street were visible across the river. Callie delighted in everything she saw. She expressed enthusiasm for the self-sufficiency and charm of New Augsburg while also commenting on how small and quaint everything was. Lydia felt that she expressed herself with all the curiosity and interest of a tourist but never as if she would consider *living* in such a place herself. It seemed that seeing New Augsburg inspired her, but toward her current course, not toward any kind of life modeled after the one Micah and Lydia had experienced within its borders.

"This kind of community is impossible in most states now," Callie commented with a spark in her eye. "I think there are only ten states where public education is not compulsory. It's honestly surprising to me that Wisconsin is one of them. Wisconsin and Indiana are the only states left in the Midwest where such a community is plausible, and I can't imagine this will go on for long if things don't change."

Lydia couldn't say she disagreed, but she did wonder how Callie could maintain her high level of energy for political discourse. They had spoken of little but national politics since she arrived. Every subject seemed to circle back to this one, and no matter how bleak Callie's prognoses were, she never appeared discouraged by them.

"There have been many times in New Augsburg's history where we thought our way of life might be threatened," Lydia agreed. "Yet, the dire outcomes never seem to come to pass. Something always comes up. I believe a new family recently moved to town precisely for the right to homeschool. They are from Pennsylvania." She realized she was thinking about David again and their brief meeting.

"Ah, yes," Callie spoke quickly. "It's a tragedy the rapid changes that have taken place in Pennsylvania over the past two years. Entire communities of Amish families who have lived there for centuries have been forced to consider moving. I think a large number of them are migrating to Montana rather than put their children in the public schools, and I don't blame them."

Talking continued on this way through the evening. Lydia excused herself to bed by nine, partly because she was exhausted from the weighty subject matter of their discourse and partly to allow Micah and Callie some time to speak alone together. Surely, they had things to process about Callie's introduction to Micah's hometown, which would be simpler to share without her.

On Thanksgiving morning, Mrs. Thomas and Danielle arrived at breakfast time to help with food prep. The conversation was light as they got to know Callie. Their questions about her upbringing, hometown, favorite Thanksgiving foods, and family traditions kept the conversation carefree. After breakfast, Micah dismissed himself to participate in the traditional annual pickup football tournament while the women all worked together to make Lydia's cooking schedule a reality.

The warmth and companionship that permeated her kitchen as they worked filled Lydia's heart with contentment even as the contrast with everyday life saddened her. This beautiful home, before always filled with loved ones, had been too empty and quiet lately. She was good at pushing away the feelings of loss in her day-to-day routines, but something about the holiday and being surrounded by laughter and friendship again made her chest feel tight.

As she stood in the corner peeling potatoes and trying to ignore her rapidly increasing heart rate, Danielle softly touched her arm. "Lydia, would you like to go for a walk? I think things are in a good place here, and it's going to be a long day. You wouldn't be missed if you took a half-hour for yourself." She paused, "Or I can come with you if you like."

Lydia could feel the tears coming. She resented them. *There is no good reason for me to cry right now,* she thought, *but that doesn't seem to matter. It's happening.* "Thanks, Danielle. I'll be right back." Grateful for her friend's thoughtfulness, she slipped out the kitchen door and started toward her favorite walking path through the woods that ran along the back of their property. Once she reached the tree line, she sank to her knees in the middle of the path and let herself weep. Twenty minutes of crying later, she felt better. Calmer, more at peace. She stood and began to walk north along the path.

It curved around the other estates and would eventually let out near the river. She could take the road back home.

As she walked, she noticed for the first time how cold she was. Despite her homemade knit sweater, the brisk November morning had caught up with her. In her haste to escape the kitchen before Mrs. Thomas and Callie observed her emotional distress, she'd neglected to take her coat.

It would be smart to turn back right away, but the mental image of what she must look like after all those tears kept her out as she worked to compose herself. She had only been walking along the path for a few moments, watching her shoes and thinking about the terrible inconvenience of grief, when she looked up and was startled to find David Schaeffer on the path approaching her, already no more than two paces away. Her eyes widened, and she almost tripped as she attempted to slow her pace. His face registered equal surprise.

"I'm sorry," he managed. "I didn't mean to startle you."

"Oh, no, I . . ." she trailed off, conscious of how red her eyes must be and how cold and disheveled she must appear.

He was obviously thinking along the same lines. With a look of sincere concern, he asked, "Are you all right? You must be freezing."

"Oh, yes." She still couldn't put together a thought. "I live back that way," she offered, pointing behind her as a feeble explanation for her appearance. Then, wondering how he came to be on a path that was usually deserted, she asked, "What are you doing here?" He looked a bit affronted, so she added quickly, "Are you lost?"

"I was looking for the football field," he said. "I must have missed a turn or overshot it somehow. I thought it was across the river from the mill, and I found this path, but . . ." He trailed off, still watching her with obvious concern.

She had started this exchange already red from cold and crying, but she could feel her face growing still redder, and found herself unable to meet his eye as she replied, "The football field is tricky to find. There is a branch off from this trail, and it's over a hill, but you passed it. I would be happy to show you."

His composure seemed to be returning, and he thanked her for her offer. "If I'm to keep you out longer, though, let me lend you my coat for the walk."

Lydia's first instinct was to refuse, but she was truly quite cold now and gratefully accepted the gesture. As she put on the warm, fleece-lined jacket, she couldn't help but notice its comforting scent. She led the way down the path, back the way David had come, until they reached a small branch off, easy to miss if one didn't know where to look. It was uphill and narrow enough that they had to walk single file through the underbrush. They walked in comfortable silence.

The noise of the football game grew more distinct as they ascended. At the top of the hill, the tree line broke, and the ground sloped down away from them to reveal a grassy plain filled with at least thirty men and boys of various ages playing a casual but spirited game of football. Lydia noticed Zach had managed to secure the coveted role of quarterback. He was currently looking out toward the end zone, marked by jackets along the base of the hill, searching for an open receiver. Just as he was about to throw, he saw her and David starting toward them and missed the pass.

Before she could be forced into a conversation that included both David and Zach, Lydia stopped and took off David's jacket. "Here you are," she said as she handed it back. "Thank you very much."

"Thank you for your help. I would never have found my way on my own," he said. He was looking at her intently, as he had the other day in town. "Lydia, right?"

"Yes," she said. "We met outside the press office yesterday." She noticed out of the corner of her eye that Zach was watching them, and she started to fidget with her hair nervously.

"It's a pleasure to meet you, Lydia. I hope you have a wonderful Thanksgiving." David seemed to sense that she was not prepared for further conversation, although she thought he might be debating whether he should say more.

"Thank you again for lending me your coat. Happy Thanksgiving." She offered him a smile and her hand and then turned and started back up the hill toward the path as quickly as possible. As she retreated back into the woods, Lydia realized she should have at least waved to Zach. He had been watching her from the bottom of the hill the whole time, and he knew she had seen him. Yet as she walked back toward home, her thoughts quickly turned from Zach to the comforting smell of David's jacket and the brief touch of his hand as they parted.

Fifteen minutes later, Lydia walked back into her kitchen to be greeted by warmth, the delicious smell of roasting turkey, and the sight of Mrs. Thomas, Danielle, and Callie gathered around a pot of coffee with slices of coffee cake. "Everything is right on schedule," Danielle reported. "And it's time for a break. Grab a cup and a slice!"

"I was just telling Callie that this coffee cake was your mother's secret recipe," said Mrs. Thomas.

Lydia took a seat. "I'm surprised that you have it," she said. "I never knew Mother to share it with anyone."

"She gave it to me last Thanksgiving and made me promise to make it for you this year," Mrs. Thomas said, reaching for Lydia's hand and giving it a squeeze.

Lydia felt that familiar catch in her throat as she smiled. "That's just like her," she managed as she helped herself to a big slice, scooping extra crumble topping from the bottom of the pan onto her plate.

"I wish I could have met her," said Callie softly. "I can tell just from being here in her home that she must have been a wonderful person."

Lydia nodded but did not speak, and the four women observed a brief moment of silence before picking up their conversation with a discussion of various coffee cake recipes, different coffee brewing methods, and listing out what still had to be done to prepare the holiday meal.

Thanksgiving dinner was a success. Micah, Zach, and John arrived on time, all of the food was delicious, and the conversation was easy and upbeat. Lydia had entertained a moment of anxiousness upon Zach's arrival, wondering if he would mention her appearance at the football field. He had looked at her curiously at their initial greeting, but she seized that moment to introduce him to Callie for the first time, and his charming, outgoing nature was at once on display as he asked her all the typical questions of first acquaintance. Lydia contemplated more than once over the course of the afternoon and evening what a blessing it was to have new people added to their gathering for the first year after her mother's death. The conversation flowed consistently, and as there was enough getting-to-know-each-other material to fill the time, it never got uncomfortably deep. Most of their relationships did not have the necessary longevity to permit too much self-divulgence.

When the gathering drew to its natural conclusion, the consensus was that it had been a wonderful dinner party and that they were all eagerly awaiting the dance the following day. After their guests departed and Callie had gone up to bed, Lydia and Micah exchanged a knowing look. They had done it. Their first holiday without either of their parents had passed, and they had survived. In a rare moment of open affection, Micah pulled Lydia in for a hug. It was too much to expect either of them to find appropriate words, but Micah managed, "Great job with the dinner, Sis. Mom would have been proud."

# CHAPTER NINE

The following afternoon, Callie emerged from Lydia's walk-in closet, enveloped in a sea of pink satin, and gratuitously twirled for her audience. Lydia applauded appreciatively and stepped behind her to tie the sash. "I feel like I've gone back in time!" Callie giggled as she ran her hands over the full A-line skirt.

"We get that a lot here," Lydia replied, expertly managing the sash and adjusting Callie's skirts. "This dress fits you perfectly. It's amazing that you and Danielle are so close in size."

"I don't know what I would have done if she hadn't brought it over this morning," Callie said as Lydia reached for her own gown and moved to take her turn in the closet. "Micah didn't say anything about needing a formal ballgown, although it would hardly have helped me if he had!"

"But I'm sure this isn't your first dance?" Lydia called from behind the door as she dressed. "Micah mentioned dances at college."

"Yes, of course. But I've never worn anything like this. This dress has about ten times the amount of fabric as the last dancing dress I wore."

Lydia blushed as her imagination constructed a dress to fit this description.

"And there's never any real dancing at a college dance," Callie went on.

Lydia came out of the closet, turning so that Callie could fasten the lacing of her dress. "What do you mean, no real dancing?"

"Surely you've seen modern dancing?"

"In the movies, I suppose. Although the movies we see here are always over fifty years old."

"Well, the state of dancing hasn't improved in the past fifty years," Callie said as she worked the curling wand through her hair.

"What do you think of New Augsburg?" Lydia asked impulsively.

Callie's look was thoughtful. "Honestly, it's not what I expected. From Micah's description, I thought it would feel . . . stifling? Controlling?" Lydia focused intently on her hairstyle and waited for Callie to continue. "It just feels like a regular town, but in a way that is completely unusual. It's as if the whole world forgot what real life is supposed to feel like, and this is the only place that remembers."

Lydia smiled. "That's not how Micah would describe it."

Callie laughed. "No, going by Micah's description, I was expecting to step into a fundie right-wing cult or some such thing."

"Yes, he's been throwing around the 'cult' label rather liberally as of late."

"But tonight, I'm just going to enjoy the fairytale!" Callie spun around the room, relishing the way her skirts moved, and Lydia joined her in a twirl.

A sharp knock on the door interrupted the girls, and Micah's voice informed them that it was time to go.

It was six o'clock when Micah, Callie, Zach, and Lydia walked across the river toward the community center. While her demeanor throughout the day had been lighthearted and carefree, now that the moment was upon them, Callie's nerves manifested themselves in constant chatter. She asked about the style of dancing, if she would be the only person there who did not know the line dances, whether there would be any currently popular music played, and whether she would stand out if she did not dance the entire evening. Lydia was kept busy reassuring her that all would be well.

"Micah is a great lead. Just follow him. He may be a bit clumsy conversationally, but on the dance floor, he knows what he's doing," Lydia teased. "Plus, not everyone dances the whole time. There will be plenty of people talking, playing cards, or enjoying refreshments at any given time if you don't want to dance."

Callie expressed her relief. "The only dances I've ever attended were school dances, and no one knows any formal dance steps anymore. I thought social dancing was a thing of the past! I never imagined I'd find myself wearing a floor-length gown and waltzing with a man in a crowded dance hall. It's like in a movie!"

"Here in New Augsburg, social dancing is a tradition," Zach stated with pride. "I'm glad resurrecting the practice was something the founders incorporated into our town's culture right from the start. Tonight, marks the ninetieth annual Thanksgiving dance if you can believe it."

Callie shook her head in wonder as they joined the cluster of other couples and families entering the community center.

Entering the hall on Zach's arm, Lydia marveled again at the distractive power of Callie's constant company and conversation over the past few days. This was by no means Lydia's first dance, but it was her first dance with a date, and she would have expected her heartrate to be elevated and her mind racing. *Not just a date, a boyfriend,* Lydia thought to herself. They were officially a couple, this was their first public appearance as such, and the whole town was here. *I should have been rehearsing this over and over again in my head,* thought Lydia. *Why don't I feel more nervous?* Music played softly, and a sign next to the band informed the group that the dancing would begin with English country dances at six-thirty.

A New Augsburg dance typically consisted of a chronological tour of historic dance styles, starting with country dances, moving to waltzes and fox trots, then ending the night with Latin dances or swing. Although the music was not loud enough to warrant it, Zach leaned in familiarly, placing his hand on Lydia's back, and whispered something about getting drinks in her ear.

Lydia noticed Danielle standing a short distance away and, moving ever so slightly to increase the distance between them, assured Zach that he would find her with her friend.

Danielle was simply glowing as Lydia approached. "I have a feeling about tonight, Lyd! I think this might be it!"

Lydia leaned in conspiratorially. "Why?" she asked. "Does John seem nervous?" Danielle and Lydia had been expecting John to propose for a few months now, and the dance would be as good a time as any.

"Oh, I don't know." Danielle waved her hands in a giddy motion as if to shoo away Lydia's pragmatism. "There's no evidence; I've just got a feeling."

Before she could reply, Danielle pointed toward the door discreetly, "Look, Lydia! Who is that with Elizabeth Schaeffer?" Standing awkwardly inside the door were David and Elizabeth. They had just entered and were looking around the room as if scanning for familiar faces.

Lydia smiled at them and waved them over, whispering to Danielle, "That's David, Elizabeth's older brother. He's in seminary, home for the holiday." Lydia prepared to introduce David to her friend, but there was no need.

As soon as they were within hearing distance, Elizabeth called out, "Danielle, Lydia! So nice to see some familiar faces here! This is my brother, David. He's the oldest and the smartest in our family and is in his fourth year at seminary right now!" David smiled with embarrassment at his sister's effusive praise.

"Actually, I've already had the pleasure of meeting Miss Klein," David said as he extended his hand to Danielle in greeting.

"Oh! Well, I don't know when that could have happened, but it is a small town. I suppose you could have run into each other anywhere!"

Lydia colored slightly as the memory of their last meeting crossed her mind.

"Good evening, Lydia," he said, turning toward her. "I hope the rest of your Thanksgiving was . . ." He struggled to finish the sentence, but his look was warm and sincere.

"Thank you. It was an idyllic holiday gathering," she replied, returning his smile and exerting herself to make acceptable small talk. "How was your first Thanksgiving in New Augsburg?"

Before he could respond, Zach burst upon the group with John in tow, calling out, "Look who I found already scouting the refreshment table!" John gestured toward himself guiltily, and the men handed Lydia and Danielle the drinks they had brought them. Without a pause, Zach went on, "Ah! The Schaeffer sibs! Welcome, welcome, to your first New Augsburg dance! You're gonna love it." Then, tempering his intensity for a moment, he said, "David, we were sure lucky you showed up for the second half of that football game yesterday. I think our team would have been done for without your catching skills."

"Oh, I doubt that very much," David said modestly. "Between the two of us, you are clearly the superior player. I would have to work hard to *not* catch your passes." Zach shook his head but looked pleased by the compliment. "If you must thank someone for victory, it would be Lydia," David suggested. "I would never have found the field without her assistance."

Instead of responding to this, Zach took Lydia's hand rather suddenly, emptied his glass, and started for the dance floor. "Well, we'll see you all out there!" he called behind him. Danielle reached out and rescued her friend's wine glass as she was whisked away, calling after them that she and John would join them shortly. But within seconds, they were beyond the hearing of their group, joining the lines forming up as the musicians played the overture to the first dance.

From her position on the floor, Lydia could see the Schaeffers still engaged in friendly conversation with John and Danielle, and she wondered at Zach's hasty departure from their cluster of friends. She did not have long to wonder, however, for between the figures and maneuverings of the dance, he clearly intended to engage her in conversation.

"I have some news, my dear, that I think you will find very exciting."

His term of endearment caused her momentary discomfort, but brushing past her unease, she asked, "What news?"

"My father brought to my attention a potential business deal this morning. I think you'll be quite interested."

"A business deal? I didn't realize there was much in the way of business maneuverings in power plant management."

"No, not for the plant," Zach corrected her, "for the press!"

"The press?" Lydia's stomach lurched, but she waited to hear what he would say next.

"You've heard of Nova Publishing?" Lydia nodded. Nova was a fairly young religious publishing company that produced a significant quantity of popular inspirational books each year. "Well," Zach went on, "my dad heard that they are looking for a new exclusive printer, and he has a contact in their company."

"Okay," Lydia said slowly. "I don't understand how that's relevant for our press."

Zach looked incredulous. The dance choreography separated them for several seconds, but not long enough for Lydia to formulate a better response. When they were together again, Zach said, "I don't get it. Obviously, I was thinking of making them a client of our press."

Lydia bristled a bit at the word *our* but decided to give him the benefit of the doubt. Perhaps he was not familiar with Nova's work. "I'm sorry, but did you know . . . ?" she searched for the words. "Nova Publishing is not a confessional publishing house. They don't uphold Scriptural inerrancy or any of our theological convictions. I'm not even sure I'd call them Christian."

"Sure, but you're reprinting classic literature. Don't tell me those authors were all *theologically aligned.*"

Lydia detected a hint of sarcasm in this last pronouncement, but his forced smile told her that he was trying his best to remain congenial. "That's very different. We don't print current popular nonfiction or fiction that goes against our values and beliefs. We're selective about which classics we reprint as well."

The dance separated them once again, and as Lydia's gaze passed the group of friends they had left, she met David's eyes. He looked away quickly as if he didn't want her to know that he had been watching her.

They came together again as Zach said, "I don't get what the problem is here. They market themselves as a Christian publisher, and they have a lot of business. A contract like that could double our profits."

Lydia looked down in confusion. Did Zach really not understand? "Zach, they accept the mainline publishing standards. They've taken the pledge. They're not a company we'd consider working with."

An uncomfortable silence hung between them as they finished the dance. Lydia avoided Zach's eye, but she could tell from his rigid dancing that he was frustrated. As the music ended and he offered his arm to escort her off the dance floor, he whispered, "Let's keep talking about this, honey. I'm sure we can work something out." While this comment was obviously meant to soothe her, it had the opposite effect, and Lydia found her frustration rising to a boiling point as they crossed the room and returned to their friends.

Danielle claimed Lydia from Zach immediately and pulled her aside. "Lydia, help me out. We are going to teach David, Elizabeth, and Callie some moves. None of them know any of the dances, of course. What do you think we should start with? Should we save the country dances for their next dance and show them the waltz so they're ready for the second hour?" Before Lydia could respond, Danielle leaned in closer and whispered conspiratorially, "How much of a done deal is this relationship with Zach, Lyd? David has been watching you pretty much the whole time you've been dancing."

"I'm sure that's not true." Lydia's cheeks warmed even as she denied her friend's assertion.

Danielle was insistent. "I mean, he hasn't been staring at you in a creepy way. He's been polite, funny . . . quite a good conversationalist, but he . . . Look, he's looking over right now." Sure enough, David was looking their way.

Lydia shook her head and moved to rejoin the group. "I think you're right that we should start with the waltz," she said, a bit louder than was necessary for the sake of the rest of the group. Then to her brother, "Micah, will you help me demonstrate?"

The next twenty minutes or so were spent teaching the newcomers enough dance moves to get by. Lydia and Micah demonstrated the waltz; then Lydia and Danielle took Callie and Elizabeth aside and talked through the women's part while Zach, Micah, and John attempted to coach David in the men's role. Lydia couldn't help but notice that David tolerated the corrections and rather boisterous coaching of his three instructors with laughter and good humor. Watching him step on his own feet and laugh at himself was a welcome distraction from her uncomfortable conversation with Zach.

"Time to pair off and give it a try!" Danielle moved through the group, making matches as she spoke. "Okay, Micah and Callie, John, you dance with Elizabeth, and Lydia, dance with David." She grabbed Zach's hand. "Zach, you and I will show them how it's done, and they can try to copy our moves."

"Let's do it," Zach took the lead. "You all only dream of looking this good!" He proceeded to lead Danielle through a much more advanced series of steps than those they had been practicing. The other couples watched, laughed, and applauded before making their own more elementary attempts.

David smiled at Lydia. "I guess you're helping me acclimate to this town for the second time this week."

"The third, if you count our run-in at the press office." Lydia couldn't help but smile back. He took her hand. "Like this," Lydia said, repositioning his left hand to be underneath her right. She tried not to be distracted by the way her hand felt in his.

"Is this right?" he asked, placing his hand on her back. She slid it up a bit until it was in the correct position.

"Right there," she said. "And remember, hold your frame."

His first step was with the wrong foot; it caught in her skirt, and they both nearly toppled to the ground. He somehow managed to keep her from falling, and they righted themselves, laughing nervously. "Okay, let's try this again," he said.

The next attempt went much more smoothly. Lydia thought he was catching on quite fast, even as he expressed the opposite opinion. "It will be easier with the right music," she reassured him. The main dance floor was still dedicated to country dances.

Before long, they all agreed that they had the steps down as well as was necessary at this point, and the group moved toward the refreshment tables. Lydia wanted to have a conversation with Danielle (topics would include the exchange with Zach on the dance floor, and details of her run ins with David), but before Lydia could reach her, John whisked Danielle away out a side door.

"Wonder where they're going," Zach said, winking suggestively. Lydia pretended not to notice his comment, but she was also envisioning the alluded-to proposal. Elizabeth and Callie were hitting it off, exchanging observations about life in New Augsburg compared to the lives they had lived elsewhere. Micah was in a particularly good mood and never strayed from Callie's side. David was charming and funny, and Zach seemed determined to outdo everyone else in vivacity and merriment. He did not broach the topic of the press with Lydia again, but he did coax her away for a few more dances before the music switched to a waltz.

At that moment, Danielle and John reappeared, and Lydia knew immediately from the glow on her friend's face what had happened. She hurried to her side to exclaim over the ring and offer congratulations.

"It was John's grandmother's ring!" Danielle gushed, grinning from ear to ear and rotating her hand so the modest but delicately cut princess diamond caught the light.

After a few breathless moments of celebration and a toast, John took Danielle to the dance floor for a waltz. Micah and Callie followed them out, and Elizabeth, with a tilt of her head and a flutter of eyelashes, asked Zach if he would help her practice her steps. He gallantly agreed, leaving Lydia and David alone.

"Care to see if your teaching is any good?" David asked, offering his hand.

Lydia had no desire to refuse him, but her stomach performed flips as they made their way to the dance floor. When she thought back to this dance later, Lydia could never remember any of what had been said between them. It had all been lighthearted and inconsequential, but there had been laughter, his jokes were sincerely funny, and his self-deprecating charm had put her completely at ease. Her feet had been trampled on more than once but laughing at their mishaps only served to make the dancing more enjoyable. His eyes particularly captivated her. They were a soft brown, but with flecks of gold in them. When he smiled, they sparkled, and it seemed to her that she had never noticed anyone's eyes that way before. At the end of the dance, Lydia was startled when Zach and Elizabeth materialized beside them.

"Switch it up for the next one?" Zach asked as the music changed.

Lydia obligingly accepted his hand and noticed with pleasure as the next dance began that David was dancing with his sister, and they both appeared to enjoy each other's company. Too late, she realized she had not been listening to what Zach was saying and had to ask him to repeat himself.

"It seems that you and David were enjoying each other's company," he said, clearly irritated with her for not having heard him the first time, and for once, he made no efforts to mask his frustration.

"Yes," Lydia replied honestly. "He's quite the gentlemen." His jealous look told her that further justification would be necessary, so she continued, "He stepped on my feet a few times and joked to lighten the mood. I didn't want him to feel bad."

Zach said nothing for a moment. Lydia watched him, trying to discern what he was thinking. It seemed that he was waging an inner debate as they moved skillfully around the room. Of her two partners, Zach was certainly the more experienced dancer. He kept to the outside of the floor, dancing faster than most of the other couples. Lydia loved a good waltz and found the way her newly styled dress swirled around her as they spun to be quite satisfying.

Zach seemed to sense that she was enjoying his leading skills, and instead of resuming their conversation, he focused all his attention on impressing her. He managed to incorporate every possible waltz maneuver, from twinkle steps, to grapevines, to a plethora of underarm turns which showed Lydia's lace skirt to great advantage. When the music concluded, he twirled her into a lavish dip—perhaps a bit too much embellishment for a proper waltz. David and Elizabeth had stopped halfway through the song to watch them and applauded as they concluded. Zach smiled at them gallantly and bowed. Lydia curtseyed, playing along.

Before a conversation could prevent them, Zach took Lydia's hand again and started the next dance. This time, he kept his moves simple, staring deeply into Lydia's eyes. *He's made his point,* Lydia thought. *I'm to infer from his superior dancing skills that he has nothing to be jealous of from David.* Lydia decided that she would speak first this time. Hoping to reestablish their relational peace, she bravely revisited the subject of the press.

"I want to apologize if I wasn't very enthusiastic before when you brought up the press. I realize that you were only trying to help, and it was thoughtful of you to pass along your father's potential connection." He watched her intently, apparently waiting for her to go on. "I appreciate your interest and thoughts," she tried. Unsure of what else to say, she threw in her most winsome smile.

Zach gave her a forced smile in response. "Thanks, but I admit, I'm confused," he said. "I thought that we were going to try out this relationship as a real partnership. I thought you welcomed my involvement in the management of the press. Aren't we hoping that, someday soon, we'll be running it together?"

The intensity of his gaze made Lydia uncomfortable. For a moment, she thought she detected insecurity, like he felt that he needed her. *Or needed the press?* She looked down at her feet. Always a mistake, she ended up tripping over the next step. He caught her with ease, steering her back into the correct pattern. Turning the charm on as if by a switch, he smiled warmly at her. "See? I've got you. You need me around." His eyes twinkled mischievously, but all that Lydia could think was that although he was objectively charming, his eyes did not make her heart skip a beat like someone else's had that evening.

David stood on the steps of the community center, waiting for Elizabeth and watching his new friends walking away into the night. Callie hung on Micah's arm, limping along in her ridiculously high heels. Lydia and Zach trailed behind them. As Zach wrapped his arm around Lydia's waist, David felt a surge of irrational jealousy and turned away from the sight to look for his sister. He spotted her in the midst of a flock of young ladies, bidding everyone goodnight. *How does she already have so many friends?* He shook his head, extending his arm to her as she came toward him and trying to force memories of Lydia's smile and shy gaze from his mind.

# CHAPTER TEN

From the moment her eyes opened the next morning, memories of the dance flooded Lydia's thoughts. Conflicting emotions swirled together as she replayed the events of the night before, confusing her on multiple fronts. Normally such an event would warrant an extensive debrief with Danielle. Lydia ached to have a long sit-down conversation to talk through all that had transpired with Zach. For a moment, she imagined she could also use help interpreting her feelings for David, but she suppressed such reflections. *David is a lovely young man, but he doesn't live here; you won't see him again. What his eyes do when he laughs is immaterial.* With this practical counsel, she told herself that David was not something that needed to be discussed and focused all her mental energy on the conversations that had taken place between herself and Zach.

Danielle, however, was no doubt enveloped in the happy bubble of a newly engaged young woman. Surely it would be selfish and silly for Lydia to steal Danielle's moment with her own less significant relationship drama.

It was Saturday, and Micah and Callie left for college immediately after breakfast. Lydia could not endure sitting around the house alone with her thoughts, so she finished tidying up the kitchen and prepared to go into town. Perhaps she would stop in the press office and work on some new layouts, or if Danielle was home, she could hear the entire proposal story again and help her friend strategize for wedding planning. As she put on her mother's coat (which she had been wearing consistently since the day she happened to find it first in the closet), she couldn't help but dwell on her parting exchange with David from the night before. What was it he had said before they all parted ways?

*"I'm looking forward to seeing you again over Christmas break."*

She had replied with, *"I won't make you wait that long to hear back about those book reprints."*

The look he had given her had been one of inquiry, and she had noticed him briefly glancing back and forth between her and Zach before they had started for home. *Did he realize that Zach and I are together?* She couldn't help but wonder. As she walked toward town, she began again to replay conversations from the previous evening to see if their relationship status had been explicitly stated by anyone. But a moment later, she shook her head as if to clear away such thoughts. *What does it matter? I am with Zach. Why would what David knows or doesn't know change anything?*

She walked to the library first, intent on procuring a coffee before making her way over to the press office. As she entered, Elizabeth looked up from the counter and smiled widely in greeting. "Lydia! Good morning! The dance last night was the most fun! Don't you agree? I had such a great time! Thank you so much for all your help learning the waltz! Maybe before the next dance, we could get together, and you could teach me some other steps. I'd love to learn swing next." Lydia smiled. Elizabeth's enthusiasm was contagious. "Oh, I'm sorry!" Elizabeth continued. "Here I am just rambling on! What can I get for you?"

"I'll take a large latte, please. No extra flavor. And yes, that sounds fun! I'd be happy to have you over some evening to practice."

"That would be lovely!" Elizabeth beamed. "Or if you come over to my house, I can coerce my younger brothers into learning too. If they're going to live here now, they'll want to have the necessary skills!" She winked. Before Lydia could respond, Elizabeth bent forward over the counter and spoke in a lower voice: "Can I ask you a personal question?"

Too curious to say no, Lydia leaned on the counter in response and nodded in agreement.

"Are you and Zach together? Like, in a relationship? I'm sorry if that's awkward to ask!" Elizabeth turned pink as she spoke, but her eyes gleamed with curiosity.

Drawing back a bit, Lydia's first inclination was to refuse to disclose her relationship status. "Why do you want to know?" she said, trying to keep her tone light.

"If I can be completely honest?" Elizabeth's voice stayed low, as if she was afraid of being overheard, "He'd kill me right now if he knew I was asking, but I think my brother might like you."

"David?" Lydia tried to sound surprised, flattered, and indifferent all at once, but her heart was beating a bit too fast to pull it off, and her voice came out sounding higher than she would have liked.

Elizabeth nodded. "He didn't say that to me exactly, but a sister knows these things. He asked me at one point during the dance if I thought you and Zach were a couple, and I can't think of why else he would want to know that."

Lydia felt that the only way through this conversation was with honesty. "Well, yes, Zach and I have been courting for a few weeks now, but it's still a bit new."

"So, you're not serious?"

"Well, no, I think we are serious," Lydia had to admit. "It's new, but we are both taking it seriously."

"Oh! Well, okay then. I will find a way to convey that information to my brother, so he doesn't lose too much sleep over you." Elizabeth's eyes danced with fun as she spoke. She seemed to think the entire conversation rather entertaining. "Zach is ever so handsome!" she went on. "And such a good dancer! And doesn't his family own the power plant? Their estate must be . . ." she trailed off, as if realizing she was still talking out loud.

Lydia didn't know quite what to say, so she said nothing.

"Well, here you go!" Elizabeth handed over the finished latte. "We will have to get together soon for those dancing lessons!"

"I look forward to it!"

*Wow,* she thought when she was alone again, *that girl sure can talk!* Despite her forwardness, Lydia liked Elizabeth. Her transparency was both refreshing and disarming. Still, what a conversation! David had asked about her? She didn't know what to think. *I'm going to go get some work done. It will be relaxing to turn off my thoughts and just do some proofing for a few hours.*

L ydia,

It's Wednesday afternoon, and the press jammed up and won't run. I took a quick look, and I've made a list of the parts I think need replacing. We won't have time to fix this before the holiday weekend, but I'll be back on Monday to take a second look at it.

John

Lydia set the hastily scrawled note back on her desk where she had found it and glanced over the list of parts that accompanied it. Her heart sank as she scanned the list. She wasn't completely sure, but if memory served her, this could be an expensive repair. And the parts might not come in right away, meaning that their schedule would likely be affected. She took a long drink of her coffee before heading into the back room to have a look for herself.

Half an hour later, she crawled out from the belly of the offset printing machine, wiping her hands clean on the hastily donned oversized apron. John's diagnosis was accurate. Several of the rollers had finally come loose from the frame, and she could see the deterioration of the metal pieces. This printing machine was over one hundred years old. Generations of her family had taken painstaking care of it, even stockpiling replacement parts when the model became obsolete. Before Lydia was born, her father had purchased a digital printing press, which was more compact, efficient, and easier to maintain, especially for their smaller print runs. But since her father left, she and Micah had been unable to keep the software up to date without triggering a content review process. She had gone back to using the old faithful offset press, pouring through the relatively ancient manuals and teaching herself how to prepare the aluminum plates. But there were no replacement rollers left, and if the frame of the machine itself was starting to go. . . .

She took the list of parts John had compiled and started back toward the library—the only place in New Augsburg with an internet connection. In the communications lab she could research the cost of these replacement parts. Perhaps some of her publishing clients would have connections to software engineers or repairmen who could work on the digital press under the radar. And she'd send Micah a message, too, just in case he had any brilliant ideas. There weren't that many people around who knew the press well enough to problem-solve with her. John was probably the only person who understood the mechanisms better than she did. *Why didn't he say something yesterday?* Lydia wondered. But then she reminded herself that *obviously he was preoccupied with his proposal plans — and rightfully so!*

Back in the library, Elizabeth was gone, and Lydia's friend Maybelle had replaced her at the counter. "Hello, Maybelle," Lydia greeted her. "I'm sorry I didn't get a chance to chat with you at the dance last night. I noticed you sitting by the windows towards the end of the evening."

"Oh, no need, child!" Maybelle smiled warmly. "You looked like you were having quite a lot of fun with the other young people. I was glad to see Elizabeth and her brother drawn into your circle. And that must have been Callie with Micah!"

"Yes, it was. I'm sorry. We should have made our way over so you could have met her." Talking with Maybelle surfaced memories of past Thanksgiving dances. In past years, Maybelle Whittier and Lydia's mother had sat together, talking fast and furiously throughout the evening and watching the young couples dancing.

Maybelle appeared engrossed in similar thoughts. After a pause, she said, "I missed your mother last night."

"Me too," Lydia spoke softly as her shoulders relaxed with a feeling of instant relief. No need for further discussion: The simple acknowledgement of what they had both been thinking was healing.

With a maternal tone but with a hint of fun in her eye, Maybelle said, "I spent the evening wondering which of your two suitors your mother would have been rooting for."

"Zach and I have been . . ." she trailed off, blushing and looking away.

"Well, from my observation, Zach is certainly the superior dancer, but what David lacks in dance moves, he seems to make up for in his ability to make you smile."

Lydia said nothing. She did not know what to say.

Maybelle, ever perceptive, adjusted her approach. "Zach is a perfect gentleman, is he not? How was your time with him at the dance?"

"We had fun," she responded with minimal hesitancy. "As you said, he is an excellent dancer. And he included David and Elizabeth in our group, which was chivalrous." Feeling that this was not effusive enough praise for a man she was supposed to be in a relationship with, she added, "I always have a great time with Zach."

If Maybelle was unconvinced, she kept it to herself. "I've always thought that Zach was a charming lad," she said, "and you two make a lovely pair together. He's not the only one whose dancing is a delight to watch! But, between the two of us, my dear, you might want to consider David. It looked like you two were really . . ." She seemed to have trouble selecting a word. ". . . connecting."

Lydia smiled and nodded. "Well, I'm having some trouble with the press," she said, changing the subject. "I'm here to use the communications lab to do some research on replacement parts."

"Oh, I'm sorry to hear that!" Maybelle said. "Let me know if you need anything."

Lydia made her way to the Comm Lab in the back of the library, setting up her tablet at one of the internet stations to complete her research task. Hours later, tired, hungry, and discouraged, Lydia headed home. Her findings were not good. There was a chance she could buy replacement parts secondhand and have them shipped, but to do so would cost tens of thousands of dollars, take a month or more, and there would be no guarantee that the parts would work upon arrival. No one was making the necessary pieces for such an old press anymore. She had spent the rest of her time looking into the possibility of getting the digital press back online and found that equally mystifying but for different reasons. The software updates were all from mainstream companies that would want to send out a technician: obviously a "no." With a sense of dread, she acknowledged that this problem was fast rising to the level of something that she might have to bring before the town council.

What had Zach said to her at the dance? That he wanted their relationship to be a partnership, and he hoped she would let him help her with the press. Too tired to seek out his company, Lydia promised herself that she would talk to Zach about the press tomorrow. In the meantime, her refrigerator was stuffed with Thanksgiving leftovers, and her couch and novel were waiting for her.

# CHAPTER ELEVEN

Lydia gave a resigned sigh and pushed the covers back. The night had passed, but sleep had proved elusive. Even now, with the cold winter sunlight angling through her window, the house was too quiet and her thoughts too loud. It would not take long to dress and eat before church, and she needed to do something to take her mind off her worries. She remembered it was the first day of Advent. Reaching for her robe, she slipped her feet into her house shoes and headed for the basement. There on the shelf in the storage room sat the old box of Advent decorations. Retrieving it, she padded back up to the eat-in kitchen to open it. Gingerly she lifted out the old wreath, setting it on its usual placemat in the center of the table. This was the first year that she would be alone in the house for the Christmas season. Last year she and Mother had read through Isaiah together each evening, lighting the candles and singing their favorite Advent hymns. She tried to picture herself singing hymns at the table alone, and instinct told her it wouldn't happen. It would be both too awkward and too sad.

Reaching back into the box, Lydia unwrapped a fresh set of candles that had been stored next to the wreath and put each in their place: three blue candles, one pink candle, and a white candle in the middle. She smiled, remembering the spirited debate Micah had instigated last year over the proper liturgical color for Advent candles. Apparently, when he went away to college, he discovered that many churches used purple. This had set off an intense fact-finding mission to track down the history of the various liturgical colors. Klein family debates could be passionate at times, but she loved the way each one inevitably ended in a research session. *There's no one here to argue with this year*, she thought sadly. *I'll just have to research whatever I'm curious about on my own.* She left the Advent wreath and her lonely thoughts at the table and went upstairs to dress for church.

S itting through the Divine Service was grounding. *Mother may not be here with me this year*, Lydia thought to herself as she prepared for Communion, *but she is here in the family of God with me. The fellowship of the saints transcends time and space—when we receive Jesus' body and blood, we are united to Him and to each other.* The tears she shed through most of the service were tears of relief. *Even if my problems are waiting for me right outside those doors,* she thought, *they are temporary. I need to do a better job of trusting it all to God: the press, Zach, Micah and Callie . . . all of it.* How often in her life had she resolved to just trust God more or better? It sounded so simple, but she still found herself, as Jesus had accused Martha, "anxious and troubled about many things." *"Only one thing is necessary,"* she reminded herself as she walked out of the church to the sound of the organ playing a medley of Advent hymns.

She turned instinctively toward her favorite spot by the river but only made it a few steps before Zach's voice calling her name caused her to stop and turn. She waited for him to catch up to her.

"Hey there!" Zach spoke in his smooth, carefree manner, giving her a nonchalant smile. "We haven't spoken since the dance! How have you been?"

*That was only two days ago,* Lydia thought to herself. *I'd hardly consider it a long separation.* Choosing not to respond with the snarky thoughts running through her head, she went with, "I'm good. Well . . . actually, yesterday was frustrating."

Zach reached for her hand, interlacing his fingers with hers, and purposefully started walking along Main Street toward the river. "How about having lunch with me and telling me all about it?"

Lydia looked down at their hands joined together, then nervously glanced over her shoulder to see if anyone was watching them. She saw the Schaeffer family congregating outside the church and preparing to walk home, and to her embarrassment, met Elizabeth's eye. Elizabeth smiled widely at her and gave her a quick wave before heading in the opposite direction up the street with her little sisters in tow. Zach squeezed her hand, apparently trying to return her attention to himself.

"Yes, lunch sounds nice," Lydia responded. "Thank you."

"Let's do my place today," Zach spoke confidently. "I asked our cook to prepare something special."

"Oh, you had already planned on my acceptance?" Lydia wasn't sure if she should feel flattered and cared for or offended by his presumption.

"Well, let's be honest, you don't have much of a social life right now, do you?"

Lydia glanced up at Zach's face. It appeared that he had meant this as a joke, but the comment stung. She said nothing, quietly walking with him toward his family home, trying to decide whether or not she liked the feeling of her hand in his.

The Barrett family estate was the largest in town. It was a waterfront property with a beautiful view of the river and the woods on the opposite bank, south of the cemetery. Positioned perfectly at the widest part of the river, it was the only estate that boasted a sandy swimming area sheltered from the current. Naturally, this was hardly an attraction in November, but Lydia had been to the Barrett estate several times as a teenager. Zach's famed swim and cookout parties had been a summer highlight for the whole town ever since he'd been in high school.

Although she knew the grounds well, Lydia had never been in the house beyond the walkout rec room in their basement that overlooked the swimming area. She had to exert herself to keep from gasping as he led her up the grand front steps and through the imposingly tall double doors into the foyer. Zach watched her face as she took it all in—the double staircase, the archway underneath them open all the way through to the back of the house, revealing large, latticed windows with a river view. On either side of the entryway, doorways led to different rooms; a study on one side, a sitting room on the other. He led her through the archway under the staircases to the back of the house, which was a large open-concept space with a lavish eat-in kitchen on one side and a fireplace and seating area on the other.

Lydia crossed the room to the windows and looked down on the lawn sloping away from them toward the riverbank.

Zach watched her, satisfied with her obvious awe. "This house was already here when the founders built the town, you know. It belonged to the owners of the old mill. None of the other founding families wanted to invest their capital in its upkeep, but my great-grandparents were young, romantic, and a bit crazy, so they went for it. It took generations to get the whole thing structurally sound and fully renovated."

Lydia had heard this bit of town history before but appreciated it anew in the presence of the imposing home itself. Zach sauntered to the refrigerator, took out a pitcher of fresh lemonade, and filled two glasses that sat on the counter—the only items out of place, they had clearly been set out at an earlier point. He handed her a glass with one hand, while simultaneously moving to push a button on the wall by the stove with the other. An intercom crackled, and he said, "Abby, you there?"

"Yes, sir," replied a voice.

"Lydia and I are ready for lunch whenever it's convenient."

"It will be up momentarily, sir."

"Very good, Abby. Thank you." He winked at Lydia, gesturing toward the high-top counter and the upholstered bar stools where they could sit in the kitchen overlooking the river.

"How can she prepare lunch if we're in the kitchen?" Lydia looked around with confusion as she took the seat indicated.

"This is the family kitchen," Zach explained. "There is a commercial kitchen downstairs for staff use."

"Oh." Lydia sipped the lemonade. It was delicious. She had not realized that anyone in New Augsburg was this rich. She felt rather intimidated but also had the nagging feeling that perhaps that was the point. *No,* she reassured herself. *This is where Zach lives. It's genuine. He can't orchestrate his entire ancestry just to impress me*. Nevertheless, the date struck her as having a tone of performance.

They fell into small talk while waiting for Abby to bring up the food. Within fifteen minutes, she appeared with a tray carrying two bowls of buttermilk soup, fresh homemade dinner rolls, and Caesar salads. Lydia thanked her warmly, offering compliments on both taste and presentation. Abby nodded and smiled but said nothing and retreated down the narrow stairway to the side of the kitchen that had initially escaped Lydia's notice.

As they began their meal, Zach returned to their initial post-church conversation. "So, you said yesterday was not great. What happened?"

"I went to the office to get some work done," Lydia began, "and it turns out our main press needs repair. John left a note, but I suppose with the excitement of his proposal he forgot to mention it when we met."

"Bummer," Zach spoke quickly, with his mouth full but with a look of concern. "Will you be able to repair it?"

"Actually, it isn't just a repair. It needs several new parts. I did the research, and those parts are not being manufactured anymore. I would need to buy them secondhand, which is expensive and risky. I wouldn't want to front the money for those out of the press' budget and have them arrive unusable." Zach furrowed his brow in concentration as she spoke but kept eating. Lydia continued, "I also looked into getting our digital press up and running again, but to do that, I'd need to have some software programmers come out, and I'm concerned that might trigger a content review. Our press flies under the radar because we don't technically have a business license, but if someone comes out and sees what the operation is, they won't believe that this is a private hobby enterprise, and it could be trouble."

Zach nodded, and Lydia added with embarrassment, "I'm sorry . . . you probably know all that."

He admitted awareness of the content review concerns, but he had not known that there were two different press machines. Lydia spent a few minutes explaining the difference between digital and offset printing and telling the stories of how both presses had come to New Augsburg. Zach listened with interest, nodding his head thoughtfully as he chewed.

When she finished her explanations, he spoke confidently: "Sounds rough, but don't you worry about it anymore. I think I can help."

Lydia bristled at his apparent dismissiveness but tried to be generous in her thoughts. "What would you suggest?" she asked quietly.

"I mean, I could just buy those parts for you," Zach spoke casually, as if offering to buy his girlfriend thousands of dollars of equipment for her business was standard procedure for a one-month-old relationship. "If they end up not working out, we can cross that bridge then or just try again from a different seller."

Lydia looked at him incredulously. He met her eyes, a twinkle in his own, making no effort to hide his amusement.

He was having fun. "I . . . that would be . . . wow, Zach, I'm not sure what to say."

His expression softened into a more earnest one as he took her hand in both of his. "Lydia, we are a team—aren't we?"

She nodded automatically. How could she deny such a leading question?

"I care about you, and I want to make you happy. I know our relationship is still fresh and new to you, but you know I've had a thing for you for years now." He looked down at her hand in his, his voice cracking with emotion as he went on. "I also care about this town, and I think that together we can be the leadership around here. We're the next generation of New Augsburg—you and me. If we combine our families' assets . . . if we work together . . . if you let me help . . . " he trailed off, looking up into her eyes again.

Something in Lydia began to relent. Here he was, talking about matters of the heart in the same breath as combining financial assets again, just as he had that day at the library when she'd agreed to be his girlfriend. And yet, maybe she was the one whose notions were too romantic. Who was she to assume insincerity in him? Surely her passion for the press and the work she did there was a big part of who she was. Perhaps he was making a grand romantic gesture. She met his eyes, studying his face. He was remarkably handsome. She had never seen his sandy-brown hair out of place, and his grey eyes were quite uniquely becoming, she had to admit. Why couldn't she let him help her? What was it she felt that she needed to prove by doing everything on her own?

She took a deep breath and responded, "Thank you, Zach. You are truly generous and kind, and this town is blessed to have you care about her . . . as am I." She blushed.

Zach visibly relaxed, leaning back ever so slightly. "Please let me help you, Lyd," he pleaded, copying Micah's nickname for her. "Give me the parts specs, and I'll order them first thing tomorrow. And then, can I come by sometime this week and look over the business plan with you? I'd love to find ways we can act now to make the press more profitable. It will only help make it more secure for the future."

Lydia stiffened ever so slightly. She instinctively resisted what she perceived as an insinuation of her incompetence but reminded herself that his offer was not intended to imply any such thing. "Let's meet at the library tomorrow morning," she said, "and I will bring the list of parts. We can order them together, then you can come over to the office with me, and I can show you around."

Zach agreed, and their conversation fell back into lighter topics.

As they conversed, Lydia wondered if she had overreacted to his Nova Publishing suggestion the other night at the dance. He seemed so sincere today, and he had completely backed off that particular business proposition. Walking home a few hours later, she couldn't help but think of the effect seeing Pemberley had worked on Elizabeth's opinion of Mr. Darcy. *Perhaps I'm having my own Elizabeth Bennet moment,* she thought as she gazed back at the beautiful Barrett mansion receding in the distance. Zach had been the perfect gentleman, his interest in her was kind and sincere, and his home was breathtaking. Mostly, though, Lydia welcomed the feeling of not being alone.

The next morning, Lydia and Zach met at the library's Comm Lab promptly at nine o'clock. Settling in at one of the internet stations, Lydia produced the list of parts and navigated to the online marketplace where she had located the secondhand seller the other day. Their order was quickly completed. Shipping would take a few weeks, but Lydia felt a great deal of relief at the prospect of this particular hurdle being behind her. As they gathered their things to depart, Zach surprised her by saying, "I did some more research on Nova Publishing, and while I respect your reservations, I'm not sure they're founded. Can we reopen that conversation, *business partner?*"

Lydia's stomach lurched. "I . . . what did you find?" she managed.

"I actually reached out to them and asked some questions," he said. "They were very interested in what we offer and seemed to like the idea of working with a small press and a dedicated contact person, instead of trying to navigate one of the big-name printers or one of those careless mass-produced presses."

"You . . ." Lydia's heart was racing. "You reached out to them without talking to me? After I explicitly told you I wasn't interested in working with them?"

Zach looked at her with nothing but surprise. "Yes. I thought we were business partners. I thought you wanted to let me into your life . . . to let me help you!"

Lydia didn't know what to say. She started to weave her way through the stacks toward the door.

Zach followed her, still talking. "If you would just listen. . . . They are prepared to offer us a huge contract. Up to half of their line could be printed here as soon as January. It's a big opportunity!"

"Oh, and I suppose it's just that simple?" Lydia said through gritted teeth.

"Well, they did say they won't work with a printer that's not federally regulated, so there are some hoops we'd need to jump through there. I know that's a concern of yours, Lyd, but honestly, I feel like it could work out well. I know some of our religious materials will probably have to bear the red mark, but that's a small price to pay for long-term organizational stability. And it could actually be a sales tactic . . ."

She whirled on him, unable to hear any more. "You don't get it at all, do you? How can you live here your whole life, talk so much about caring for this town, and yet not have any concept of what our founders stood for?" She turned again and charged through the library doors.

Zach followed her, grabbing her arm outside the library, and willing her to look him in the eye. "How dare you question my loyalty!" He was practically shouting. "We cannot always think like the founders. They are gone! This town is ours now, and they had no idea what we would face in this world. We have to make our own way. Make our own decisions. I am just trying to do something good for this place . . . for these people . . . for *you*!"

Lydia looked around, realizing that they were shouting at each other in public. Hopefully, no one was watching. "Maybe we should call it a day and do the office tomorrow," she countered, pulling her arm away from him.

"No." Zach's tone was quiet again but firm. "We are not fighting. We are fine." He gave her a forced smile and offered his arm. "I'm sorry for raising my voice. We're new at this, perhaps, but I'm sure we can learn to navigate our differences of opinion with grace?" This last was intoned as a question, and Zach reached for her hand, gently wrapping it around his arm and beginning to walk.

Lydia could make no sense of her feelings and did not know how to argue with his assertion. With some confusion, she relaxed her arm into his, and they made their way toward the press office. Zach went on to speak calmly of the financial advantages of his suggestion. He spoke of the long-term sustainability concerns he had for both the press and the town as a whole and expressed both unease and urgency in a way that was eloquent and difficult for Lydia to argue against. It was clear to her that he had put a great deal of thought into this, more perhaps than she had initially realized. And yet she couldn't help but feel certain that his philosophy was antithetical to the founders' vision for the town and her family's legacy at the press.

As they entered the office, Lydia reached for mail in the inbox out of habit. Glancing down, she saw a single sheet of paper folded in half. On the back half was written:

*Thanks, Lydia! It was nice to meet you this week.*
*~ David S.*

She knew it must be the list of books that David was looking for, but instinctively she set it underneath the other messages and returned her focus to Zach.

"In summary," he was wrapping up his case, "I think it's better to put more books out into the world and create more content that can be a witness to others, even if we have to do so under the red mark. Better to have people read it than not, right? A day will come soon when this whole operation may be illegal. If that day comes, it will be shut down. If we cooperate, play by the rules, we live to fight another day."

Lydia studied him. He had finished his argument and stood confidently. *As if waiting for applause,* she thought. She focused on responding in as calm a manner as possible: "I hear what you are saying, and I understand you are concerned for the future and want to position us well to weather whatever comes, but I feel this is a complete departure from generations of how this town and press have operated. I cannot agree to such a radical rethinking of our mission between now and January. That's impossible for me to contemplate." She hoped that her words would strike him as reasonable and put off any further attempts to convince her, at least for the moment.

Zach looked a bit deflated but managed to shrug off her reply without argument. With the seemingly forced enthusiasm that Lydia was coming to expect from him, he changed the subject and asked for a tour. They spent the next hour exploring the entire operation. Lydia showed Zach how the equipment worked, the room where she did layout and proofing, the warehouse space where inventory was stored, the business office with its file cabinets of records and computing station, and the modest on-site library, where sample copies of all the books they had printed recently were displayed neatly and accessibly.

After the tour, Zach invited her to have lunch with him, but Lydia declined. As her excuse, she explained that she had not spoken with Danielle since her engagement, and she was sure there was much to discuss and plan. Zach made no objection to her refusal, and they parted ways.

As he exited, Lydia reached immediately for her stack of mail, leafing through to the note from David and glancing over the list of titles he had given. The list consisted of mostly early church fathers. All of these works would have been available through the seminary's digital repository, and there were probably hard copies in their library, but getting personal physical copies had become more challenging lately. Ancient Christian writings had been all but pulled from mainstream retailers, and there wasn't a big enough market to make them profitable to reprint on any kind of scale. Lydia cross-referenced David's list with her digital files, pleased to discover she had access to the proofs of everything he wanted. She could have these printed on her regular printer and spiral bound for him by the time he returned for Christmas break. Typically, she would message customers from the library, but for some reason, she found herself reaching for the office phone and entering the contact code he had provided.

She was equal parts relieved and disappointed when he did not answer, but she left a succinct message letting him know that the works he had requested would be printed and ready for pickup by mid-December when he returned for Christmas break.

# CHAPTER TWELVE

Lydia spent the afternoon with Danielle, talking about all things bridal and marriage related. She kept waiting for an opportunity to discuss Zach and his ideas about the press, but no natural opening presented itself. Danielle was in euphoric wedding-planning mode. A few times, she referenced Lydia and Zach's relationship, hinting that perhaps their wedding planning would be shortly underway as well, but Lydia never managed to segue such hopeful comments into a deeper discussion of her fears and concerns. The afternoon passed without any serious conversation about Lydia's life.

*That's okay. This is a big moment for Danielle. I shouldn't make it all about me.*

Danielle and John had set their wedding date for New Year's Day, conveniently a Saturday this year. It would be a short engagement, but Danielle and John had been together for three years, and weddings in New Augsburg were all the same and came together very quickly. Mrs. Thomas had been not-so-secretly working on her daughter's wedding dress for months, and it would take only a few afternoons to do final fittings and finish the project. Flowers had been ordered from the florist in the next town over, and Main Street Café was enlisted to supply the catering.

"The church will already be decorated for Christmas." Danielle spoke with enthusiasm. "I can't believe we will be married so soon!" Catching herself, she laughed and said, "I mean, *I know* that was my plan, but still! It's finally happening!"

Lydia's own excitement for her friend provided some level of distraction but not enough. She tried to picture herself being equally thrilled to plan a wedding with Zach, but it was hard to conceptualize. *I've always been the overthinker,* she mused. *If only I could hold things as loosely as Danielle. If only I could be as carefree and joyful as she is.* Ruminating on her friend's exceptional qualities, Lydia started for home.

The next few weeks, Lydia kept busy with office work while waiting for the new press parts to come in. She spent her time preparing the custom books for David as well as an assortment of other custom reprint orders from community members. A rush of such orders always came in preparation for Christmas. With no presses to operate, Lydia gave John extra time off, which he gratefully utilized to spruce up his apartment and prepare for the wedding.

Zach and Lydia continued to spend time together, all the time maintaining the charade of a peaceful relationship. Zach behaved as the perfect gentleman. He was thoughtful, punctual, took the initiative in planning dates, and seemed genuinely interested in continuing to build their relationship. He began sitting with her in church and issued an open invitation for her to join his family for meals. When the first snow fell, there he was outside her house shoveling her walk before she was even dressed.

Even as Lydia grew used to Zach's company—at times, she genuinely looked forward to seeing him—she could not help the nagging feeling that something was off. She kept going over the chain of events in her mind, remembering when he said he'd reached out to Nova and conversed with them. Between the Friday of the dance and the Sunday afternoon when he'd revisited the topic, no office would have been open for him to contact. Lydia felt sure that he must have reached out to them before mentioning the idea to her. She thought about confronting him and asking him about it directly—in fact, she rehearsed this conversation many times in her head—but as it never went well in her mind, she was unable to find the courage to try it in real life.

Lydia expected both the new parts for her press and her brother Micah to arrive in town by the eighteenth, but on both counts, she was disappointed. The parts arrived on Wednesday, the week before Christmas, and Zach came over to help John with the installation. When the rollers were unboxed, Lydia was dismayed to see that they did not look any newer than the old ones they had removed. "Of course, they must be about the same age, because no one makes rollers for this press anymore," John spoke hopefully. "Let's see how they work."

But after hours spent installing the new parts and cleaning the machine, the press still would not run. With an exasperated sigh, Lydia slammed down the instruction manual and marched back into her office. Just as she sank into her seat, the phone rang. It was Micah calling to tell her that he would be spending Christmas with Callie's family.

"This is our first Christmas without Mother, Micah," Lydia said softly. She did not want to appear needy or to complain, but her heart sank when he delivered the news.

"I know, Lyd. I'm sorry. I am coming home, though. I didn't want to miss John and Danielle's wedding. Callie and I will be there by the twenty-ninth and can stay until the second. Can we do a second Christmas together when I'm in town?"

Lydia agreed. It was reasonable, she told herself. They would want to visit both Callie's family and Micah's, and the wedding meant that this was the most logical arrangement. "I'll miss you," she said, rallying to sound as upbeat as possible, "but we will have a great Christmas together when you do arrive." When she hung up the phone, she looked up to see Zach in the doorway, watching her.

"Want to come to my house for Christmas?" he offered, smiling sympathetically.

"Sure." Lydia attempted to return his smile. *This Christmas will be nothing like Christmas,* she thought, mentally running through all the family traditions that she would miss. She knew from experience that her sadness wasn't about traditions, though. It was about her mother's absence. Zach came in and sat down in the chair that faced her desk.

"So, those parts are worthless," he said without preface. "And I'm not going to be able to return them and get the money back."

Lydia nodded. She had realized this already. "We're not going to be able to fill our orders for January. When we don't meet those orders, we won't get paid for them. We could have to shut down within a month or so."

Zach nodded in agreement. "I think we should work on getting the digital press back up and running," he said. "I'll make a call and get a software guy out here as soon as possible."

"I don't know if we have the budget for that," Lydia said. Budget was not her biggest concern with the idea of bringing in an outside software company, but she didn't want to start a fight.

"I have some ideas about that," said Zach.

"You can't just give me money all the time, Zach," Lydia said tiredly, with a wry smile.

He grinned in return. "Of course not. We need a realistic business model and an investor—an influx of cash." Zach must have observed Lydia's exhaustion and sadness because he did not continue to go into detail about his business plan. Instead, he offered to take her home.

"Let me help John finish packing up those parts, then I'm taking you out to dinner." He stood decisively and moved toward the office door. "I'll go over the numbers, and we can talk about everything again tomorrow morning." Lydia hesitated, but Zach insisted. "Not every problem has to be solved immediately. We've got time to sleep on it."

The next morning, Lydia hurried to arrive at the press office earlier than usual. With the press still offline and Christmas only a week away, she needed to complete all the custom Christmas orders and go through the larger outstanding orders to see if any of them could be done on the regular printer. If any were too close to the production deadline, she would have to contact the purchaser to inform them of the delay. She also wanted to go over business financials before Zach came in and have time to think of alternate plans so she would be prepared to counter anything unreasonable that he might propose.

First, she checked in with John. He was in the back of the warehouse, where, with the presses down, he finally had time to begin an intensive deep cleaning and organization that was long overdue. She then started the printer humming on some custom print jobs while she went through the outstanding orders and made a list of customers to call. Finally, she pulled up all the financial records, opened a notebook, and started running different scenarios and taking notes. Lost in thought, she did not realize how much time had passed until the bell rang, indicating that someone had entered by the front door.

Lydia looked up with surprise to find David standing before her. "Oh, it's you!" she exclaimed awkwardly, immediately wishing she could redo the moment with more composure.

David smiled. "Hey, how have you been since Thanksgiving?"

"Well, it's been an eventful few weeks," Lydia admitted. "You must be here for your books."

David nodded. "I got in late last night and was eager to start reading Saint Augustine as soon as possible." Lydia studied his face, expecting to see that he was joking, but while his eyes were playful, it was clear he was in earnest.

"*City of God* did take forever to print," Lydia said, standing and moving to the shelf where his order was waiting in a box. "And I'm sure it will take even longer to read. I was surprised you didn't request *Confessions*. It's the one I reprint most often for Augustine readers."

"I already have a copy of that one," David admitted. "My mother tracked it down for me during my high school years when I started to show an interest in theology."

Lydia placed the box of books between them. David leafed through them, commenting on how nicely they were printed and thanking her for her help. He took an envelope containing payment out of his pocket and set it on her desk discreetly.

"Are you looking forward to your first Christmas in New Augsburg?" Lydia asked to make conversation.

"I am," he replied. She expected the exchange to fizzle out, but he seemed in no hurry to go. "I will miss our old Christmas traditions in Pennsylvania, though. Our town had a big skating rink. Every year they would put up a huge tree, and my family would always skate there together on Christmas Eve after church." He looked thoughtful for a moment and then asked, "What are your favorite traditions?"

Lydia studied him for a moment. He didn't seem interested in mere small talk. She could have picked any tradition, but she found herself wanting to match his openness with her own. "I'm pretty sure this year won't be a traditional one for me either." David met her eyes and waited, so she went on. "Micah won't be home for Christmas, so I think it will be just me. I can't see myself putting up a tree or cooking any of our favorite dishes by myself."

"I didn't realize it was just you and Micah," David said. "Has it been just the two of you for a while?"

"No," Lydia answered, forcing herself to hold his gaze. "My mom died in May."

"I'm so sorry," David said with compassion in his voice. Something about the way he said it sparked Lydia's curiosity. "My mom died when I was three," he said.

*That's why,* Lydia thought. *He gets it.* "I'm sorry too," she said.

"My dad remarried a few years later, a widow with two kids. We all grew up as a happy family, but even though I can't remember any Christmases with my mother, there's something about holidays that magnifies loss, I think."

Lydia nodded and looked down, unsure of what to say next.

David's eyes brightened with an idea. "Hey, do you have a little time?"

"I suppose so. Why?"

"Let's go get a coffee, and you can tell me all about your mother and your favorite Christmas memories of her."

Lydia was shocked by his openness. She could feel her eyes moistening. "I . . . Are you sure you don't mind?" She longed to talk about her mother. She knew that people avoided mentioning her, probably because they didn't know what to say and wanted to respect Lydia's feelings, but all she wanted to do sometimes was talk about her. She felt acutely how generous David's offer was and knew she would be unable to refuse it.

David smiled and gestured toward the door. "I'd honestly love to hear them, and I'm guessing that talking about her will help."

"Well, okay," Lydia said, reaching for her coat. "But only if you promise to tell me about your mother too."

"I don't remember much," David admitted, "but my father has told me about her." They walked down the street to the library together, conversing easily the whole way. An hour later, they were still sitting in the library coffee shop, their coffee cups empty, talking about family traditions, childhood, and the strangeness of grief. Lydia was the first to notice how quickly the time had gone and move to go. Pointing out that he had left his box of new reading material behind, David accompanied her back to the office. As they walked, Lydia wondered out loud if she would find Zach waiting when they got there.

"I hope he hasn't been there waiting for me this whole time," she said, dismayed to find that she had forgotten all about their plans for the day.

"Has Zach been helping out with the press?" David asked politely. Lydia thought he was trying to appear disinterested.

"He has," she replied. "We've been having some trouble with the presses lately, and he spent all day there with me yesterday installing replacement parts which ended up not working." She explained the situation with their equipment and shared her concern that they would not be able to meet orders or stay afloat if they couldn't get the presses running again soon.

"I'm sorry to hear that," he said as she concluded her account of the past week's struggles. "The work you do printing books and Bibles for the Church is so valuable too. I hope you'll be able to figure something out. You should definitely reach out to the district if you need additional support or financing. I don't think anyone wants to see this press go under."

"You may be right," Lydia agreed. "Zach seems to think he has a business plan that will take care of everything, but I'm not sure." She stopped herself before going on. David had a way of putting her completely at ease in their conversation. It was easy to open up to him and say exactly what she was thinking, but she didn't think it would be right to speak negatively about Zach.

David said nothing for a moment, then asked, "Are you concerned about this new tax resolution making its way through Congress?" Noticing Lydia's complete confusion at his question, he elaborated, "You know, the move to increase the property and income tax rates on businesses and nonprofits that work against the interests of the people through the promotion of so-called hate speech? I forget what they're calling it . . . the Freedom from Intolerance Act or something like that?"

Lydia shook her head, internally rolling her eyes at the irony of the name. "No, I haven't, but I don't often seek out the news. What do you think it would have to do with the press?"

"I was just wondering if you were worried about the increase in taxes here at all," David explained.

"Oh, well, technically, we aren't a business. The press is owned by my family, and we don't employ anyone. The whole community is set up to avoid the oversight that comes with taxation. John works at the press, but he doesn't get paid for it. He also doesn't pay rent, though. The McKenzie family owns almost all the private residences in town, and John lives in his apartment for free. As long as you can show that you contribute to the town by working somewhere, whether that's at the mill, on the farm, at the press, or wherever, you have a place to live. I think your family bought one of the only lots of land available for private sale. Food is shared and allocated similarly. Many families do have money from the businesses they run, such as Mrs. Thomas' seamstress work, but for the most part, the five founding families own . . ."

". . . the land and the means of production?" David finished her sentence. She nodded. "So, feudalism then?" he asked, and she laughed.

"Yes, I suppose so." They had reached the press office as Lydia talked, and as they walked in, Zach emerged from the print room, wiping his hands on a towel and looking like he'd been working on the equipment for a while.

"Hey, guys," he greeted them. Lydia thought she saw a flash of jealousy cross his face. "I didn't know you were back in town, David. Where have you two been?"

Lydia looked up at David, lost for words. He smiled at Zach and looked like he was about to respond, but Zach waved his hand dismissively and went on, "I just came in early to give these parts another go, but they're just as useless today as they were yesterday." Without giving David a second glance, Zach addressed Lydia. "We should go over the business plan now, if possible. There are some things to consider that are time sensitive."

David took this as his cue to pick up his box of books. "Thank you for your time and help with these, Miss Klein," he said. "Zach," he nodded in his direction, "good to see you again."

"You too, Schaeffer." Lydia felt there was a hint of coldness in Zach's reply. But then Zach's natural charisma resurfaced: "Hope to see you at my Christmas party this Sunday! Ask Elizabeth for the info. Everyone should have gotten an invitation." David nodded to Zach and gave Lydia a somewhat longer parting look before heading out the door and down the steps to the street. Before the door had swung shut, Zach had spun on his heel and marched into her office.

Lydia followed Zach and took her usual seat. He came around to her side of the large desk and perched on the edge of it facing her. With a flourish, he flung a file folder onto her lap and crossed his arms, waiting.

"What's this?" she said automatically as she opened the folder. She glanced at the contents. The top page was on letterhead from Nova Publishing. Not wanting to read it, she closed the folder quickly and looked up at Zach, the cold look in her eyes daring him to explain.

Instead of answering her question, he countered with his own. "What were you and David doing?"

"Nothing . . . getting coffee. We were having a conversation," Lydia's voice sounded defensive, even to her, but she wasn't sure how else to respond.

"It kind of looked like you were on a date," Zach said. His voice had an edge to it that made her uncomfortable.

"No, Zach, we weren't on a date," Lydia replied stoically, setting the offensive file on the desk and pushing it away from her. "We were just talking." Zach waited, studying her face and obviously expecting further explanation. She admitted to herself that he probably deserved one, so she said quietly, "David has also lost a mother. He asked me if I'd like the chance to talk about her. This is the first Christmas . . ." she trailed off.

Zach visibly relaxed, leaning in and placing a hand on her shoulder. "I'm sorry, Lydia. I should have been the one to ask you that. I'm glad you had someone to talk to."

Lydia nodded, expecting him to ask her more about her mother or how she was handling the holiday season, but instead, he sat up straight, redirecting his attention to the folder. "This is the business deal I managed to secure with Nova. It's a good deal. Normally, this would probably need to be presented to the town council, but I've already talked to my dad about it, and he doesn't anticipate any issues. I want you to look it over, let me know if you have any questions or concerns, and if all is in order, we can have Micah sign it when he's here for New Year's."

Lydia was stunned. She felt her stomach tightening into knots as he spoke. "I . . . Zach . . . We did not talk about this," she managed. "I did not agree to this." She waited for him to respond, but he didn't. He continued watching her in a way that looked both patronizing and teasing. After a few more seconds of silent waiting, she exploded. "This is my press!" she almost shouted, rising from her desk and pacing in the space between the desk chair and the bookshelves that lined the back wall of the room. "You do not own this press. We are not married! You do not have any authority to converse with publishers, broker deals, or talk to members of the town council about any of this! I've spent every day working here for as long as I can remember. You just started helping me out in the past month! Who . . . who do you think you are?"

She stopped to catch her breath and, to her dismay, saw that Zach was smiling at her. His eyes were laughing even. He stood up and crossed the room to where she stood with her back to the window.

Reaching down, he twirled a lock of hair that had escaped from her French braid around his finger and spoke softly, "Man, you're irresistible when you're mad." She looked at him with confusion, a bit flustered by his proximity. "You're right," he said. "We're not married." Dropping his voice even lower, he all but whispered in her ear, "I think maybe we should be."

"Zach!" Lydia felt her anger being replaced by equal parts confusion, frustration, and embarrassment. It was infuriating how he could pivot the conversation so swiftly.

He stepped back, considering her for a moment before relaxing and saying repentantly, "Don't worry, dearest, I'm not proposing to you today. And I won't put you on the spot about the Nova deal, either. I know this is your domain and your family's legacy. I think you know that I'm becoming more and more smitten with you each day. I genuinely desire nothing but to be helpful to you."

Lydia continued to eye him with suspicion. Zach went on, "Just think about it, Lyd. Take the file home, read it over, and if you hate it we'll start from scratch. I don't want to do anything to jeopardize what we're building here together by losing your trust." He reached for her hands, lifted them both to his lips, then picked up the file and handed it to her. "Don't be mad at me, Lyd. I love you."

Lydia was speechless. Zach gave her a final, teasingly gallant bow and left without another word. Looking down at the file in her hands, she robotically reached for her bag and placed it inside. Then, forgetting that it was mid-morning on a workday, she locked up and left the office.

# CHAPTER THIRTEEN

Not wanting to run into Zach, Lydia turned east, walking away from the river. Her thoughts were racing, and she knew her typical fifteen-minute walk home would be insufficient to process the conversations that had already happened that day. The contrast between her emotional state after an hour with David versus an hour with Zach was not lost on her. She could not help but compare them in her mind, remembering David's thoughtfulness and genuine care for her feelings juxtaposed against the fury she felt at Zach's narrow-minded interference.

Zach's response to her outburst had left her feeling doubtful of her own perceptions. *Did he say he loved me?* She had been so incensed by his meddling, but what if he was sincere, and his only motivation had been to help her?

Maybe he knew that she was struggling with the holiday season and had chosen to act without consulting her in an attempt to take work-related pressures off her plate. She had never been in a relationship before. She'd never had anyone look at her the way Zach looked at her. If she was honest with herself, it was deeply flattering. It boosted her self-esteem in a way that nothing else ever had. She had always had this secret, nagging fear that she might be unlovable, unable to attract a husband. Zach's attentions made her feel safe, in a way. And yet . . . she had imagined love as being . . . *more fun?* She was thankful Zach had left so swiftly after his declaration, making a response from her unnecessary.

Looking up, Lydia realized she had walked almost to the edge of town. The Schaeffer farm was to her left, and as she took in the view of the fields, barren and dusted with light snow, she noticed David and his two little sisters out cleaning the chicken coop that sat across the field from her. From such a distance, she could not hear what they were saying, but they clearly enjoyed each other's company. David appeared to be making a joke, then, dropping his bucket, he chased the girls around the coop as they laughed with glee. *I wish it was David.* The inescapable clarity of her own feeling took her by surprise. David looked in her direction, and for a moment, she thought he saw her. Quickly, before she could be sure whether or not she'd been spotted, she turned and walked purposefully back toward town.

The next day was Friday, and Lydia reluctantly went in to work to finish up the previous day's abandoned printing projects. Zach did not make an appearance, and she did not find the courage to open the Nova file and review the contract. Instead, she filled her day with other tasks and convinced herself that she had not had time. When she got home in the evening, a bouquet of deep pink roses sat on her porch in a vase with a note attached.

> *My dearest Lydia,*
> *Please accept this gift as a token of my sincere*
> *apology for upsetting you yesterday. I did*
> *not mean to blindside you or make you feel*
> *unappreciated. You are everything I've ever*
> *wanted, and I hope you'll forgive me.*
> *Yours, Z. B.*

She took the flowers into the house and closed the door.

Saturday was devoted to wedding preparation. Without discussion, both girls knew that Lydia would be Danielle's maid of honor. Mrs. Thomas had found a bridesmaid dress in a donation bin a year ago and set it aside, thinking it looked exactly like Danielle's style. It was navy blue chiffon, hanging straight down but with volume in the skirt that would swish and twirl nicely. It had an off-the-shoulder neckline and short sleeves. Lydia sat with her friend, stitching an ivory lace belt onto this gown to tie it in with Danielle's dress. The girls sipped sparkling water (to avoid the risk of stains) and worked away at their respective dresses. Lydia's update on the equipment struggles at the press had been succinct. She then listened and responded appropriately as Danielle shared all her thoughts, dreams, and wedding-related plans. But after a long, unbroken discourse on her designs for John's apartment, she took notice of Lydia's unusual quietness.

"You seem a bit off today, Lydia. What has been going on with you this week?" Danielle asked.

Lydia hadn't realized she'd been tensing, but she felt her shoulders relax at the opening that Danielle's question presented. Unsure where to start, she sighed and asked, "What do you think of Zach?"

Danielle smiled slyly. "I think the more important question is, what do *you* think of Zach, Lydia."

Lydia kept her eyes focused on her sewing. "Yes . . . but it would be nice to have your opinion. I feel confused about him, and I'd value some objectivity." Danielle nodded, and Lydia went on: "Yesterday, he said he loved me."

"He what?" Danielle lowered her sewing, looking up at Lydia eagerly.

"Yes, he did!" Lydia affirmed. "But it was right after he ambushed me with this business contract for the press that he had pursued on his own without my knowledge. I was angry and yelled at him, and then he basically told me that I was adorable and he was in love with me."

Danielle's eyes sparkled with delight over the juiciness of this disclosure. "Well, are you still angry with him, or did his profession of love win you over?"

Lydia shook her head slowly. "I don't know. I haven't even read the contract yet, so I suppose I don't know how much of my anger was warranted. The publisher he wants to contract with is not one I want to work with. I'm afraid one of the terms might be federal regulation, which of course, we couldn't do. But I suppose I should look at the document before I speculate about it."

"But do you love him, too, Lyd?" Danielle always went straight to the point.

"I don't know," Lydia responded. "I don't think so. I haven't been in love before, but my guess is that I would know for sure if I was in love. Wouldn't I?"

Danielle shrugged. "Maybe . . . probably. What do you feel for him?"

"Well," Lydia tried to compose her thoughts. "He's handsome. He has a beautiful house. He's kind, attentive, and generous to me with his time and gifts. He likes me, which is flattering. It makes me feel more secure in this world, in a way. Like I have options. Like I'm not alone. But I don't know if that's love."

Danielle nodded with understanding. "It sounds like it could turn into love. Or maybe you know you don't love him, and you're too scared to admit it because then you're alone again."

Lydia laughed uncomfortably. "Yep, I think you nailed it. It's one of those. If only I knew which one!"

Danielle attempted to tactfully change the subject. "I ran into David and Elizabeth at the store yesterday. Did you know he was back from seminary for the holidays? I asked them if they'd be at the Barretts' party on Sunday, and Elizabeth said they were planning on it. Won't that be fun!"

"Yes," Lydia answered carefully. "I actually had a long conversation with David on Thursday." Danielle looked at her quizzically. "He came to pick up some books he'd ordered, and we talked for a while. Did you know his mother died when he was three? Mr. and Mrs. Schaeffer are both on their second marriages." Danielle expressed surprise and interest at this news. "Anyway, we talked about our mothers and family traditions."

Danielle looked like she had more to say but chose silence. A few minutes later, she said, "Elizabeth said that the bill passed both houses of Congress yesterday. The tax bill . . . what was it called?"

"Oh, David told me about it the other day," Lydia said. "That can't be good. What do you think will happen?"

Danielle shrugged. "I think we'll be okay here. It could have a trickle-down effect for the press though if the publishing houses are negatively affected." The subject naturally dropped. Neither of the girls was accustomed to conversing about national politics, and they simply did not have enough information to speculate further. Lydia enjoyed the rest of her time at the Thomas', finished her dress alterations, and started for home.

On the way back, she stopped at the press office. Mail for the press was fetched from the P.O. box in the neighboring town every Friday evening by a delivery boy. She picked up the mail parcel on the porch, unlocked the door, and stepped into her office, intending to leave the mail on her desk. A large envelope was on the top of the stack with a return address from the IRS. Feeling nervous, she opened it and scanned the contents. The cover letter began:

*To Micah Klein and Lydia Klein,*

*This letter is a formal request for additional documentation regarding your individual income taxes. There has been an indication that you may be operating a business enterprise, and to prevent an audit, you will need to submit. . .*

She didn't read any further. Stuffing the letter back into the envelope, she took it with her and started hastily for home.

# CHAPTER FOURTEEN

By the time Lydia walked into church the next morning she had read the contents of the Nova file and the IRS letter. The publisher contract was exactly what Zach had pitched to her in his plan three weeks ago over lunch. He had helpfully included copies of the forms necessary to file for federal regulatory approval, as doing so was a condition of the contract. Certain that she had already made her objections clear, it still seemed wise to give him the benefit of the doubt. She did not want to make a scene at church or the Christmas party later in the day, so she resolved to find an opportune time to discuss it with him later in the week. The thought had crossed her mind that she did not technically need to discuss it with him: She and Micah could refuse to sign the contract without any explanation necessary. But if she wanted her relationship with Zach to work out, that meant talking through these decisions together.

The IRS letter, however, scared her. She was required to submit complete financial records for the past several years within the next month, and there was no knowing what might happen when they were reviewed. *If they are not satisfied with our records, we could be audited. If the press is flagged as a business operation, we would be required to apply for a license. Not only would we be forced to file for regulatory approval, but we could owe years of back taxes.* Contemplating the worst-case scenario was too terrifying, so Lydia had set aside the letter and contracts and come to church.

Zach greeted her with a smile as she approached their pew. "You look lovely today, as always," he began. "I can't wait to see you decked out in your holiday finest and on my arm all evening as we host the grandest party of the season tonight, *together*." The last word was whispered into her ear and made her squirm with discomfort as she glanced around to see who was watching them. "Did you get a chance to look over that file?" he whispered again. The service had not yet begun, and the prelude music provided enough volume so they could speak privately.

"Yes, I went over it last night," Lydia replied. "Let's not spoil today by talking business, though. We can get into it on Monday." After a moment of hesitation, she decided to add, "I also received a letter from the IRS yesterday. I have to submit a bunch of paperwork, otherwise, Micah and I might be audited." Zach exhaled sympathetically. Before he could say anything, Lydia hastily went on, "I really don't want to talk about it now. Monday for that topic, too, if you please." She tried to make this last remark sound upbeat and light.

Zach put his arm around her shoulders, gave her a comforting squeeze, and gently kissed her hair. "I'm sure we'll be able to work all of that out. Monday it is."

Lydia felt that this display of affection in front of what essentially amounted to the whole town was not quite called for by her news, but she tried to suppress her discomfort. *What is wrong with me?* she wondered. *Why am I always so uncomfortable with the thought of people watching us? Why can't I let Zach in?*

Pastor Pedersen entered from the chancel area, motioned for the congregation to stand, and all began to sing the opening hymn, "O Come, O Come, Emmanuel." Lydia did her best to set aside her thoughts and worries and focus on her Savior and His gifts to her in the Divine Service.

The Barrett family Christmas gala had been a tradition in New Augsburg for generations, yet this year marked Lydia's first attendance. Traditionally an adults-only evening of fine dining, dancing, and live music, for the past two years, Lydia had remained home with her mother, who had not felt well enough to attend. This year would be different. Lydia tried to ignore the queasiness in her stomach as she contemplated her dress options, torn between the new dress that she had worn to the Thanksgiving dance and a lace top with her full, floor-length crimson skirt. The skirt had raised floral embroidery and swung about when she danced to reveal the ruffles of a white underskirt. It was not technically as formal as her ball gown, but it did have Christmas flair. Plus, it seemed wrong to wear the same dress to two dances in a row in one holiday season. She settled on the red skirt outfit, curled her hair and pinned it up in a loose updo, put on a scarf and her mother's coat, and started on the short walk down the street to the Barrett home.

Zach had asked her to arrive a few minutes early, and as she walked up the grand steps to the entrance, he greeted her warmly, first removing her coat and handing it off to an attendant, then taking her hand and tucking it protectively around his arm. "You look amazing tonight," he said. "I'm the luckiest guy in the whole state of Wisconsin! Come, stand with me while we greet our guests."

Lydia greeted guests for the next hour, standing with Zach on one side of the entrance while Mr. and Mrs. Barrett stood on the other. It seemed the entire town had turned out for the occasion, including John and Danielle and David and Elizabeth. When the Schaeffer family arrived (David and Elizabeth's parents were also in attendance), Elizabeth greeted both Zach and Lydia effusively. David's greeting was reserved, but when he took her hand, Lydia could not help feeling that the gesture and his look into her eyes were a fraction longer than politeness warranted. There was something irresistible about him. His eyes drew her in, and she thought for a moment that they betrayed a sense of longing. Upon withdrawing her hand, she would have convinced herself that it must be her imagination, but Zach's arm tightened possessively around her shoulders at just that moment, telling her that he had sensed something too.

After the guests had arrived, a three-course dinner was enjoyed by all. Tables and chairs had been placed throughout all the main level rooms and living spaces. As the meal concluded, drinks and light snacks were placed in the family kitchen, and staff removed the furniture from the large living area that overlooked the river. Twinkling lights glittered to life overhead, and a string quartet situated itself by the fireplace to play as the guests started to dance.

Throughout the evening, Zach kept Lydia at his side. Thoughtful and attentive, he complimented her on everything from her beauty to her wit to her fine dancing. Although constantly occupied with him and his friends, she felt that she could sense people talking about them. At one point, she overheard a couple of older women discussing "Miss Klein and young Barrett," and she wished she could know what they were saying.

After the first several dances, Zach led her to a high-top table at the side of the room. "Wait here," he whispered. "I'll be back in a few minutes," and he slipped away. Lydia stood patiently, looking out the windows at the frozen river below, framed by snow-covered trees.

"Would you like a drink?" She looked up suddenly to

find David standing before her, holding two champagne flutes.

Scanning behind him and seeing Zach nowhere, she nodded gratefully and accepted the offered glass.

David stood beside her for a moment in silence, looking out the window with her. "You look beautiful tonight," he said finally.

"Thank you," Lydia replied, surprised to find that his compliment had not ruffled her. The way he said it was not suggestive of anything; it was as if he was observing a simple fact, the same as if he had admired the view.

"This house is quite impressive," he offered as his next attempt at conversation.

"Yes," Lydia agreed. She didn't know what else to say. She thought that he looked quite handsome as well. He was wearing a dark grey suit with a gold bow tie. She would have thought it a bold choice, but it complemented the golden flecks in his deep, brown eyes and became him perfectly.

After another long pause, he said, "Elizabeth has been making me practice dancing with her. Would you do me the honor of a waltz? You can see if you think I've improved since Thanksgiving."

"I would love to," Lydia admitted honestly, sipping her champagne, "but Zach asked me to wait here for him."

At just that moment Zach reappeared, two more glasses of champagne in hand, weaving his way through the crowd to where they stood. Lydia thought he looked frustrated, but before David turned to face him Zach had put on his generous host smile. "David! Thanks for getting my girl a drink. I hope you've been enjoying the party," he said, casually setting both the glasses he'd been carrying on the table.

David smiled politely. "Yes, thank you. This is easily the finest party I have ever had the privilege of attending." Zach glowed with pride, placing his arm possessively around Lydia's waist. David was unfazed by this thinly veiled message and went on, "I was just asking Miss Klein here if I could have the pleasure of a dance, but she told me she was waiting for you. Could you spare her?" Zach was unable to refuse such a direct and courteous request, and David offered Lydia his hand and led her to the dance floor.

They danced in silence for a few moments, laughing once or twice as they tried to find their common rhythm. Overcoming the occasional missteps, they soon fell into a comfortable pattern, weaving their way around the perimeter of the room. Lydia found herself relaxing and to her surprise, realized it was the first time that evening. David startled her out of her thoughts with a question: "Are you happy here, Lydia?"

"Happy where?" She tried to think what he meant, but his eyes were distracting her again, and instead of responding intelligently, she merely stared at him, trying not to lose herself in his gaze.

"New Augsburg is new to me. It's a very unique place. I've never lived anywhere like it—well, I don't suppose I technically live here now. I guess I was just wondering what you thought of it as a life-long resident."

Lydia managed to regain her focus and consider his question. "It is home to me. I love it the way I love my parents. I suppose I don't know anything else, though." She thought about the times when she'd been jealous of Micah attending a university, experiencing new places, encountering new ideas, and granted the gift of years devoted to study. "I've always wanted the chance to broaden my experiences and knowledge of the world, but I've never seriously pictured myself living anywhere else."

David looked thoughtful. "When I graduate from seminary this spring, I could end up living anywhere."

She nodded slowly, wondering where this conversation was going. "Where would you like to go?" she asked.

David's eyes met hers with intensity, but before he had the chance to respond, the music stopped. He stepped back and bowed awkwardly as if performing a movement he'd never attempted before. Lydia smiled at him, curtseying as smoothly as she'd done all her life. The dance had concluded with them on the opposite side of the room from where they'd left Zach. Suddenly and with a quick survey of the room, David took Lydia's hand and drew her off the dance floor into the living room.

Here guests who were not dancing sat and stood about in conversation or gathered around board games. He led the way to a quiet corner and, without dropping her hand, asked, "Are you planning to marry Zach, Lydia?"

Startled, Lydia stared at him for a moment before responding. Inexplicably feeling defensive, she lifted her chin and said, "He has not asked me to marry him."

"That's not what I asked," David spoke softly, nonthreateningly, but the tone of the conversation sent Lydia's heart racing.

"I'm not sure that I can answer your question," she finally replied, standing tall and trying to exude confidence. For some reason, she did not want him to sense the conflict within her. He looked at her seriously for several seconds, and she sensed his own internal battle. He made less effort to hide his struggle than she did hers.

At the same moment they both observed Zach approaching again from across the room. Before he came within earshot, David leaned close and said, "With all due respect, Miss Klein, if you were single right now, I would be asking you out on a date. I just wanted you to have that information at your disposal." Taking a step back, he said, "Enjoy the rest of your evening" and walked away.

Lydia did not have time to process this revelation before Zach arrived at her side, claiming her hand and steering her back toward the dance floor. She had been afraid he would mention David, but he refrained from the subject entirely, and Lydia was grateful. After a few elegant, sweeping passes of skillful waltz maneuvers around the outside of the dance floor, Zach slowed their movement and gravitated toward the center, where the couples who were better described as "swaying in time with the music" danced. Pulling her close, he whispered, "I've been waiting impatiently to have you to myself all day."

"We're hardly by ourselves now," Lydia said with a laugh.

Zach smiled at her. "You truly are the most beautiful woman in all of New Augsburg. Lydia, I have been waiting for you to return my attention for years. Now, we've only been officially dating for a month, but we've known each other our whole lives. I know you might think this is impulsive or fast, but I'm ready to take this step."

Lydia's breath caught in her throat. She had not expected this to happen so soon. She felt a surge of panic but forced herself to breathe deeply and wait.

"Everything about you delights me, Lydia. Everything about our future together excites me to my core. I can't wait to lead the next generation of this town with you. I can't wait to see you as mistress of this home. I can't wait . . ." he trailed off, his voice betraying a hint of nervousness. The hand that had been on her waist reached for his pocket, and as he issued the question, "Lydia Klein, will you marry me?" he held up a glistening diamond ring, easily three times as big as the one Lydia's mother had worn.

Lydia gaped, trying to catch her breath and think as the room spun around her. "Can we get some air, Zach?" she asked after a moment.

As if he had anticipated her exact response, Zach smoothly dropped the ring back into his pocket, took her by the hand, and led her out through the French doors facing the river onto the balcony. It was a freezing evening in December, so naturally, the balcony was deserted. Zach took off his suit coat and placed it around Lydia's shoulders, then leaned against the rail with his back to the river and watched her expectantly as she stood before him, desperately trying to gather her thoughts.

"Zach, I . . ." She couldn't figure out what she wanted to say. She had assumed that she would accept his proposal when it came, but she had not expected it so soon. And then there was David and what he had told her moments before Zach's declaration. It was all too much. "Zach . . ." she tried again.

Smiling at her with amusement, Zach saved her from embarrassment. "I know, honey, I get it. I'm desperately handsome, the best thing that's ever happened to you, you're thrilled about our future, too, but it's all happening too fast, right?" There was a twinkle in his eye, and she was grateful for his sense of humor.

"Something like that, I guess," she acknowledged with a begrudging smile.

He crossed the distance between them and pulled her into a hug. "I don't want to rush you, Lydia," he spoke softly. "I know what's going on with the press right now is a lot. You've been through so much this year with losing your mom, and Micah planning to move away permanently. I know I may have moved too quickly, but I wanted you to have a sense of stability. I wanted to give you something you could count on. I wanted to help you solve all your press-related problems, but also, I wanted to be there for you. If we were married, I'd be able to help with all of those things. I'd be able to support you financially, emotionally . . . someone you could trust and fall back on." The last line he whispered in her ear, "You wouldn't be alone."

She melted a bit into his embrace, allowing him to hold her as she pondered his words. All she knew for sure in that moment was that he was right; she didn't want to be alone, and yet, she did not know if she wanted to marry him. Her thoughts were too jumbled, her gut feeling obscured.

"Zach," she said finally, "you are a good man. Thank you for caring about me and being interested in me. I am deeply honored by your proposal." He said nothing in response but reached out and touched her hair as she spoke. "I want to be honest with you, as you have been with me. My feelings and thoughts are not clear tonight. May I give you my answer later?"

"Of course," he said softly. "Take all the time you need." He kissed her on the forehead and looked for a moment as if he wanted to do more than that, but, as if sensing her desire to pull away, he let her go.

As they walked back into the house, she felt his hand reach for hers and the diamond ring press into her palm.

"Take this with you," he said softly. "When you are ready to say yes, put it on."

Once back inside, Lydia was immediately intercepted by Danielle, who pulled her to the side with a quick nod to Zach that said without words *you've had her all night, and it's my turn.* "What just happened, Lyd?" her friend asked eagerly. Danielle was nearly bouncing with excitement. With her back to the room, careful to shield the view from all eyes but Danielle's, Lydia opened up her hand to reveal the ring. Danielle gasped, started to giggle, and looked like she would begin jumping up and down.

Lydia quickly grabbed her arm and shook her head. "Shh!" she whispered frantically, slipping the ring into her pocket and trying to calm her friend. "I haven't given him an answer yet."

Danielle's eyes widened, and she immediately tried to calm herself and appear casual. Linking arms with her friend, she began to walk about the room so they could speak less conspicuously. "I don't know if this is relevant, but David was watching you. He was sitting right there by the fireplace, pretending to participate in the conversation Elizabeth was having with some of the others, but he kept looking toward you and Zach the whole time you were dancing. When you went out on the balcony, he headed to the kitchen, presumably to get another drink, but I think he was trying to see what was going on. When you and Zach embraced, he set down his drink untouched and left! I think he's gone home!"

Lydia shook her head slowly in amazement, trying to take it all in. "He told me he was interested in me," she said, a dazed expression on her face, "not five minutes before Zach proposed!"

"Oh, Lydia!" Danielle appeared to find it all very dramatic and exciting, but after seeing her friend's apparent distress, she moderated her tone to one of sympathy. "I'm sorry! That's a lot for one night. What are you going to do? Wait, do you like David, Lyd?" Danielle looked like she was genuinely trying to keep up.

"I don't know!" Lydia admitted. "Maybe I do. Zach has done so much for me, though, and . . . I just don't want to talk about this right now."

Danielle nodded, stifling about a dozen comments that threatened to burst forth, and finally settled on, "Would you like to come over and talk about it tomorrow?"

"Maybe," Lydia was hesitant. "I think I must give Zach an answer before your wedding. Waiting any longer than that seems inappropriate. And it would never do to attend a wedding together with something like this hanging between us."

"It sounds like you're leaning toward refusing him," Danielle pointed out, trying to sound neutral.

"I am not," Lydia defended herself. "Zach has been nothing but wonderful to me. He is everything I always thought I wanted. He is perfect."

"Then why didn't you accept him?" It was an obvious question.

"I don't know," Lydia answered honestly before defaulting to her preferred deflection practice of self-deprecation. "Perhaps because I like to overthink things."

# CHAPTER FIFTEEN

The next several days were a blur of paperwork as Lydia combed through all their financial records in search of the ones requested by the IRS. Upon entering the press office early Monday morning with a file box of her family's tax returns brought over from the house, she found a mid-size live Christmas tree in the narrow hall, positioned perfectly so that it could be seen from the entrance, her office, and the layout room. At some point over the weekend, John and Danielle must have snuck into the press building and decorated. She had to squeeze past it to go anywhere, but it warmed Lydia's heart. Decorating her own house was out of the question this year. The memories there were too poignant. Since the presses weren't running, she used the large table in the layout room to organize all her documents.

Her goal was to complete the paperwork before Micah and Callie came to town so that the odious task would not impinge on their family time.

The work was not immersive enough, however, to keep her mind off of all that had happened at the Barrett party. To Lydia's surprise, Zach kept his distance for the first half of the week. He'd actively sought reasons to spend time together nearly every day for the past two months, making his absence stark by contrast. But putting herself in his shoes, she could not find fault. What else is there to say to someone after you propose? Nothing remains to be said or done until an answer is given.

Danielle had invited her over on Monday, but Lydia had declined. She told herself it was because of the tax paperwork, but if she was honest, it was because she didn't know the answers to the questions Danielle would certainly ask. Not that she couldn't talk to Danielle—she knew she could tell her friend anything and find compassion and support—but she didn't want to confront her own uncertainty.

On Thursday, the day before Christmas Eve, her friends apparently grew tired of giving Lydia space. When she came out of her house to walk to work, Zach was standing there, hands in his coat pockets, waiting for her. "Good morning, beautiful," he said gallantly. "I've missed you."

"Good morning, Zach," Lydia felt nervous but also relieved to see him again. The amount of comfort she could derive from being alone with her thoughts was limited, and she had been running up against that limit. They fell in step together and walked in silence for a few minutes, enjoying the unusually warm thirty-plus degree temperature and the bright morning sunlight.

After a few moments, Zach spoke first. "I resolved to give you your space, Lydia. I wanted to respect your need for 'more time,' as you put it. I'm only disturbing you now for two reasons. First, because I know that the Nova contract proposal has an expiration date of January first, and I wanted to make sure we'd have time to make a decision on that. And second, because I am hoping you'll still come over for Christmas, and I felt I should re-extend the invitation, given the circumstances."

Lydia nodded. "I am still planning to spend Christmas with you and your family. Thank you for re-extending the invitation." She thought for a moment, then asked, "Do your parents know that you proposed?"

Zach shook his head. "No, I didn't want to tell them until I could tell them of your acceptance as well. I know they will be so overjoyed to welcome you to the family." Noticing Lydia's mixture of relief and discomfort, he went on, "Don't worry. If you haven't given me an answer by then, you are still welcome to come, and we don't have to tell them anything until you're ready. You can just be my girlfriend for Christmas if that's what you want."

Lydia said nothing. Zach's invitation struck her as both selfless and generous, prompting a fresh wave of guilt that she had not given him an answer. Determined to change the subject and already uncomfortable enough that another contentious topic could do little to worsen things, she mentioned the Nova contract. "As I told you at church on Sunday, I did read over the contract." Zach nodded, waiting. "I feel that I still have all my original reservations with the idea, Zach. I can't imagine willingly accepting federal regulation. It's true that at this point, we could still publish whatever we wanted, as long as we printed it with the mark, but what if printing our books in any way isn't legal anymore in a few years, or a decade, or even in fifty years? I feel that it's irresponsible, like asking for trouble, to invite in government regulation just for a publishing contract."

"But Lydia." Zach tried to keep his voice steady as they approached the office. "Right now, as things are, you can't afford to print anything. Without a deal, you won't be printing next month, let alone next year or in twenty years. If you accept regulation you can apply for a business license. You'd be able to open a line of credit to buy a new press. You could do whatever you wanted. It would be security."

"Security is not everything," Lydia responded slowly, but as the words left her mouth, she found herself wondering how many of the decisions she'd made in life had been made with nothing further in view than her own comfort and security. All she'd ever wanted was to live in this town, be involved in her family's business, have a husband and a family, and raise her children in a safe bubble of truth, beauty, and goodness. Zach was offering her that, and she wondered if the only reason she was struggling with the decision was because he didn't seem to share her views on the family business. Maybe she was the one who needed to let something go. Maybe she needed to trust him with her security instead of trusting herself and her own perceptions and ideas.

Lydia was lost in thought as they arrived at the press. Feeling the need to extend something to Zach in exchange for his patience and kindness, she impulsively invited him in. "I'm wrapping up the documentation I need to submit to the IRS. It's kept me completely occupied these past three days. It would be helpful to have a second set of eyes on everything before it's mailed off. I think John is working in the back today, so it won't be just the two of us."

Zach's shoulders relaxed with visible relief as he followed her inside, and they spent the morning talking about tax forms and filing systems before he excused himself to oversee a repair at the power plant.

No sooner had Zach left than Danielle burst through the door of the press office, eagerly in search of her friend.

"Lydia," Danielle spoke without preface, "you must spend Christmas Eve at our house with Mother and John and me. I saw Zach on my way over, and he said that you were still planning to spend Christmas with him. I assumed that meant that you'd accepted him, and I was about to congratulate him, but he told me no, that *you haven't answered him yet!* So, I imagine spending two days in a row with the Barrett family might be too much for you, and therefore, I think you must spend Christmas Eve with me."

Danielle concluded triumphantly, sure that there would be no objection, and there was none. Lydia was grateful both to have a place to go for Christmas Eve and not to have been asked to make a decision. She hugged her friend and accepted warmly.

Lydia started scanning paperwork for electronic submission while Danielle perched on a stool to watch. As she scanned each document, she could feel her friend's gaze boring into her back. She knew what Danielle was thinking and finally spun around. "You want me to talk about Zach, don't you?"

Danielle nodded emphatically. "Yes, I do! I want to know every thought that's run through your head these past three days. All the times we pictured getting engaged as kids, I don't think either of us imagined receiving such a romantic proposal and *not responding!*" This last exclamation came out in a high-pitched feminine squeak.

Lydia smiled ruefully and nodded. "True. I never imagined myself in this situation. I think I need to accept him. It feels like the right thing to do."

"Then, I ask you again, Lyd, *why didn't you?*"

"And as I said before, I just don't know! I'm so confused by all this!" Lydia finished scanning the last sheet and sat down on the stool beside her friend, feeling as though she might cry.

Danielle sat still, sensing the serious turn the conversation was taking. She altered her approach to match

Lydia's distress: "Have you prayed about it?"

Lydia shook her head, staring at her lap. "Not really. I mean, I think I did once in the past three days. I know I should pray more. That would probably help."

The next question came out barely louder than a whisper. "Do you think part of this is about your mother?"

At the mention of her mother, Lydia began to cry. "I hadn't thought about that," she managed in between tears, "but oh, how I wish I could talk to her about it! She would help me know what I wanted. She would tell me exactly what to do."

Danielle walked around to Lydia and rubbed her back. "Your mother was such a wise woman. What do you think she would say if she were here?"

"She'd probably tell me that marriage is an important decision. She'd tell me I should be sure. She'd also tell me to pray about it and not to make a choice out of fear, one way or the other."

"All great advice," Danielle said.

"She and Daddy didn't date. They had an arranged marriage. Do you think they were just lucky? To be happy and to love each other?"

Danielle shook her head. "I mean, maybe they were a little lucky, but I think marriage is about making a choice to love no matter what. It's about work and sacrifice as much as it's about warm feelings and companionship."

Lydia smiled through her tears, elbowing her friend playfully. "It looks like you and John have lots of the warm feelings, though. You two don't make love look like work."

Danielle laughed happily. "Perhaps it's not work right now. I mean, I *adore* John! He is the best. I don't want him out of my sight for a second! But someday, in thirty years, if I begin to grow tired of him . . ." she winked to indicate that she was speaking in fun, ". . . I'll still choose to be with him and to love him every day. That's the commitment." She looked thoughtful for a minute before adding, "But I don't think I'd commit to that if I wasn't head over heels in love with him now. Maybe that's just me."

Lydia watched her friend's gaze become distant and starry-eyed. She couldn't see herself feeling that way about Zach, and this self-awareness filled her with guilt and frustration. Wiping her tears, she stood up and finished packaging up her tax forms.

Christmas Eve was peaceful and uneventful. Zach and his parents were out of town, visiting his mother's family in the twin cities. Lydia spent the day at the Thomas home, making cookies, enjoying a traditional turkey dinner, and playing board games. The family went to church at 6:00 p.m. As the congregation filed out of the sanctuary after the service, Lydia noticed John conversing with David and Elizabeth. Danielle leaned over to her friend and whispered, "David has been helping John out this week with the apartment renovations."

John finished his conversation and returned to Danielle's side. "I've invited David and Elizabeth to come over for a few hours," he said. "They are planning on coming back for the vigil service, too, and I thought they might like to play cards and help us with our mountain of Christmas cookies in the meantime."

And so it was that Lydia found herself spending the night of Christmas Eve with David seated next to her, playing a rowdy game of cards and enjoying herself much more than she had thought possible. As she and David were never alone together, and Lydia and Danielle were the only ones who knew about Zach's proposal, the evening proceeded unmarred by awkwardness. Lydia was able to genuinely relax and enjoy the company of friends.

Christmas Day began with Zach escorting Lydia to church, followed by an elaborate Christmas dinner at the Barrett home and a gift exchange that surprised Lydia with its extravagance. Mr. & Mrs. Barrett had gone all out, lavishing both her and Zach with at least a dozen gifts each. Lydia received two bottles of wine, several boxes of fine chocolate, a few books, a new pair of leather gloves, a cashmere sweater, multiple scarves, and an ornate crystal vase. Lydia's instinct was to be embarrassed by the imbalance—she had brought Zach's parents simply a poinsettia plant and a tin of her family's signature homemade cookie bars. They were gracious hosts, however, so she tried to relax and be at ease.

After the gift exchange, Mrs. Barrett brought out cake and coffee as they sat around the fireplace. Leaning back in his armchair and surveying the group, Mr. Barrett politely asked Lydia about the situation with the press.

"I haven't heard much from you since the council meeting, Lydia," he began. "I hope all is going well. Have you and Micah spoken any further about his plans for the future?"

Lydia gripped her coffee cup a bit tighter and shook her head. "No, sir, Micah has not changed any of his plans as far as I know." She paused, unsure if Zach had told him anything about the mechanical issues they'd been facing. She was suddenly self-conscious, wondering if she should have communicated with someone on the town council already about the repair costs. She glanced at Zach, who shook his head ever so slightly, indicating that he hadn't told his parents anything. "We have been facing some challenges, actually. Our offset press needs repair, and the replacement parts that we ordered did not end up working." She did not mention the threat of an audit, deciding the repairs alone were enough bad news for casual Christmas Day conversation.

Mr. Barrett nodded sympathetically. Turning to his son, he abruptly asked, "So, Zach, are you planning to propose to Miss Klein any time soon?" Lydia nearly choked on her coffee. Zach smiled slyly, and she marveled at his uncanny ability to never appear ruffled or uncomfortable.

"I really should, shouldn't I, Dad?" he said, winking at Lydia.

Mr. Barrett smiled at Lydia approvingly. "We'd love to

have you in our family, Lydia. And I'm sure I wouldn't be the first person to point out to you the obvious advantages to the town and the press of such a match."

Lydia didn't know how to respond. She settled on a mid-sip half-nod, hoping it was a reaction that betrayed nothing.

"If that's what our future holds, then I'd be one lucky man," Zach said. He rose from his seat and retrieved one of the new board games he'd given his father for Christmas. "Let's see if I can beat you at this, Dad, before you have a chance to study the strategy, and I never win again." Lydia fully appreciated the generosity of his conversational redirection.

# CHAPTER SIXTEEN

The following Monday morning, Lydia's breakfast was interrupted by a knock at her front door. Answering it revealed the two youngest Schaeffer girls on her porch with an envelope in their hands and happy smiles on their faces. "This note is from Elizabeth," Allison, the older sister, said, handing the envelope to Lydia.

"She sent us on a very important mission!" little Marta chimed in.

Lydia smiled. "Why, thank you! Would you girls like to come in and warm up?"

"Oh no, we cannot!" Marta's eyes opened wide with self-importance.

"Our mission is not complete," Alison jumped in. "We still need to visit Miss Danielle!" She waved a second envelope in the air as evidence.

"I see. Well let me, at least, give you each a cookie for the road then." Lydia stepped quickly into the kitchen and returned with two gingerbread men, which the girls accepted with juvenile delight before bouncing away down the drive.

Lydia examined the contents of the envelope. It contained a floral-printed card with a simple message:

> *Lydia,*
> *Please join me for a proper "Third Day of*
> *Christmas" ladies' tea. I look forward to seeing*
> *you today at our home at 2:00 p.m.*
> *Your friend, Elizabeth*

Naturally, Lydia had no other plans. The week between Christmas and New Year's was generally understood to be a week of rest and relaxation, and she had intended to do some light housework and then read all afternoon. But an invitation to tea sounded infinitely more interesting, and it was obvious from the Schaeffer girls' mission details that Danielle would be there as well. She was more than happy to go.

At two o'clock, Lydia approached the Schaeffer farmhouse, ascended the steps of the wrap-around porch, and knocked at the door. Allison answered her knock with the same bright-eyed enthusiasm she had exhibited that morning. Standing as tall as her eight years would allow, she very properly said, "Miss Klein, please allow me to escort you to the sitting room."

At that moment, Marta came tearing around the corner to see their guest, but one look from Allison caused her to pull up suddenly and walk toward Lydia with prim dignity. "May I take your coat, ma'am?" Lydia obliged Marta by offering her coat before following Allison down the narrow hall and around a corner into the indicated room.

The sitting room was in a corner of the house and sunlight streamed through four generously sized windows divided between two of the walls. There was a couch and two armchairs with a tea table between them covered in a lace tablecloth. Elizabeth was nowhere to be seen, but David was kneeling at the wood-burning fireplace, arranging logs and attempting to start a fire. Lydia stood uncomfortably for a moment, unsure what to do. Allison gestured toward the table and said, "Please sit," with the air of a little girl who has set her mind on events proceeding exactly as planned out in her head. Lydia obliged her, taking a seat on one of the chairs. Allison spun on her heel and ran out of the room, evidently satisfied that her task had been completed.

David looked up at her and nodded in greeting but remained focused on his task. After watching for a minute, Lydia was quite sure he had no idea what he was doing. She felt a strong urge to step in and do it for him but resisted the impulse.

After another moment of awkward silence, Lydia spoke first: "How was your Christmas?" She knew it wasn't a strong conversational opener, but it was the best she could manage.

"I like Christmas in New Augsburg," David responded, looking up from the fireplace. "How was yours?"

"It was nice," Lydia replied. For some reason she didn't want to bring up the Barrett family with David, and she didn't have anything else to say.

"Elizabeth is still in the kitchen finishing things up," David offered as explanation, "and I don't know why Danielle isn't here yet."

Lydia nodded. They both watched the fire for a moment. The kindling had finally caught, and it looked like the logs would follow soon. "When do you go back to seminary?" she asked, glad that another question had come to mind.

David's shoulders slumped in disappointment as he repositioned the screen in front of the fireplace and stood up. "Actually, I received some bad news this morning," he said. "The seminary is closing for the next semester. There won't be any classes, and the students have been advised not to return to campus."

"What?" Lydia's jaw dropped in surprise.

"It's that new tax bill," David explained with a frown. "The property taxes at the seminary are increasing to an alarming rate. And while the new rates wouldn't technically affect the tax bill due this spring, the renewed focus on taxing religious organizations is prompting the local government to try to collect years of back-dated taxes. The state hadn't enforced them in the past, so they had never been paid.

Apparently, to keep from losing the property, the seminary needs to cut all operational costs for six months."

Lydia shook her head slowly, taking it all in. The seminary had been part of their church body for almost three hundred years. She couldn't imagine the property being seized over a tax bill. It seemed unbelievable.

David watched her reaction. "I'm so sorry to hear that," she finally managed to say. Before David could reply, Danielle entered the room with Elizabeth and the tea tray close on her heels.

"I'm sorry to keep you waiting, Lydia," Elizabeth said with hurried enthusiasm. David stood up, greeted Danielle politely, and then excused himself. Elizabeth arranged the tea things on the table, then hurried back to the kitchen to get a plate of sandwiches, scones, and a little crock of lemon curd. "I used to have friends over once a week for high tea in Pennsylvania," she explained as she poured. "I was hoping you ladies might be interested in resurrecting this practice with me. I've so missed my teatime chats."

Danielle and Lydia exchanged looks with each other before nodding and assuring Elizabeth that they were honored to share in her tradition and be friends. Conversation flowed easily: from recaps of their respective Christmases, to Danielle's upcoming wedding, to their family traditions and upbringings, and anything else that came up. They discovered their shared love for British literature and considered the possibility of turning their tea times into a book club.

"I still can't believe you have the original version of *Jane Eyre* here!" Elizabeth exclaimed. "I'd always loved that story, but when I found the unedited version in the library my first week here, I devoured it in one week! I couldn't believe how many parts were missing from the red mark edition we'd had before."

"I know!" Lydia agreed. "And since you love Jane Austen, I'll have to find you a copy of *Mansfield Park* as well. Entire conversations were removed from that one in the red mark version."

"There's a handful of copies of these books around town," Danielle chimed in. "But I can't wait for Lydia to get her classics line going so we can circulate hundreds of them!"

Lydia blushed slightly and sipped her tea as Elizabeth and Danielle sang her praises.

"Yes, we simply must have a book club," Elizabeth reflected, "but not every week. I also like to have time to just talk with no agenda or schedule. Maybe once a month or every other week, our tea could be a book discussion."

As the conversation began to wane and the refreshments were depleted, Lydia mentioned the news David had shared. "I was so sad to hear about the seminary closing for the semester," she began. "Do you think David will stay here? What will he do if he can't finish his degree and be ordained this spring?"

Elizabeth waved her hand disinterestedly. "It really is terrible news for the Church," she conceded, "but I wouldn't worry about David. He will be just fine no matter what happens to the seminary."

"Doesn't he have student loans?" Lydia asked with surprise. "And surely that's how he's been planning to make a living. It will be almost impossible to find a job in the business world with a seminary degree on his record, even though I'm sure many of his skills would be transferable."

Elizabeth looked at her a bit quizzically for a moment, then rolled her eyes as if at her own foolishness. "I always forget that people in New Augsburg don't know our whole family story." She leaned in conspiratorially, obviously enjoying her chance to divulge something of interest. "David is filthy rich," she said without ceremony. Lydia and Danielle looked appropriately shocked, and Elizabeth tried not to show how pleased she was to have been the means of shocking them. "Yes, it's true! His mother—you know he has a different mother than the rest of us? She was an heiress and left him a fortune. He could probably buy this entire town!" She sat back, glancing toward the doorway as if to make sure he hadn't heard. "He doesn't talk about that. He doesn't want people to think differently of him."

"Wow!" Danielle exclaimed. "I never would have imagined . . . Did you know this, Lydia?"

"No," Lydia shook her head slowly. "I mean, I did know about his mother but not about the fortune."

Elizabeth smiled but then, appearing to have some misgivings about having shared her brother's secret, added hastily, "Don't tell him I told you! Maybe I shouldn't have said. I just didn't want you worrying about him, Lydia. You *should* worry about the rest of the Church and how we will train pastors, but my brother David? He'll be just fine."

As Lydia and Danielle were leaving a few minutes later, David approached them from the direction of the chicken coop. His worn denim jeans and oversized work jacket gave his appearance a rugged charm that sent Lydia's thoughts racing in surprising and uncomfortable directions. He looked down at his soiled work clothes with embarrassment, then up at them awkwardly for a moment before blurting out, "Lydia, forgive me for asking, but I heard that Zach proposed to you at the Christmas party last week?" It was intoned as a question.

Lydia and Danielle exchanged a sidelong glance. "Yes, Zach proposed to me," Lydia said, working to keep her tone neutral.

David looked at her for a moment, and when she met his eyes, she thought that he was trying to conceal his emotions. "I wish you both the very best," he said. "My sincere congratulations." He moved to offer his hand but, realizing in time that it was dirty from his efforts in the coop, simply nodded at her.

Lydia nodded in return, unsure of what to say. She did not want to explain that she was probably going to marry Zach but hadn't made up her mind yet, so she simply said, "Thank you." He headed toward the house, and she and Danielle continued to the street.

Danielle looked back over her shoulder as David disappeared inside and closed the door, then grabbed Lydia's arm and whispered, "He clearly likes you! He's disappointed, I think! I feel so sorry for him! Why didn't you tell him you haven't accepted Zach yet?"

Frustrated, Lydia declared, "Because if you're right and he does like me, I don't want to lead him on! I also don't want people to think I don't like Zach, especially if I end up marrying him. I didn't say anything untrue . . . It was rather awkward of him to ask me, don't you think?"

Danielle squeezed her friend's arm comfortingly. "I don't know, Lyd. I think it would be hard for him to think he saw you getting engaged and still not have heard any definitive news. If he does like you, that could be its own kind of agony." They walked in silence until they reached the Thomas' house, where Danielle turned aside. Lydia continued home alone.

David entered the farmhouse through the back door, kicked off his boots in the breezeway, and headed for the nearest sink to scrub the evidence of farmwork off his hands. Several minutes passed before he realized the task had been more than sufficiently performed. He shook his head at his own foolishness and dried his hands on the towel, turning away from the utility sink to find his sister leaning against the kitchen doorway, watching him with an amused smile.

"What?" David returned her loaded expression with

his own as he brushed past her to the kitchen and helped himself to the leftover tea spread.

"You're pining for her, aren't you?"

"For who?" David shook his head, feigning cluelessness.

"You know full well *for whom*." Elizabeth was laughing at him.

He grimaced, ignoring her correction of his grammar. "I honestly don't know what she sees in this Zach guy."

"I mean, I can tell you what a girl might see in Zachary Barrett, but I doubt that's what you're looking for right now." Elizabeth followed him over to the counter and helped herself to a leftover scone.

David didn't respond. He silently poured the remainder of the tea over ice and searched through the fridge for a lemon wedge. He could feel his sister watching him and knew she wasn't ready to let the conversation drop.

"Zach is a good match for Lydia. Her life is here. I don't think she'll ever leave New Augsburg."

"*So, your pursuit of her is pointless,*" was what she was trying to say. David knew she was right, but in the weeks since Thanksgiving, during which he'd been unable to get Lydia's smile or intensely focused blue eyes out of his head, he'd allowed himself to fantasize. She might think she wanted to stay here forever, but what she really loved about New Augsburg was serving the Church. She would always be able to do that with him. Couldn't that be enough?

"Her family isn't here anymore," he said finally.

"That's true, but only in a technical sense. The press is

all she has left of her parents. In a way, their absence ensures her connection to her family will always be here."

David nodded. He couldn't deny it. "Well, it doesn't matter. What kind of man would I be to be 'pining,' as you put it, over an engaged woman?"

Elizabeth gave him a look of mock pity. "A mere mortal, like the rest of us, big brother, unable to control your every emotion."

He looked at her sharply but saw the teasing sparkle in her eyes. "Well, as a mere mortal and an exceptionally slow reader, I suppose I should begin my prereading for next semester now."

"I thought that semester was canceled," she retorted, but he sidled past her and escaped to the stairs before she could interrogate him further about his heart.

# CHAPTER SEVENTEEN

Micah walked through the door at eight o'clock on the evening of the twenty-ninth to find Lydia sitting in the living room, waiting for him with a pot of coffee and a plate of cookies. Dropping his two bags on the floor in the entryway, he looked at her with forced cheerfulness and wished her a merry Christmas. Lydia knew her brother and did not miss the sadness and frustration behind his eyes. He dropped into his favorite armchair, kicked up his feet, and stared at her.

"Where is Callie?" Lydia asked, surprised not to see her with him and knowing that was the question he was waiting for.

"She couldn't come," Micah stated the obvious. "There was a big event—a networking opportunity she felt she couldn't miss." He gazed out the window as if he was not planning on elaborating; then, he did something unusual in Lydia's experience. He told her how he felt. "I'm sad that she's not here, Lydia. I also feel used, like she's taking advantage. I missed Christmas with you in our home to be there for her, and she couldn't return the favor."

Lydia nodded sympathetically as her mind searched for a response. But Micah quickly leaned forward and changed the subject.

"Let's talk about you. I heard from Zach a few weeks ago. He called me, asking for my blessing to marry you."

"He did?" This was news to Lydia.

"Yep. He also asked me if I'd sign over the press to him if he did. I kind of expected that I'd have heard something from you about it by now. Has he proposed?"

Lydia smiled, "If he hasn't, you just ruined a surprise."

Micah looked at her with amusement. "I take it then that he has. Shall I congratulate you, future Mrs. Barrett?"

"He proposed on the nineteenth at his family's Christmas party," Lydia began, her cheeks warming with embarrassment.

"Wow, you've been engaged for ten days and haven't found the time to shoot me a message?" Micah's tone was teasing.

"Actually," Lydia replied, "I haven't given him an answer." She waited nervously to see how he'd respond to this admission.

Micah's eyes widened. "You what? You've made a man wait ten days for an answer to his proposal?"

"Well, Micah, what do you think I should do?" Lydia shot back. "Did you give him your blessing?"

"I mean, yeah, I guess so," Micah shrugged. "I told him if that's what you wanted, I would be happy for you both. I assumed it was what you'd want."

Lydia gazed down at the book lying untouched in her lap. *If only I knew what I wanted*, she thought. Looking up, she asked, "Are you in love with Callie?"

Micah looked a bit surprised at the conversational pivot but answered without hesitation. "Yes, I am. How is that relevant to you and Zach?"

"I think I haven't accepted Zach's proposal because I'm not sure I'm in love with him," Lydia said slowly. "I wonder if I'm supposed to be. It seems like I should be if I'm going to marry him."

Micah nodded, beginning to see where she was going. "I think about Callie all the time. About the way she laughs. The sparkle in her eyes when she's teasing me. Anytime someone walks into the room, I look up, hoping it's her. I picture the way her hair falls in waves down her back. Every time I talk to her, I think, subconsciously, I'm trying to get her to smile. When I imagine my future, she's always there. . . ." He trailed off, staring into the distance.

Lydia watched her brother thoughtfully. "So why haven't *you* proposed?"

"Actually . . ." Micah leaned forward, his knee shaking up and down the way it always did when he got excited, "I was going to ask you if you thought it would be right for me to use Mother's engagement ring. I thought I'd take it back with me. This is our last semester of college, and it's going to happen sometime before graduation."

"I mean, I suppose one of us should have Mother's engagement ring," Lydia said. She reached into her pocket and pulled out the huge diamond ring Zach had given her, holding it out for Micah's inspection. "This is the one I was offered."

Micah's eyes widened. "Wow, Zach! I'm impressed!" he said, taking the ring and holding it up to the light. "You should obviously marry this guy, Lyd," he joked, handing back the ring. "Love or not, I'd lock down this offer while it's on the table!"

Lydia laughed, knowing that he was at least mostly joking. "I'm probably going to marry him. I don't know what else to do with my life. On paper, it's what I've always wanted, and it seems like it will be good for the town."

"Do you think I should prioritize what is *good for the town* over my heart too, Lydia?" Micah asked, a new layer of tension in his voice. "Or do you speak only for yourself in that?"

"No, I . . ." Lydia stopped, replaying what she had said and seeing it through his perspective. "I wasn't trying to make any statements about you, Micah. I was speaking for myself," she said humbly. "I've always pictured my life here in New Augsburg, and I've always loved the press. I want to get married here, raise my children here, and keep the vision of the Founders alive for another generation. You know that's always been my desire."

Micah softened. "I guess I was defensive there. Sorry, Sis." He reached for a cookie and a cup of coffee, indicating to Lydia that the serious part of their conversation was over. They chatted lightly for another hour or so, then went to bed.

As Lydia went through her evening routine, she replayed Micah's words about Callie over and over in her mind. The fact was inescapable—she did not feel that way about Zach. It was touching that Zach had called Micah to ask for his blessing. But then Zach's behavior was always so . . . *correct.* If there was a book on proper courtship, he certainly had studied it and was following it to the letter. She considered what Micah had said about the rest of the phone call. What if Zach's real purpose was merely to verify that the press transfer would occur smoothly? Again, she faced the nagging feeling that Zach's behavior toward her was less than sincere: a pretense for something else.

*Does Zach want me or the press?* she wondered. *Would he want to marry me if it weren't for the press?* But surely, this was a hypocritical train of thought! Lydia knew she had seen Zach as a means of saving the press from the beginning. His expressed interest in her predated the press situation, and she could not say the same thing for her interest in him. Could his enthusiasm for the press simply be part of his pursuit of her, an attempt to romance her by caring about what she cared for? No, surely not, or he would not be pushing contracts and plans that she was so strongly against. *Perhaps he's just so invested that he's willing to fight with me about it.* She did have a tendency to respect strong male leadership, but this thought produced a wrench of guilt. If the love he expressed for her was genuine, she knew she did not yet return it. What she didn't know was if that was enough of a reason to refuse his proposal when every material circumstance pointed toward their alliance.

The next morning Micah went to help John and the rest of the men in the wedding party with the reception setup. Lydia planned to head to the community center in the afternoon when the other women would be there to help with the decorating, which left her a few hours to catch up on housework. The sound of footsteps on the front walk interrupted her sweeping. Looking out her front window, she saw Maybelle Whittier approaching with a basket on her arm. She quickly set down her broom and went to open the door.

"Maybelle!" Lydia greeted her warmly. "What are you doing here this morning?"

"Well, my dear, I wanted to have a chat with you if you have some time," Maybelle replied. "And I brought you some muffins . . . well, us some muffins. We can't have a chat without sustenance," she said with a wink.

Lydia welcomed her inside and led her to the kitchen table. She started a pot of coffee to accompany the muffins before sitting in the seat next to her friend. Maybelle did not stand on ceremony. She reached into the basket, took out a muffin, and handed it to Lydia as she started speaking.

"My dear, I intend to insert myself here where I have not been invited because I believe that you could use someone to talk to and a bit of advice. Do you disagree?"

Lydia shook her head slowly. Maybelle was correct in her assessment.

Maybelle nodded acknowledgment before diving in. "I've been watching you since the Thanksgiving dance—well, since before then, probably—and I've seen some things. I saw the way David made you laugh at that dance. I saw the argument you had with Zach that day you came by the library to order press parts. I may be wrong, but I think he proposed to you at his family's Christmas party. It was clear to everyone in attendance at that party that he believes you are his future wife. I saw you in church on Christmas, and I saw no ring then. I see none now, either." She paused, meeting Lydia's eyes unwaveringly. "So far, do I have it right?"

"Yes, ma'am, you do," Lydia answered. She could feel her cheeks turning red. Her stomach was churning with discomfort, but part of her was relieved to have been seen. Maybelle was like family to her, not to mention wise and experienced. Yet at the prospect of talking this through with

Maybelle, Lydia felt an overwhelming surge of sadness that it wasn't her mother sitting across the table from her.

Maybelle was quiet for a moment, watching her. She reached out and covered Lydia's hand with her own. "I wish it was your mother here, too, my dear child," she said quietly. "I know that she would want me to step in and help you make sense of it all."

They sat in silence for a moment. Lydia wiped the few tears from her eyes and was grateful when the coffee pot interrupted the quiet with its shrill beep. She stood up to retrieve it and some mugs. She poured the coffee, bit into the moist, flaky muffin, and after chewing for a moment, said, "So, where would you like me to start?"

Lydia told Maybelle all about the past few months. About Micah's decision to leave New Augsburg, what that meant for the press, the cost of repairs, her relationship with Zach, and about his proposed publishing deal with Nova. Maybelle listened, asking clarifying questions here or there but primarily receiving the story as Lydia shared it.

"In conclusion," Lydia said when she felt she had wrapped everything up, "I need to give Zach my answer in the next day or two. I can't think of any good reason to refuse him, and I obviously have several reasons to accept him. So, I'm thinking that's what I should do." She eyed Maybelle questioningly, obviously looking for validation.

"You disagree with Zach on some fairly fundamental issues that will lead to immediate conflict in your marriage," Maybelle remarked after a moment.

"Yes, I suppose that's true," Lydia agreed.

"Starting off a marriage in a fight is not ideal. It can work if the two of you love each other and have a strong foundation. Do you?"

Lydia's eyes widened in surprise. Her mind jumped back to the conversation with Micah from the night before. He had been mad at Callie one minute and talking of his imminent proposal the next. But Micah and Callie had a foundation of years spent together and the consciousness that they both loved each other.

Maybelle went on, taking the look on her face as an answer. "What would happen, my dear, if you didn't marry Zach?"

Lydia looked down at her half-eaten muffin, fidgeting with the wrapper in her hands. "I don't know," she said softly. "I guess I assume that we'll lose the press. Not just me, but the town."

Maybelle let the words hang in the air without responding.

"I love the work that I do at the press, Maybelle!" Lydia went on. "I believe in it. The only hope for the world is the Truth, and truth is hard to come by these days. God chooses to reveal Himself to us through the written word, so we know that He cares about what we write and what we preserve for the future. I feel like we are living in a second dark age, and our world needs the press. I don't want to compromise it by contracting with a publisher that doesn't respect God's Word, but I also don't want to lose it through my fear or negligence."

Maybelle nodded in understanding. "You feel responsible," she summarized.

"I *am* responsible!" Lydia corrected. "Micah doesn't want this responsibility, and there is no one else! I'm the only one who has the power to do anything about it." She heard the words she was saying as they left her mouth and was instantly embarrassed by them.

Maybelle's eyes sparkled with the faintest hint of amusement, but she waited for Lydia to make the correction herself.

Shaking her head at her own foolishness, Lydia amended her statement, "I'm *not* the only one who has power here."

"That's right, dear," Maybelle said. "Your worst fear is that you will let down your family, your community, and (dare I suggest it?) all of Christendom if you do not manage your little press judiciously." Her eyes twinkled as she spoke, and Lydia knew the last part was added to lighten the mood.

She smiled wryly in response. "Well, when you put it *that* way . . . "

"Tell me about Zach," Maybelle asked. "If it weren't for the press and your positions in the town, would you want to marry him?"

Lydia furrowed her brow in thought. Had she really never asked herself that question? It had been an emotionally trying year: her mind and heart so often flooded. She tried to think about Zach and the times they had spent together. All the memories mingled with anxiety about her family business and her role in the town, her grief over her mother, and . . . *David*.

Maybelle watched her for several minutes before speaking again. "Lydia," she said softly. "When you marry someone, it should be for a good reason. It shouldn't be out of fear. Marriage is a gift from God. It is a beautiful thing: a picture of Christ and His bride, the Church. It is based on self-sacrifice, respect, and a shared vision for a life lived to God's glory. Many happy marriages have begun without feelings of being in love, but few happy marriages have begun based on lies.

"You are not in love with Zach, and that's obvious to both of us, I think. Does he know that? Is he in love with you? Would you be marrying him because you don't trust God to provide for you or the press if you don't? These are the questions you need to consider."

An hour later, after Maybelle had left, Lydia still sat at the kitchen table, staring out the window into the snow-covered yard, lost in thought. She had always known that her parents' marriage was arranged and that love had grown gradually over time. On some level, she did not think that she had ever considered romantic love as a main motivator for marriage. Maybelle's words were convicting, though. Zach had declared love to her, and if she accepted him, he would assume she felt the same. She needed to be honest with him.

She tried to picture the conversation. *I'll marry you, Zach, but it's just for the sake of the town and my own sense of security. At this point, I don't love you, and I wanted you to know that.* She winced. That was not something she wanted to hear herself say out loud.

She realized that even if she were willing to admit that to Zach, she still had to grapple with Maybelle's other question. *Did she not trust God to provide for her without Zach?* But what if God was providing for her by sending Zach?

She stood up from the table in frustration, realizing that she would be late to help Danielle with the reception setup, and prepared to leave. *I will pray about this,* she resolved, *and I will talk to Zach tomorrow. One way or the other, I'm going to talk to him. He's waited long enough.*

As she set out for the community center, she realized with chagrin that her thoughts were not of Zach. David's words echoed in her ear, and she found herself (not for the first time) replaying that final moment with him at the Christmas party. *"If you were single right now, I would be asking you out on a date."*

# CHAPTER EIGHTEEN

The next day was New Year's Eve and the day before Danielle's wedding. Lydia's decision was made, and the time had come. Her stomach was in knots, making her reluctant to eat anything. Knowing from experience that failure to eat would only exacerbate the situation, she choked down a piece of toast and a cup of mint tea before bundling up and heading out. She was supposed to be with Danielle by noon, and the rehearsal was at the church at 4:00 p.m. Turning toward the Barrett estate, she silently prayed that she would find Zach at home.

When she reached the fork in the road, she was surprised to find David walking toward her on Main Street, his hands shoved in his pockets, looking aimless and carefree. The trees had hidden him from view until they were mere paces away from each other. Her already anxious stomach did a summersault as she realized that it would be impossible to avoid talking to him.

"David," she exclaimed, nodding and pausing awkwardly in the middle of the road.

"Hello, Miss Klein." He appeared so much more composed than she, tipping his hat to her in a way that was completely charming.

"How are you today?" she managed, holding her hand up to her eyes to shield them from the sun rising behind him.

"Actually, I've had some rather good news," David admitted, looking pleased.

"Oh?"

"I received word from the seminary that the entire faculty has decided to donate their time for the next semester. We will not be able to use the facility, but our classes will be held online, and I will still be able to complete my degree in the spring as planned."

"That's wonderful!" Lydia said with feeling. "How generous of the professors. That must be quite a sacrifice for them."

"Yes," said David, "but that's what it means to be the Church. No matter what goes on in the world, no matter what the public policy may be, Word and Sacrament ministry will go on. Jesus has promised us His faithfulness, and it makes us bold to be faithful in response."

Lydia made no answer but nodded. She knew he spoke

the truth, but there was nothing she could add to such a statement. "Will you stay in town then or . . . ?" She trailed off, realizing that appearing too eager might send the wrong message.

"Yes, I am planning to stay with my family this semester. I'll probably be holed up in the communications lab at the library pretty much all day every day, since it's the only place in town I can access my coursework."

"Well, I wish you a smooth semester then."

He nodded to her politely, tipping his hat again. "See you around, Miss Klein."

They parted ways, and she continued up the road towards the Barrett home, wondering if there had been any graceful way that she could have told him what she was on her way to do.

When Zach answered the door, he looked pleased to see her, if a bit nervous. They both recognized the fated moment had arrived. He led her into the sitting room, and she politely sat in the armchair he indicated. "Should I get us some tea or coffee?" he asked, his eyes never leaving her face as if searching there for clues.

"No, thank you, Zach. Would it be okay if we just talk?"

Nodding, he perched on the edge of the couch facing her. The tension in the room was undeniable. Lydia had never wanted to be anywhere less in her life. She knew she had to speak first. Reaching into her pocket, she took out the ring he had offered her and, fingering it nervously in her hand, she began.

"Zach, I've had a few weeks to think about this. You have been so generous to me. I can't believe how thoughtful you've been, not requiring an immediate response, deflecting your parents' inquiries at Christmas, including me in your family meals and celebrations . . ." She looked down at the ring, unable to meet his eyes. "I have prayed about this and contemplated it . . ." She was stalling. And she ought to look at him. Taking a deep breath, she looked up. His steel-grey eyes were cold and met hers with an intensity that did nothing to calm her nerves. Gritting her teeth in determination, she forced the statement she had rehearsed from her lips: "Zach, I thank you for the honor of your proposal. I wish I felt that I could accept your hand, but I find that I cannot. I am very sorry." She reached out, placing his ring on the coffee table between them, then withdrew her hand back to her lap and dropped her gaze, waiting uncomfortably for whatever came next.

Zach sat motionless, his stare unwavering. He did not even glance at the ring. After several painful seconds, he stood abruptly and walked past Lydia to the window, looking out over the porch and front lawn. Lydia sat in silence, wondering what, if anything, she should say next. She had just about decided to stand up and show herself out when he spun on his heel and took two steps toward her chair until he towered over her. He said only one word, but his tone was icy and sharp: "Why?"

Lydia rose to her feet and moved away from him before

responding. "I suppose the biggest reason is that I don't love you, Zach. You told me you loved me that day in the press office, and when you proposed . . ." She trailed off, but her resolve strengthening, she met his gaze firmly. "I don't love you, and I think that you should marry someone who does. I never meant to hurt you, and I'm very sorry. I thought perhaps our love had time to build and grow, but at this point, I don't think I can give you what you want."

Zach's stony stoicism was fast stripping away. He appeared to be positively enraged now. He began to pace in front of the windows as he spoke, his voice rising to a shout: "I don't love you, Lydia. I never did. God, Lydia, you are the most thoughtless, ungrateful girl I've ever had the displeasure to waste my life wanting! After all I've done for you and for your stupid little press, how could you even think of refusing my offer? What do you think is going to become of you or your family legacy now?"

Lydia stood rooted to the spot in shock. She had pictured many different reactions but had never expected him to yell at her and berate her. She had never seen him like this. He stopped pacing, ran his hands through his hair, and Lydia thought she detected a look of panic. But his explosion was fast strengthening her confidence in her decision. "Me and my family legacy, as you put it, are in God's hands, Zach. They never were yours to save. I will be just fine. Just because I don't know how exactly I will be fine doesn't mean God won't provide. I thought He might have been providing for me through you and this potential marriage, but it is fast becoming clear to me that that is not His will."

He glared at her, once again crossing the room to intimidate her with his towering height. When he was inches from her face, he said through gritted teeth: "Mark my words, Miss Klein, you have no place in this town without me. You are a conniving, ungrateful, scheming girl. Don't think for a moment that I don't see how you've strung me along, just for my money, with no intention of ever honoring my investment in your press. I assure you I am no fool, and you owe me. Especially after taking my money for your precious machines. Well, I don't need to marry you to acquire your press and work whatever business deals I want around here. The Strauss and McKenzie families are without heirs. Your brother has both feet out the door. I am the future of this town. You will live to regret this day, I promise you."

"You mark *my* words, Mr. Barrett," she responded, now fully furious in her own right. "This is a day I will never regret for as long as I live. This is the day where I made a wise decision and saved myself from a lifetime of misery." And without a second glance, she swept past him, chin high in the air and stormed out of the Barrett home, slamming the door behind her.

She maintained her purposeful and indignant retreat until she rounded the bend in the road and was out of sight of the house. At that moment, the pressure that had been building in her chest burst, and she began sobbing uncontrollably, her body shaking all over. She glanced around, and seeing no one, ran blindly toward home.

Minutes later, she burst through her own front door, tore up the stairs to her room, and threw herself across her bed. But the tears were mostly spent at that point, and she gingerly sat up after a few minutes of deep breathing and looked toward the doorway. Micah stood there, watching her with concern.

"What happened?"

Lydia wiped the tears away and smiled nervously at him. "I refused Zach."

"It looks like it went poorly."

"You could say that." Lydia's thoughts were jumbled, and she didn't know how much she wanted to share.

"What did he say?" Micah pressed, crossing the room and sitting beside her on the bed.

"He was mad. I'm not sure I am up to repeating it all just now."

Micah's eyes narrowed. "It seems to have been pretty bad—you're . . . Do I need to beat him up or anything?" he asked, and Lydia knew he was only half joking.

"No," she said, trying to smile. "He threatened our family, though. He said I had no place in this town without him and that he'd take the press if he wanted to. Or it was something like that." Seeing the look of alarm and anger growing in her brother's eyes, she hastily added, "He was probably just hurt and posturing." She nodded as she spoke, as if trying to convince herself as well: "He was just angry.

His pride was hurt. I'm sure he didn't mean me to take any of that literally." She fought to combat the fear threatening to take hold inside her with rationality and optimism.

Micah's eyes were dark, and he paced angrily, his hands balled into fists. Lydia closed her eyes, rallying. The last thing she needed was Micah to make a scene with Zach on Danielle's wedding weekend.

"Micah, it's fine. It's between him and me."

"Not if he's bringing our family into it! Plus, it's my job to look out for you."

Lydia grinned in spite of herself at this attempt at chivalry. Even saying the words, Micah looked uncomfortable. She knew he wasn't the "defending the family honor" type.

"Micah, I promise, if I need you to defend us from Zach, I'll tell you. Now, I need to get ready . . . " Lydia got to her feet and reached for her hairbrush to tidy up her appearance. Micah's shoulders relaxed. He appeared at least somewhat placated by her assurances and, after asking one final time if she was sure she was all right, left her alone to prepare for the day's festivities.

As she brushed her hair, Lydia's heart sank as she imagined encountering Zach at the wedding the next day. *And honestly, the whole town,* she thought. *Everyone is going to be gossiping about us after that Christmas party.* She coiled her hair into a soft bun and put one of her mother's silver combs in to hold it in place, reflecting on two conflicting feelings after the morning's events. She was intensely grateful that Maybelle had come over the day before and helped her find the courage to refuse Zach. And yet, despite having friends like Maybelle, she struggled against the familiar fear that she was utterly alone.

# CHAPTER NINETEEN

Lydia did not want to detract from her friend's big day by rehashing the events of the morning, but she knew that Danielle would desire an update. So, after the rehearsal dinner, she found a moment alone with Danielle and told her simply that she had refused Zach, that they were no longer together, and that she was doing fine.

Curious as always, Danielle pressed for details, and Lydia briefly related the substance of her conversation with Maybelle, along with her conviction that it would have been wrong to accept Zach's offer because she would have been doing so not out of love and care for him, but out of fear. Danielle was sympathetic and supportive, as always, but their conversation was soon interrupted by the demands of out-of-town relatives, and Lydia found herself alone with her thoughts. The rest of the evening and the following day were busy and eventful. There were no additional opportunities to speak with her friend, but the wedding events provided a welcome distraction.

Standing beside John and Danielle in front of the congregation, listening to Pastor Pedersen read from Ephesians Five, Lydia could not have been more confident in her decision to refuse Zach: "*Husbands, love your wives as Christ loved the Church and gave Himself up for her . . .*" She could still hear him shouting at her. "*I don't love you, Lydia. I never did . . .*" The venom in his voice . . . the scorn . . . she couldn't believe she had been seriously intending to accept him just a few days ago. In her mind, she knew he had been gracious and generous to her; the positive memories of their relationship had not been her imagination. He had told her he loved her. She hadn't made that up. But when she remembered those words and the way he had looked at her, her heart had felt foolish, embarrassed, *worthless.* . . . Watching Danielle and John gaze into each other's eyes with such joy-filled love and hope for the future, she sent up a silent prayer of gratitude that God had spared her from what she was sure would have been a disastrous marriage.

Her certainty and gratitude to God (and to Maybelle) did not keep her from feeling emotionally worn down as the wedding festivities stretched on into the evening. The juxtaposition of her friend's happiness and her own narrow escape, paired with Zach's words still playing in her mind, was more than overwhelming, and she found it was all she could do to go through the motions of the reception and make the required small talk. The few times she caught Zach watching her, he would glare at her and turn away, and she lacked the energy to insert herself into any of the groups of young people talking or dancing at the party.

From her seat at a table in the corner, she instinctively watched David as he danced with his little sisters, laughed and chatted with Elizabeth and his parents, and mixed with the other young people. She never caught him looking at her, and he never approached her. When she felt she had stayed long enough, she said a final goodnight to Danielle and John and went to find her coat.

As she stood by the door donning her coat and gloves, she scanned the room for Micah. She finally located him on the dance floor with Callie. His arm was wrapped possessively around her waist, his hand buried underneath her long, wavy hair, and his eyes danced in a way that Lydia had never seen before. Callie was laughing at something Micah had said, the pair a perfect picture of romantic bliss. Lydia wondered with amusement when Callie had arrived. The grand gesture of flying across the country for one night together was clearly having its desired effect on her brother. As they were obviously enjoying their reunion, Lydia felt no remorse for slipping out without disturbing them.

The next morning, Lydia entered church behind Micah and Callie and followed them to their usual pew. Her spine tingled as if tactilely feeling the inevitable stares of her fellow parishioners, trying not to imagine the gossip and speculation taking place at her expense. Zach was already seated in his family row and did not turn to look at her. Reaching for her hymnal and searching for the first hymn listed on the hymn board, she resolved to put her personal life and all of its challenges out of her mind. This was a moment to reflect on Jesus and His incarnation, not for her to worry about who was whispering about why she and Zach were no longer sitting together.

As Lydia scanned the verses of the hymn, she had almost succeeded in putting her intrusive thoughts to rest when David walked up the side aisle in a hurry, dressed in a black clerical shirt and preacher's white collar, and ducked into the sacristy. He reappeared a few moments later as the congregation was rising to begin, this time wearing an alb (with no stole, as he was not yet ordained), and took the typically vacant seat next to Pastor Pedersen. Although still resolved to focus on the service, Lydia could not help but realize two things: First, that David was going to be preaching this Sunday, and second, that he looked strikingly handsome in his clerical. This last realization caused her some discomfort. *Is it okay to think a man attractive in a clerical?* She didn't know, but she did know that she had missed the opportunity to meditate on the words of the opening hymn, and she hastily redirected her thoughts to the Divine Service as Pastor Pederson rose to begin with the invocation.

David's sermon was everything a sermon should be—aptly drawn from the Scripture reading, explicit in its application of the law, sweet and powerful in its administration of the Gospel, passionately delivered, and exactly twenty minutes long. Lydia was impressed. When Pastor Pedersen had given the benediction, Lydia reached for her handbag while mentally attempting to compose an appropriate compliment to offer David on the way out. She almost missed the fact that Pastor Pedersen was still standing before the congregation, doing what everyone had given up on expecting years ago: He was announcing his retirement.

Monday morning began with Callie, Micah, and a leisurely breakfast. Callie's visit had been so short that they delayed beginning their trip back to campus as long as possible. But at eleven o'clock, when the inevitable could be no further postponed, they said their goodbyes and left. Lydia tidied up the kitchen and headed to the office, feeling both anxious and eager to get back to work after the intensity of the holiday season. She contemplated her next move for the press with Zach no longer in the picture and composed a mental list of calls to make and messages to send. The next town council meeting loomed at the end of the month, and she needed to have some good news to offer by then.

The press office was quiet. John would be out of town for the next few weeks on his honeymoon, and no hum of working equipment broke the silence. Lydia pulled out the Nova contract, looking it over to see if refusing it would require a response. While it appeared as if she could just toss it, she composed a brief letter indicating that Klein Press was no longer interested in working with them. She worded it as graciously as she could while still sounding final.

Next, she drafted a letter to her bishop, asking if he knew of any funding that could be used to pay for new machines or any other resources of which she might be unaware. She wondered as she worked on the wording why she had not considered this immediately. How tempting it was to think of herself and her beloved New Augsburg as an island, and yet the entire founding principle of her hometown was that the Church stands together, sharing what resources it has in common. She reflected on the description of the first church in Acts Two while she typed. *Satan always wants God's people to feel alone,* she mused. *That's how he gets us.* Determined to no longer believe that lie, she resolved to also talk to Pastor Pedersen and reach out to some of the publishers she had printed for in the past to see what resources or connections they might have. With her communications drafted and ready to send, she closed up the press and headed to the library to make use of the internet connection before heading home for the day.

As she entered, Elizabeth waved her over to the coffee counter with a smile. "Hey, Lydia! You just missed Zach. He's spent all day in the Comm Lab doing who knows what! He literally just left a minute ago."

Lydia breathed a sigh of relief. What a welcome coincidence. *I wonder how long I'll feel nervous about running into him,* she thought. It was a small town, and she couldn't avoid him indefinitely. She tried to give Elizabeth a noncommittal response, but her friend was too clever and persistent for that.

"We're friends now, right?" Elizabeth was leaning over the counter, eyes dancing with interest.

"Of course!" She approached the counter, realizing that they were going to have a full conversation before she could head back to the Comm Lab.

"Can I ask you a question, then? Zach didn't sit with you in church yesterday, and at the wedding, you two were so icy to each other."

Lydia was tempted to point out that there was no question but resisted, understanding the implicit one perfectly well. "Zach and I are no longer seeing each other," she said simply.

"Oh! I'm so sorry! What happened?" Catching herself, Elizabeth backed down a bit. "I mean, you don't have to tell me, obviously. It's okay." She immediately reached for the espresso machine and started making a latte. "You must have a coffee on the house with news like that. No matter what happened, I'm sure it's a lot to process."

Lydia nodded, appreciating both the offer of coffee and Elizabeth's understanding. While she waited for the latte, she asked Elizabeth about her weekend, successfully managing to divert the conversation to more neutral territory.

Several minutes later, coffee in hand, Lydia finally made her way back to the Comm Lab and set her tablet down on the syncing station. She didn't need to do anything; it would only take a minute for her already-written messages to send. David sat in the far corner with headphones on, apparently listening to a lecture. She remembered him saying he'd be here regularly for the foreseeable future as his classes met online. He didn't notice her coming in, and she couldn't think of any reason to interrupt him, so although her instincts urged her to talk to him, she left a moment later without saying anything.

# CHAPTER TWENTY

The next day as Lydia approached the press, she was alarmed to see the light on in the office window. Ascending the steps to the door with caution, she reached for the handle, and it gave in her hand. It was not locked. Her stomach did a somersault as she stepped into the hallway, wracking her brain for a forgotten meeting or some other explanation while simultaneously trying to remember who else other than John and herself might have a key. She turned the corner into her office and stopped still in alarm. There was Zach, looking back at her from behind her desk. All of the drawers were open, and papers and files littered the surface of the desk and the floor about him. He did not even have the decency to look embarrassed. When he saw her, he grimaced with determination and went back to rifling through her things.

"What . . . are . . . you . . . doing?" Her voice was cold with deliberation and rage.

He gave her a nasty, withering look and said nothing. He reached for a briefcase and began to stuff files into it as she watched.

"No!" She crossed the room in three steps and grabbed the strap of the bag, pulling it towards her. "You are stealing, Zach! This is wrong, and you know it!"

"You can't stop me, Lydia. You have absolutely no power or authority to do anything about it." He didn't let go of the bag.

Knowing she couldn't force the bag from his hands, she reached into it and pulled out the files, holding them tightly to her chest and stepping away from him. "Get out, Zach! Get out!" Her voice had risen to a near scream as her panic increased.

"I'll go when I'm ready," he said without raising his voice.

Lydia felt herself start to shake with anger and fear. *Why was he going through her files? What was he planning to do?* She wanted to ask, but she couldn't find the words. He placed two more files in his bag, then crossed the room to where she stood, standing just inches from her. She tried to look confident, but it was all too easy for him to rip the documents out of her arms.

"Goodbye, Lydia." His whisper as he stood so close to her frightened her. He turned and left.

Lydia remained frozen in place for a long minute, her mind refusing to process what had just happened. Her heart beat fast, and her chest felt tight. Slowly, she lowered herself to the floor, pulling her knees to her chest and trying to breathe. Then the tension within her broke, and she put her head down on her knees and cried.

Several minutes passed. When Lydia's tears were spent, she slowly rose to her feet, picked up her bag, which lay on the floor where she'd dropped it, and put a few folders of documents she'd been planning to proofread in it. Then she exited her office, locked the door, and walked mechanically back outside into the cold January air. She turned instinctively toward the library and took deep breaths as she walked, wiping her face with her mittened hands and trying to compose herself to the point where she'd be able to order a coffee. She didn't want to be alone, and she didn't think she could work in her office today.

No one was at the coffee counter when she entered the library. Certain that either Maybelle or Elizabeth would be back soon, she turned toward the café seating area and headed toward a table by the window. She pulled her work out of her bag and opened it up in front of her, but when she tried to attend to it, the words on the page swam before her eyes. She put her head in her hands and let out a sigh.

"Are you okay, Miss Klein?" She looked up with surprise

to see David. He was sitting at a large table against the far wall, books and tablet spread out before him. She didn't know how she had missed him there when she came in, but of course, she reminded herself, he would be in the library studying.

"Yes, I'm fine, thank you," she replied, but his face showed plainly that he didn't believe her, and she felt a pang of discomfort at her obvious lie. She shook her head slowly as he watched her. "No, actually, I'm not okay. I just had a rather unpleasant experience at my office, and I thought if I got away, I'd be able to focus and do my work. I'm not sure it's working." She gestured to the documents in front of her and attempted a smile, but David's look of concern only deepened.

"Would you like to sit over here?" he asked, moving aside some of his books and papers. She hesitated for a moment, but his presence was already soothing her, and she did very much want to talk to another person instead of replaying those moments with Zach over and over in her mind. She nodded gratefully and gathered her things, crossing the room and taking the spot he had cleared.

Neither of them said anything at first. Lydia was trying to decide what she wanted to tell him about Zach, and David appeared to sense her confusion and waited patiently. A few times, she opened her mouth to explain, but no words came.

It was becoming apparent to her that she found David attractive. All of their interactions had made her feel seen and valued. He had always treated her with kindness and compassion, which convinced her that he was a good man, but he was also witty and funny, and she enjoyed their conversation and the sound of his laugh. And then when he had preached on Sunday, well . . . there was something magnetic about a man who could preach the Gospel like that.

Today he sat surrounded by books, wearing a knit vest, his shirtsleeves rolled up to the elbow. This was the first time she had seen him with reading glasses, and Lydia felt it pushed him over the edge in terms of alluring good looks. He was utterly distracting, and she was hopelessly confused.

*Hadn't he said that if she was single, he'd ask her out?* It felt awkward, given her growing feelings for him and that particular circumstance, to tell him about what had transpired between her and Zach. But the news would have to come out, and if he didn't find out about it from her, he might wonder why she hadn't told him.

All these thoughts raced through her mind in mere seconds, leaving Lydia with no idea what she wanted to say. So, she broke eye contact and looked down at her work without having offered anything by way of explanation.

David must have read some of her thoughts because his next words were, "Elizabeth told me about you and Zach—that you're not together anymore."

"That's right," she whispered. If only she had clarified their engagement status when he had asked her about it the previous week. The internal tension had built up too high, and it needed an outlet. Lydia found the words tumbling out against her better judgment. "He's angry with me because he had plans for the press, and now that we've broken up, he doesn't have a hope of acquiring it. But today, when I went to work," she paused to swallow around the lump in her throat, "he was there, rifling through my office. He stole several of my files." She looked up, trying to appear matter-of-fact about the whole thing. "So that's why I'm here. John is away on his honeymoon, and I didn't want to be alone over there. I have no idea how he got in, but . . ." she trailed off.

David's eyes flashed with anger. "What are you going to do, Lydia? You can't just let him steal from you!" His voice grew louder with each word.

"Shh!" Lydia leaned in, urging him to be quiet, although she didn't know quite why. "I don't know what I'm going to do. I don't know what he's planning! I'm afraid, but I'm not sure what I'm afraid of." Sinking back into her chair, her shoulders drooped as she admitted, "Honestly, the worst of it is the humiliation. A week ago, I thought I might marry a man, and today he breaks into my office and steals from me. Is my judgment so impaired that I . . .?" Her voice cracked, and she put her face in her hands, doubly embarrassed to be sharing this with David. It seemed so vulnerable and inappropriate, but he had a way of listening that just made her *talk*. *He'll be a great pastor with that skill,* she thought with a mixture of admiration and embarrassment.

"What happened, Lydia?" David asked, a new firmness in his voice.

She cautiously met his eyes. "I told you. That's all . . . he was taking my files, I told him to stop, he told me there was nothing I could do about it . . . that's it."

"He didn't hurt you or anything?"

"No, he didn't hurt me." She didn't add that for a moment she had been afraid he might.

David relaxed slightly, his jaw clenching less intensely. "Will you report him to the police?"

Lydia looked at him incredulously. "I couldn't do that! There's no municipal police force in town, as you know, and if I report this to the county . . ." She shook her head without continuing. "It just isn't done. I could talk to the town council about it, or I could go over to his parents' house and talk to his father." As she said it, she recognized the reasonableness of such a plan, but the thought of executing it filled her with such dread that she knew instinctively it wouldn't happen.

"I could go back, look through everything, and try to figure out what's missing," she said instead. "That might help me figure out what he's up to."

"Do you want company? You said you came here so you wouldn't be alone over there."

Lydia relaxed at the offer. "Company would be wonderful. I'm not sure I'm quite ready to face it all, though." She closed her eyes, remembering the ransacked state her office was in.

"There's no rush," David said, but she could see the tension in his body language. He was exerting energy to remain calm for her benefit. "If you want me to join you, I'm free the rest of today. My class ended an hour ago."

"I don't want to take you away from your studying, though," Lydia mildly protested.

He smiled, "No matter how edifying a systematic theology text is, one can only slog through it for so long before needing a change of scenery."

Lydia stared at the two-inch thick book open before him and saw immediately that he must be correct. "If you put it that way, I suppose I'm the one doing *you* the favor," she teased.

"I mean, that's how I see it," he responded, and she found herself lost in the way his eyes twinkled when he spoke.

He moved as if to stand, but she shook her head. "Can we just sit for a bit? My heart is still racing."

For the first time she surveyed David's spread of books, noting the familiar embossing on the cover of several volumes. Silently, she fingered the miniscule KP on the back cover of a Greek Bible that was face-down near her elbow. David watched her.

"I think the majority of my theology books were printed on your press," he said.

Lydia exhaled slowly. "We ship them out by the pallet, but I don't often see them in use. It's kind of surreal."

"Imagine how I felt coming here for the first time! I never pictured the famed Klein Press as . . ."

"Being run by one young girl?" Lydia finished the sentence for him, but David looked at her with amusement and shook his head.

"I was going to say, as such an intimate operation. For a small facility in a small town, your press has unbelievable reach and impact. It's amazing. Like the fish and the loaves."

"We do ship books and Bibles all over the world," Lydia agreed. "It's a privilege to serve God's people in this way. I love what I do here. That's why it's so hard for me to understand when . . ."

"When people like Zach don't get it?" Now David was finishing her sentences for her.

"Yeah."

Maybelle had returned to the coffee shop as they were talking, and after a few moments behind the counter, she approached their table with drinks in hand. "Coffee for our resident scholar and mint tea for you, dear. I heard you say your heart was racing, so I took the liberty of deciding against caffeine on your behalf."

As Maybelle set the tea in front of her, Lydia took the chance to say sincerely, "Thank you for your visit the other day. I'm eternally grateful. I needed to hear what you shared."

Maybelle gave Lydia's hand an understanding squeeze and said, "Please do come by and visit me whenever you'd like a talk. The company does me good as well, my dear."

Lydia nodded her agreement, making a mental note to take Maybelle up on the offer on a regular basis. Before walking away, Maybelle offered David several specific compliments and comments on his sermon, and he responded graciously.

When Lydia took the last sip of her tea a while later, David looked up from his reading and asked, "Are you ready?"

"No," she replied with a grin, "but I'm sure you're itching for a break."

As they approached the press office, Lydia could feel her anxiety bubbling back up to the surface. At the library with David her calm had returned. His presence had distracted her almost completely from the distressing event, but stepping back into the building, the waves of emotion greeted her as though she'd never left. She felt violated, betrayed, anxious for the future, and the fact that it was all at the hands of a man she had trusted so recently made her nauseous.

David followed her into the office and inhaled sharply. "Oh, Lydia," he said softly but with an edge in his voice. "I'm so sorry."

"Why?" she said bitterly. "You didn't do it. I'm the idiot who almost married a thief." She slammed her bag down on her desk in angry frustration and started picking up papers from the floor with fervor. She knew David didn't deserve her attitude, and so she added the shame of her own bitterness onto the pile of uncomfortable feelings she was experiencing.

David said nothing but began picking up the folders and documents that littered the floor on his side of the desk. Lydia stormed out of her office and around the corner into the layout room. She started organizing the documents on the large table. It would be time-consuming to figure out what was missing, but she knew it must be done. Seeing what she was thinking, David started gathering up the remaining files in the office and bringing them to her. He did his best to help, but as he was unfamiliar with the documents, Lydia had to do most of it herself.

After a quarter hour of silent sorting, she remembered to thank him for his help. "You've done so much already. I think I have to do the rest, so feel free to go back to your systematic theology if you need to." She tried to offer him a smile, but the whole time they'd been there, she'd been fighting back tears.

"I can go if you'd like me to," he said quietly, "but I'm more than willing to stay. You said you didn't want to be alone here."

His mention of being alone put another thought in her head, and she looked at him nervously. "I really don't want to be alone," she admitted, "but it also may not be entirely proper for you and me to be alone here *together*." She felt her heart rate pick up as she said it and blushed.

He didn't falter. "Look, if anyone asks, you'll just tell them the truth—that you were robbed and needed someone else to be here." She looked uncertain, and he jokingly added, "We'll keep this giant table between us at all times, okay?"

The way he said it made her laugh, which did wonders for the knots in her stomach. "Okay," she said. "It's probably not quite proper, but I'll try to go quickly so we're not here too much longer."

Lydia's sense of propriety told her she should send him away, but she was equally sure her panic would return with him gone. She began explaining her organizational system, and, for a while, they spoke only of files, dates, and the task at hand. Once everything had been refiled and laid out, Lydia stepped back to take it all in, surveying the materials to see what was missing. Her hand went to her mouth, and her face turned white as realization hit, and she looked at David in horror. "It's the past three years of my family's personal tax returns," she said shakily, "as well as our customer lists, account summaries, and balance sheets."

David stared at her wide-eyed and then looked toward the front door as if he was about to storm through it with a vengeance.

Lydia's voice was a whisper as she said shakily, "He told me he would acquire the press. He said I had no place in this town without him."

David took a few steps toward her. For a moment, she thought that he looked as if he wanted to comfort her, but then his eyes shifted to the table that he had promised to keep between them, and instead of approaching her, he stormed silently out into the evening.

Robotically, Lydia began moving the files back into her office, returning them to their rightful locations. Through the window, she saw David pacing in the street, waiting for her. It took her a while to put everything right, but finally she turned out the lights and locked up, following him out into the now-dark lane.

"I'll walk you home," he said, no question in his voice. She fell into step beside him as they started toward the river. As if by unspoken agreement, they both walked slowly, prolonging the all-too-short walk to Lydia's house. For a few moments they walked in silence. David opened his mouth to speak a few times but, each time, refrained. Lydia was grateful for his company but was too stunned and confused by the day's events to make conversation.

Finally, as they were crossing the bridge, David asked, "What are you going to do?"

"Do you have any ideas?" Lydia asked woefully. "I think I must report it somehow, but I just don't know who to turn to. His father is on the council, and, well . . . " she trailed off.

"You don't know how he'll respond, and so that scares you, too," David finished her thought.

She nodded. "It's the only thing to do, though. I have to talk to Mr. Barrett. I could go to Pastor Pedersen perhaps, but I think Matthew Eighteen . . . honestly, I'm not sure how to apply Matthew Eighteen here."

"The town must have a grievance procedure," David said. "This can't be the first time someone's sinned here since the founders arrived."

Lydia smiled, nodding. "I guess I just don't know what it is. I'm not going to be able to sleep tonight."

"Let's go straight to the Barretts' home right now, that way you can get the initial confrontation behind you, and you'll know your next step."

Lydia looked alarmed, but she had to admit that knowing would make her more likely to find sleep. She wanted to say no, to admit that she was terrible at confrontation and would rather pretend none of it had happened for as long as possible, but the fact that David had witnessed the aftermath and was willing to go with her made her reluctant to appear cowardly. She nodded slowly, and they continued down Founders' Way, past her house toward the Barrett estate. She tried to put out of her mind the possibility of a confrontation with Zach. She would ask for his father and avoid eye contact. That was the full extent of her plan.

They ascended to the porch, rang the bell, and waited. David stood several paces behind Lydia, allowing her to take the lead. Lydia remembered all too well the last time she had been here, and every inch of her felt the tension that memory stirred. She was amazed that she could breathe, and it felt like an eternity before the door opened. To her horror, although not to her surprise, it was Zach.

"Zach!" she exclaimed breathlessly. He glared at her, his frame filling the doorway, arrogance and bravado exuding from his presence. He said nothing, daring her to speak with his steely gaze.

Remembering her mission, she drew herself up to her full (although unintimidating) height and said as calmly as she could, "I am here to speak with your father. Is he at home?"

Zach's eyes twinkled with scornful amusement. "He is not at home. He will be out of town until the town council meeting on the thirty-first. I'm sure he will be happy to speak with you then." He made no move to close the door, daring her to say something further. She did not take the bait. She turned, descended the steps, and started down the driveway. Behind her, she heard raised voices, and she knew that Zach and David were exchanging words. She walked as quickly as she could, not wanting to hear what they were saying. When David caught up with her at the corner of Founders' and Main Street, he looked purely livid.

"What did he say?" she asked, but David only shook his head.

"I'm not going to tell you."

"Okay then." She was both immensely curious and relieved that she wouldn't have to bear the knowledge of what had passed between them.

"Come work at the library again tomorrow," David said. "I'm guessing you won't want to be alone in the office, and if you need someone to talk to, I'll be there. If you want to strategize or figure out what to do . . ."

Lydia nodded, "That sounds like a good plan. I will work from the library again tomorrow. I might be in late. I'm going to file an official grievance. I can't remember how that's done, but I'm sure it's written down somewhere. Perhaps I should stop at the church in the morning and talk to Pastor Pedersen too."

David nodded agreement, then reached out and touched her arm. "I'm so sorry for the day you've had, Lydia. I want you to know that I'm here for you, for whatever you need." Their eyes met, and Lydia's stomach did a somersault. While it had been one of the worst days, there was no denying the connection she felt to this man. As he looked down at her, the mixture of righteous anger and protectiveness that he clearly felt on her behalf made her feel both safe and excited.

"Will you be okay alone tonight?" he asked, looking from her to the large empty house that now stood before them.

"Yes, I'm fine." She felt quite sure that the theft of documents, while serious, did not point to any physical danger from Zach. He had never been violent with her. Somehow, she knew he'd gotten what he wanted that morning. David's eyes searched hers with uncertainty, and she blushed as she considered the scenes he must be envisioning that would lead him to have asked that question. "I'm quite safe," she repeated, standing as straight as she could and smiling as if to exude confidence.

David nodded in acceptance. "Then goodnight, Miss Klein," he said softly, and walked off into the night. She turned towards home, a flurry of confusing emotions within.

# CHAPTER TWENTY-ONE

David headed for the bridge, his thoughts consumed with images of Lydia alone in her empty house after the day she had endured. Would she do housework or bake to distract herself? Would she lock all the doors and feel afraid? Would she cry? He shook his head. His reason told him that he ought to maintain at least some emotional distance. But his heart longed to protect her, to see justice done on her behalf.

He still did not understand this community. Why couldn't they just call the police? It must have something to do with keeping the extent of the press' operations off the government's radar. There was a deep-seated mistrust of secular authority here and, given the political climate of the past decades—even the past century—he had to admit it was not without warrant.

He groaned inwardly, recalling the heated exchange that had just passed between him and Zach. He hated that guy. *Hate is a sin*, he reminded himself, but it didn't take the sting out of his feelings towards Lydia's ex-fiancé. What had she ever seen in him? He commended her judgment for ending it when she had, but the relationship still mystified him completely. Lydia seemed a woman of judgment and discernment. By contrast, Zach struck him as a man with a violent temper, deep-rooted insecurities, and a generous dose of conceit.

When David had challenged him just moments ago, Zach had claimed to be the innocent party of all things! He'd used the most abusive language in description of Lydia, suggesting that she had led him on for months to think her madly in love with him, only to have her break up with him after meeting David, but not before he paid thousands of dollars to help her fix her press. David did not credit this spin on events for a second, but the fire in Zach's eyes almost convinced him that Zach believed it.

*"And as for stealing, how dare you, of all people, accuse me! I saw the way you looked at Lydia at the Thanksgiving dance. I saw you with her at the football field, skulking about together in the woods. She couldn't even look at me that day. If one of us is a thief, it's you!"*

David knew he should have stayed calm if he was to refute Zach's accusations, but in the heat of the moment he'd lost it and yelled something about Lydia not being property to be passed back and forth but a person to be treated with respect. Zach had retorted that he no longer had any use for her, but *"Mark my words, Lydia Klein will never marry an outsider like you either."* Then the door was slammed in David's face.

Something about the situation was off. David tried to control his anger and consider where Zach might be coming from, but he couldn't come up with a story that would so much as explain his behavior, let alone excuse it. He'd never been particularly drawn to Zach, but before today, he hadn't thought of him as a villain.

Clearly, Lydia lived with a deep sense of obligation as a descendant of New Augsburg founders. Zach was heir to a founding family too. Was he motivated only by selfish, mercenary ambition, or was there more to it? Was there any chance Zach felt a similar kind of responsibility to the town that Lydia did and merely disagreed with her about the steps to be taken? But David stopped himself there. It just didn't matter. At some point, actions speak for themselves, and Zach's had been deplorable.

David turned his thoughts to more pleasant material: spending the day with Lydia. She had found his presence comforting, of that he had no doubt. Might something be there between them? It was too soon to think of her that way, especially with what she was going through after breaking up with Zach, but the thoughts were hard to resist.

# CHAPTER TWENTY-TWO

By the end of the week, Lydia was exhausted from lack of sleep. Each night she would lie awake, reliving the scenes in the press office with Zach, agonizing over her own behavior and responses to his aggression.

The day following the break-in, she had sent Micah a message letting him know what had happened, and had spoken with Pastor Pedersen. She also filed a formal report, sent personally to all members of the city council, notifying them of the incident. On Friday morning, the missing files had appeared in the press mailbox with an exasperating note:

> *Per the instructions of the town council, I am returning these items to the press office with my apologies. ~ Z.B.*

Having the physical files returned to her was a formality. She already had digital copies of all of them, and at this point, surely, Zach did too. There was not a hint of repentance or remorse, and she was still just as terrified as before about what he had planned.

Each day was now spent in the library. David split his time between the Comm Lab and the café, and when he was in the café, Lydia knew they distracted each other from their work. They spoke occasionally of the events at the press, but mostly they talked of other things. They would have theological conversations inspired by David's coursework, or he would ask questions about growing up in New Augsburg. His company was more than a welcome distraction from her troubles. It was intoxicating. He had a way of looking at her when she spoke that made her feel seen and valued, and every time they were together, she learned something new.

One morning he invited her to listen in during his classes, and she found herself thoroughly fascinated by the professor's explanation of Luther's two realms theology. She jotted down at least a half-dozen questions during the lecture and interrogated David afterward.

Another week passed, and then another, and she heard nothing else from Zach. He did not appear in church, which did not surprise her. She very much doubted that Pastor Pedersen would admit him to the altar, and she liked to imagine that Zach knew this and stayed away due to a guilty conscience.

As the month wore on, she continued spending all her time at the library. As time dulled her fears of being alone at the press, on some level, she knew that David was her true motive for working from the library. She could tell he enjoyed her company, too, and Lydia occupied a good deal of her evenings going over their conversations and interactions in her mind and attempting to explain to herself why he had not yet asked her out.

The final week of January, she admitted to him that she missed Danielle's company and was fearful that now her friends were married, she would have fewer opportunities to share dinner with others. It had been weeks since she'd spent the evening with other people. David always spent his weekends studying, and she had thought it might be too forward to suggest he do otherwise. Her admission of loneliness seemed to take him by surprise.

"I just assumed that since you grew up here, you must have lots of friends and connections," he said.

"Well, most of the people I grew up with are either married and taking care of little ones in the evenings, or are off at college, or have moved away. Folks go to the community center for movie night on Fridays—have you been to one yet? I haven't gone recently because of Zach. But honestly," Lydia was surprised to hear herself confide, "I've never had more than a few friends. I don't know why."

David looked thoughtful. "Maybe we should go to the Friday night movie together this week."

Lydia's heart skipped a beat before she remembered: "What if Zach's there?"

"If Zach's there, we can either stay, and you can hold your ground, or we can leave. It's your town, too, and he was in the wrong. You shouldn't have to avoid people or places because of him."

"Well, okay then," Lydia agreed, anticipating the first fun evening she'd had all month.

"Instead of walking home and eating alone, why don't you come to our place for dinner Friday night?" David asked. "It seems like the most reasonable thing to do, and Elizabeth would like that. I think you'll enjoy getting to know the rest of the family as well, although," he added apologetically, "we can be a bit rowdy if you're used to peace and quiet."

Lydia accepted the invitation with delight. Nothing could have pleased her more, and the next two days passed slowly as her anticipation grew. All anxiety about the council meeting the following Monday was overshadowed by her thoughts of Friday. Foremost in her mind was the question, *"Is this a date?"* which ran on repeat through her thoughts.

When the day arrived, she adhered to what had become her regular routine but with an extra measure of excitement and anticipation. She wore her blue dress, which had three-quarter sleeves, an elegant boat neckline, an A-line skirt with pleats, and a black belt that accented her waist perfectly. It was a strikingly simple outfit, but it brought out her eyes. As she pulled her hair back into a loose French braid and went the extra step of selecting pearl earrings, she glanced in the mirror and smiled with satisfaction. She had never been this excited to see Zach. It was unclear if David intended this to be a date, but meeting his parents was a significant event, and she would take no chances by not putting her best foot forward. She pulled on her mother's coat. The grey fabric complemented the blue dress well as it fell an additional eight inches past the hem of the coat. Lydia selected a checked scarf to tie the look together and headed out.

First, she stopped at the press office, intending, as she had each day for the past few weeks, to gather necessary books and work items and check the mailbox before heading to the library. There was still no progress on the repairs. She was waiting to hear back from a few other organizations within their church body who had thought they might have technical support for the digital press or additional funding to repair the offset press. In the meantime, Lydia had been busying herself with proofing and translation work for books she wanted to bring back into print, although she was not sure what John would have to work on when he returned from his honeymoon.

This day, however, when she placed her key in the lock, the door swung eerily open—it had not been latched. Remembering the last time she had entered an unlocked office, Lydia's heart skipped a beat, and her breath caught in her throat. She stood motionless on the porch, the door swinging open before her. As it opened, she saw a shadow from her office door, and she knew instinctively that Zach was inside, waiting for her.

Without a second thought she turned and started walking as fast as she could away from the press toward the library. She would *not* face him alone in there again. Whatever he wanted from her, he would have to approach her in a public place with witnesses around. She heard his footsteps coming behind her, hitting the pavement in rapid succession. She was tempted to run, but he could easily catch her, and it would appear cowardly. She did not want him to realize how rattled she was, but it might be too late for that.

"Lydia!" Zach's voice sounded friendly, but she did not trust it for a second. She kept walking, knowing there was only one more block to cross before she reached her goal. She was walking along the north side of Founders' Park now, and the library was safely within view. If it were summer, the park would have been bustling, but in the cold of January, it was deserted. "Lydia!" he called out again, this time louder. She could see David coming down the street toward her on his way to the library. He was still several blocks away but knowing that she was in his line of vision gave her the courage to turn around and face Zach.

"Yes, Mr. Barrett? I trust you have an equally immoral excuse for being in my office again this morning," she said coldly, fire in her eyes as she tried to hide the anxiety in her voice.

"On the contrary, Miss Klein." He reached her and stood about four feet away. His eyes left her face and traveled down to her feet and then back up again, irritating her completely. "You're dressed up today. Who are you trying to impress?" He nodded down the street in David's direction as he spoke. David was still not close enough to hear, but Lydia could see his lips pressed together in determination as he walked quickly toward them.

Without waiting for a response, Zach took two quick steps, closing the distance between them. He now stood inches from her and spoke quickly and quietly. "I'm here today, Miss Klein, to inform you that on Monday evening, I will be presenting an offer to the town council to purchase the press from Micah. The offer is a good one, for a price that I think you will find hard to refuse. I have a contract with Nova which funds the entire proposal, including mending the presses and getting them online again. I think you will find that the advantages outweigh any scruples you may feel at the terms of the sale, but on the off-chance that you are feeling vindictively self-righteous at the meeting on Monday, I want you to know that both Nova and I have enough evidence against you to trigger an IRS audit, and we are not afraid to use it." David was close enough to hear him now, so Zach took Lydia's arm and pulled her still closer, whispering in her ear, "You are losing the press, Miss Klein. It will either be in my hands or the government's. Your choice."

David reached them at that moment, and Zach released Lydia, stepping back several feet and smiling at David as if their conversation was completely ordinary. "Good morning, Mr. Schaeffer," Zach offered with his usual charming smile, tipping his hat. "I hope your studies are fruitful and your weekend relaxing." He turned and walked away before either David or Lydia could respond. David took a step as if to pursue him and opened his mouth to respond, but Lydia put her hand on his arm and held him back.

"What happened?" he asked. Lydia sank down onto a park bench. They had been standing at the corner of the park, kitty-corner from the library entrance.

Dazed, Lydia responded, "I think he's blackmailing me. He's going to try to buy it, and if I try to stop him, he's going to . . . ruin everything."

David sat down next to her, their shoulders just touching, waiting for her to explain.

"He's planning to make a purchase offer for the press and has a contract with Nova lined up to fund all the repairs. If I make a scene or try to object at the meeting on Monday, he said that they have enough information to trigger an audit. With the new legislation, we would definitely be reclassified as a business, and even if they didn't make us take the pledge, the taxes alone would ruin us." He said nothing, staring straight ahead as he listened, but she could see his jaw tightening in anger.

"I can't believe it . . . he's blackmailing me." she said again, shaking her head as her eyes began to fill with tears. Without hesitation, David put his arm around her and pulled her close. She leaned into him and cried silently, feeling both the sadness and anger directed toward Zach as well as the comfort of David's closeness. David gently stroked her arm, doing his best to reassure her with his presence.

"He won't get away with this, Lydia. People will know the truth. They will see through him. You said that Nova's values don't align with New Augsburg's. The council will see that." She nodded, trying to believe him. "Anything you need, I'll do it. If you need me to tell them what I saw at the press office that day, or . . ." He trailed off.

Lydia knew he was racking his brain, searching for a hopeful idea or plan. She also knew they could not sit so close to each other in public for long without attracting gossip. *It's probably too late for that already,* she thought ruefully, wondering who might be watching from their windows. David seemed to read her thoughts, and without a word they both stood and went into the library.

David looked up from the paper he was writing and glanced in Lydia's direction. Ever since the events of the morning, he'd been wondering about the status of their evening plans. Now it was four o'clock, and Lydia hadn't said anything about the evening either way. It had been a quiet day. Lydia was usually eager to talk about her problems, but today she had been laser-focused on her work. They'd exchanged a sprinkling of light-hearted conversations as the hours passed, but a heaviness had settled behind Lydia's eyes, and although she made it very clear that she didn't want to be alone, he thought that she might need some emotional space. She'd been working on that page for an hour, and from the way she sighed and bit her lip, he knew it wasn't her work that occupied her thoughts.

But it was time to ask. Instinctively, he reached for her hand but stopped himself before taking it. That might be too forward. "Ahem." He cleared his throat, and she looked up. "Are we still on for dinner and a movie tonight? Or would you rather do it another time?"

Lydia straightened and smiled, but her eyes were tired. "I wouldn't want to disappoint Elizabeth. You told me yesterday how excited she was, and it wouldn't be right to back out at the last minute."

"Elizabeth would understand if you're not feeling well," he replied, trying not to read anything into the fact that Lydia's concern over the engagement was about his sister's feelings and not his own.

"I know, but I'd like to come." She began gathering her things into her bag, and he did the same. When they exited the library, side by side, and turned toward his family's farm, he thought for a moment that her hand moved towards his. He looked down at their hands, mere inches apart. The impulse to take hers in his own was magnetic.

If he closed his eyes, he could imagine the feeling of their fingers intertwined. But then he looked at her face, saw the worry that she was so obviously trying to hide from her eyes, and could not bring himself to make the move. Not today, when her mind was full of Zachary Barrett.

To distract both of them from their private ruminations, he told her about the paper he was writing for class. She leaped at the offered conversation, asking perceptive questions that demonstrated genuine interest, and they completed the walk to the Schaeffer home in pleasant companionship.

# CHAPTER TWENTY-THREE

Monday was fraught with anxiety for Lydia. She attempted to keep to her routine, but all she could think about was the meeting. That and Danielle's imminent return. Her newlywed friends were due back in town any day now. As neither John nor Danielle had ever traveled, they had decided to take an entire month for a honeymoon. Lydia felt that it had been a most inconvenient month for her best friend to be absent, but as she contemplated all the things that had happened that they would need to discuss, she marveled at the way David's presence had filled in for Danielle's absence. She had not been alone. She offered up a silent prayer of thanks, wondering at the fact that if the seminary had not been in dire financial straits, she would have had no one to turn to when Zach broke into the press.

*Surely God, you could have provided for me in a different way,* she prayed silently, *but thank you for sending him here. Whatever comes in the future, I'm so grateful for his friendship right now.*

David had invited her over for dinner again tonight, but she declined. Spending the evening with David would have been a welcome distraction, but his company had become *too* distracting lately, and the seriousness of this meeting required that she take the necessary time to mentally prepare. After her solitary meal, she rebraided her hair, touched up her light makeup, and verified that her navy dress wasn't too wrinkly from the day before heading to the community center.

Despite her intent to diligently prepare for this meeting, when it came down to it, Lydia had simply not known how to do so. There was no good news to offer the council. Her conversations with the district and with her publishers were ongoing, and while hopeful that the press would be up and running soon, she did not yet have anything concrete to present. Then, there was the blackmail. If Zach was really prepared to ruin the press, there was very little she could do about it. She would have to depend upon the shrewdness and integrity of the town council to correctly discern the situation and make the right choice. *It's in your hands, God,* she prayed again as she walked into the crowded meeting room. *Give me strength.*

The elder Mr. Barrett called the meeting to attention and proceeded with other, more mundane town business for the first half-hour or so. Lydia glanced around the room. She was sitting in the same seat that she had occupied at the meeting on November first. There was no file folder of notes this time and no Micah by her side. Zach was sitting in a chair against the wall, dressed in a smart business suit with a briefcase bulging with important-looking documents. She tried not to look at him but couldn't help herself. At one point, he caught her watching him and beamed her his most charming smile and a wink. It unnerved her more than all his menacing looks had done over the past month.

At some point, David had entered and taken a seat by the door. Now he locked eyes with Lydia and gave her an encouraging nod as if to say, *I'm here, and I know you've got this. Everything is going to be okay.*

Finally, Mr. Barrett raised the issue. "Miss Klein," he began, "it has been three months since we spoke last regarding the press. The council has been alerted that there have been several developments. If you would please, give us an update on how things are going, both operationally and also with regard to you, Micah, your ownership plans, and the press' role in the future of this town."

Lydia wondered what he really thought of her. He was always so calm and professional, but just a month ago, she had sat in his home on Christmas Day, and he had alluded strongly to her future with his son. Was he angry? Disappointed? Did he think less of her now? *Of course, he thinks less of me,* Lydia told herself. *I refused to marry his son. It's too much for me to expect his good opinion under that circumstance.*

Rising to her feet, she began, keeping her voice as steady as possible. "Since our last meeting, nothing has changed regarding the ownership of the press. It is still Micah's, he still plans to reside outside of our community following graduation, and no future plans have been determined at this point. I am praying and trusting God to reveal a path in His timing." She swallowed, taking a deep breath before going on. "Around Thanksgiving, our offset press stopped working. We attempted to purchase replacement parts and make a repair, but it was unsuccessful. The press itself is so old that new parts are not in production. As you may know, we also have a digital press which has been offline for quite some time. I have been in contact with the district and with the publishers we partner with, and we are working to find a software engineer within our faith community who can fix it. I wish I had something more definite to offer, but I am doing everything I can to get the presses up and running again as soon as possible. In the meantime, it has made the financial situation at the press less viable. We have not been able to deliver on this month's orders, so there has been no money coming in."

She glanced at Zach. He was smiling at her in a way that appeared almost encouraging. *What is his game?* she wondered, and her thoughts scattered in confusion. Redirecting her attention to the council, she concluded, "As always, the founding values of biblical and confessional purity must be upheld. Our press serves as a beacon of light in the darkness, printing works that are hard to acquire in mainstream markets. To this end, I will proceed with caution and will not contract with just any repair companies or publishers, although some opportunities have arisen in those areas that Micah and I have decided to turn down." It always felt safer to her to invoke her brother's name as the owner, even if the decision had been hers alone.

Mr. Barrett shifted in his seat as if he was about to rise, and Lydia made a split-second decision. "Also." Her voice cracked as she tried to maintain her composure. "Also, as the council members should all know, my press office was broken into and robbed this past month by Mr. Zachary Barrett. I filed a statement requesting appropriate disciplinary measures and detailing what was taken, which I believe you have all received. It goes without saying that this criminal offense has caused me both loss of time and productivity as well as significant emotional distress." Her stomach was in knots, and the room threatened to spin about her, but gripping the edge of the table, she concluded with, "I would like the council to act on this matter, if you please." She sank into her chair, fidgeting with her skirt and staring at a spot on the wall just above Mr. Barrett's head as she fought for her composure.

"Thank you for that update, Miss Klein," Mr. Barrett said. "We are sorry to hear about the difficulties that the press has experienced these past months. Hopefully, we will be able to work together to find a solution that will serve our town and the church at large well." He nodded toward his son. "Regarding your allegations of theft, the council has convened regarding that matter, and Zachary has testified as to his side of the story. He claims that he did not break into the press office at all but that you and he had been working together at the press regularly over the past month. He expressed surprise that you had found his entrance intrusive, and when he realized you no longer wished to share in the work of managing the press, he returned the files he had in his possession without delay. The council was unable to find sufficient evidence of malicious intent, and so Zachary has been pardoned in this matter. Son, was there anything else you would like to say?"

Zach rose to his feet, a look of serene innocence on his perfectly handsome face. "As I expressed to you in writing, Miss Klein, my sincerest apologies for the miscommunication and for borrowing files that you no longer intended me to have access to without permission."

Lydia felt nauseous, and her mind went blank. She could not think clearly. Should she defend herself? What was the evidence? She could not think fast enough, and the next thing she knew, the council had moved on to the next order of business.

Mr. Barrett was speaking. "Zachary has a proposition to put before us now with regard to the press. My understanding is that he has made Miss Klein aware of it prior to tonight's meeting and that we are all prepared to consider his proposal seriously."

Zach stood, making his way to the table where Lydia sat, the one that faced the council where the person presenting would stand. "Thanks, Dad. I appreciate the introduction and your clarification regarding that other matter." He spoke smoothly, buttoning his suit jacket with one hand while setting down his briefcase with the other. Watching him, Lydia thought to herself that she would not be surprised if he had come here earlier and rehearsed this.

"Town council, ladies, and gentlemen of New Augsburg, I have a humble proposition to put before you that I hope will be deemed acceptable. We live in a small town," he gestured to the room, every inch of him oozing charisma, "and we all know each other's business. I'm sure you are all aware that Miss Klein and I conducted a courtship this winter wherein we thoughtfully and prayerfully sought to discern if marriage was in our future together. Now, that courtship ended amicably a few weeks ago, at least on my end. I understand Miss Klein was upset that I continued to take an interest in the press after that point, but I bear Miss Klein no hard feelings for being less than clear during those final days of our courtship.

"However, during our time together, she and I often spoke of the future of the press, and one of our mutual desires was to see the press continue to be owned and managed successfully by a resident of this town for many years to come. Although our relationship has ended, I did not want that to cost this town or the Klein family the legacy of this fine establishment that has served the church so well. To that end, I am humbly offering to buy the Klein family estate from Micah Klein for the price listed here."

At this point, he began to pass out packets of information to the councilmen, offering one to Lydia as well. She was numb. She didn't know if she should look at it or not. Out of a desire to control her reaction until she knew what Zach would say, she turned the document face down in front of her and continued to stare straight ahead, looking nowhere in particular but putting all of her energy into remaining calm.

"Now, you may be wondering where I would get that kind of money, and it's a good question. I have brokered a contract with a relatively new publishing company, Nova Publishing, and they have agreed to contribute the down payment for the sale in exchange for a ten-year contract with prices locked in and co-ownership of twenty-five percent of the company. I've been over the numbers, and it all looks viable from a financial standpoint, but of course, the council will want time to review everything thoroughly."

Mr. McKenzie spoke next, looking straight at Lydia. "Miss Klein, has your brother reviewed this offer? Do you and he find it to be acceptable?"

Before she could respond, Zach cut in, "Actually, I spoke with Micah just earlier today." Lydia started and stared at him in shock—had he really? "He is reviewing the offer right now, but he is not against it. He and I go way back. I'm sure he'll be happy to find a way to both do his duty by the town and also live the life he seems to desire." Zach sat down beside Lydia, touching her arm gently, and said to her as an aside, "I hope you will stay and manage everything for me, Lydia. No one knows the business as well as you."

She felt that this was all a performance for the gathered town members but did not know what to do. Should she stand up and tell them everything? Should she shout and cry? Should she inform them all that he was being fake and insincere? Part of her knew that, on some level, such a reaction would be justified. These people deserved to know the truth. But she was too scared. She had no idea what he would say if she started talking. She had no idea what he would do. She was conscious of the fact that she appeared rattled and emotional tonight while he was coming across the picture of poise and professionalism. She could not risk seeming hysterical. Moving aside slightly so that he was no longer touching her arm, she slowly rose to her feet.

"Zach . . . Mr. Barret spoke with me months ago about the possibility of a contract with Nova Publishing. I must confess I was against it at the time, and I am still opposed to it now. I hope that the council will look into Nova's work and their statement of belief before approving this plan. Contracting with Nova would be a serious and complete departure from the standards under which this press and this town have operated since their inception. Without the Nova contract, Mr. Barrett cannot afford to purchase the press. And the contract, in my opinion, is a non-starter. Therefore, I believe on closer consideration, the council will not be likely to approve of this plan." She moved to sit down but then thought of something else and remained standing. "Also, I believe closer inspection of these terms of sale and Nova's share of the company will reveal that Za . . . Mr. Barrett will need to license the press as a business. Doing so may mean we can no longer print works freely without the red mark. It would also expose us to greater taxation liability."

Lydia sat down shakily and found herself looking toward where David sat. He gave her a subtle nod of approval, and she exhaled. Hopefully, she had done her duty, and the council would sort this whole thing out.

Mr. Barrett addressed his son, "Zachary, do you have a response to Miss Klein's concerns?"

"Yes, sir," Zach said confidently, leaning forward and rubbing his hands together as he spoke. "I want to assure the council that I take the confessional commitments of our faith incredibly seriously. I have already spoken at length with several representatives at Nova, and they have agreed that we will only print works that comply with our own statement of faith. Regarding the business license, I do not fear the government as Miss Klein does. Even if we do have to put the red mark on our books (which may not be the case), that will not change the timeless truth that the books themselves contain. We cannot live under a rock, afraid of everything that moves. We are a part of this world, and I believe we can participate in both the right and left-hand kingdoms here."

Lydia saw David roll his eyes, but the councilmen and townspeople seemed to be nodding in thought—maybe even agreement—with Zach. She leaned back in her seat, dejected. There was nothing else she could say.

In the end, the council agreed to read over the contract and purchase agreement as well as reach out to Micah. "Obviously, this decision lies with Micah," Mr. McKenzie explained. "The council must approve the sale, but Micah is under no legal obligation to accept it."

"Actually," the elder Mr. Barret spoke up, "I called Micah before this meeting to see where he stood. He said that he will respect the decision of the council. If the council deems this a good move for the town, Mr. Klein is prepared to sell to Zachary."

Lydia felt her breath leave her as if she'd been punched in the gut. Betrayal. *Was it true? Would Micah really say that without talking to her about it, even once?* As if it was happening somewhere far in the distance, she heard the council adjourn the meeting and felt those around her getting up to leave. Numb, she stood and made her way toward the door, her only object to get out of the room without having to speak to anyone. Thankfully, Zach did not try to interact with her. A sweet, older gentleman stopped her, telling her that he wished her the best and hoped she'd continue working for the press once Zach owned it. She nodded ambiguously and continued to make her way to the door. An overly friendly woman playfully nudged her, asking why she hadn't married that charming young man. Mr. McKenzie looked as if he was going to try to reach her, but she finally attained the door and hurried out into the night, avoiding eye contact with anyone else.

David was waiting for her right outside, and without speaking a word, he fell into step beside her, matching her rapid pace as they put distance between themselves and the community center.

# CHAPTER TWENTY-FOUR

Lydia lay awake in bed the next morning, making no motion to get up and start her day. She stared at the ceiling, the unpleasant memories from the council meeting competing with her memories of David for prominence in her thoughts.

David had walked her home, offering silent companionship as she inwardly raged and fumed. When they reached her front porch, she had sunk down onto the step, the concrete freezing cold beneath her, leaned her head against the railing, and shed silent tears. David had sat down beside her and taken her hand in his. He had continued to say nothing, but when Lydia's tears had been almost spent, and she ventured a glance at his face, she had seen that he was not as serene as she'd assumed. There was anger behind his eyes—and what she felt sure was indignation on her behalf. For a long moment, they had stared into each other's eyes, searching each other, both trying to understand what Lydia needed next. Finally, Lydia sighed and admitted, "I really do need to talk about this, but I don't think I can do it right now. Will you . . . ?" She hadn't known how to finish, but David had squeezed her hand comfortingly and promised to return in the morning and take her out for breakfast.

Breakfast . . . what time was it? Turning towards the clock, she groaned at the lateness of the hour and pulled herself upright. Her room was cool, and she reached for her robe. Tugging the soft, warm fabric around her shoulders, she was transported back to that moment last night on her front porch with David. Before parting, they had embraced, and while the hug had been one of friendship, Lydia had known in that moment that she wanted to hug him every day for the rest of her life. Now, as she closed her eyes, she could almost feel his arms around her, could remember how it felt to rest her head on his shoulder. *He's the perfect height for me,* she thought. It was the only moment in the past twenty-four hours when she had felt *safe.*

As she moved about the room, getting dressed and ready for the day, she contemplated what she should do next. *I need to call Micah.* That much she was sure of. She could not believe he had sold her out . . . *literally.* It was inconceivable that he would have agreed to sell the press to Zach without so much as a conversation. There must be some mistake. But if there wasn't . . . it was too horrible to contemplate. *I'll have breakfast with David first, then worry about Micah.* Intuitively, she reached for one of her favorite outfits. A soft blue sweater top with a charcoal grey full skirt that swished happily as she walked. The skirt's high waist was particularly flattering, and she reached for her mother's pearl necklace to finish the look. *No,* she thought, putting the necklace back, *that's too much. There's no special occasion, and I don't want to look as if I'm* . . . She didn't know how to finish her own mental sentence. As she braided her hair and coiled it into a low bun, her thoughts were of David, and a hope was starting to grow in her mind that she hardly dared articulate, even to herself.

She did not have to wait long. David appeared at her door just minutes after she came down the stairs, and they walked into town toward the café. As they walked, Lydia talked. It was always so easy with him; she could *say anything.* She vented about the meeting. She admitted how angry she was with Micah. She acknowledged how foolish she felt for ever having entertained the idea of marrying Zach.

At the café, David requested the booth in the far corner, where they would be hidden from the view of most of the dining room. When their plates of pancakes, bacon, and strawberries arrived, David took advantage of a lull in Lydia's rantings to ask his own question. "Have you ever thought of moving out of New Augsburg?"

Lydia looked at him quizzically, reaching for her coffee mug as she formulated her reply. "I suppose I've imagined it, especially during high school. I've never seriously considered it, though, especially since Micah began to express an interest in leaving."

David watched her intently. "I'm truly sorry about what Zach is doing, Lydia. I'm sorry about your press. If it all goes through, though—if Zach gets his way—would there be any reason for you to stay here?"

Her fork stopped midair. "Honestly, I don't think I've thought that far ahead." Looking into his eyes, she thought for a second that she knew what he was really thinking. She felt the color rise to her cheeks and turned her face down toward her food as she spoke. "This press is all I have left of my parents. I feel like if I lose it, I'm losing them. This is their legacy—their parents' legacy. I can't be the generation that fails them. I don't know how to live in that story."

"Hmm," David also studied his plate as if in thought. "I suppose," he said after a long pause, "that we're both trying to wrestle with what our parents left us, but in different ways." Lydia waited, knowing he would go on. "My mother . . ." David cleared his throat and gazed across the restaurant for a moment before meeting her eyes and continuing his story.

Lydia tried to focus on what he was telling her rather than getting lost in the deep softness of those brown eyes with flecks of orange and gold in the center.

"My mother was not a Christian. She came from a very wealthy family. They owned a large tech company before the Trans-Pacific Wars put them out of business. Her parents were incredibly shrewd with their money management and somehow managed to protect their capital when the company collapsed. Their wealth was made investing in things that make me sick to contemplate. The politicians they supported, the faithful believers they ran out of business and persecuted . . . My father wasn't Christian either. It wasn't until he met his second wife that he became a Christian and was baptized. Anyway . . ." David took a deep breath, "I think often about the fact that if my mother hadn't died, I might not have been raised knowing Christ. But it also torments me, you know?"

Lydia nodded, a lump in her throat. She didn't know what to say, but she could imagine that kind of inner conflict.

"Anyway, I'm determined to invest that money in building the Kingdom. My wealth was accrued at the expense of innocent lives, but I want it to be redeemed somehow. I want it all to mean something, to be transformed into something good."

"Do you know how you're going to do that?" Lydia asked.

"I don't know. I want to do pastoral ministry somewhere where there's a need for a faithful church but not enough Christians to support a pastor. I've often thought that this money gives me a chance to take the Word of God to a place where the faith is rare. Perhaps one of the coasts," he shrugged. "The seminary will place me, but they already know about me and my . . ." he smiled, trying to find the words, ". . . lack of need for a full-time salary."

Lydia frowned in thought, trying to connect all that she had just learned about David with her life story and what she'd shared about her family legacy. "So, what you're saying is, a legacy is a hard thing to live with, whether it's one you can't live up to or one you can't live down . . ."

David nodded. "Well put."

It was one of those days in mid-winter when there was an unexpected and short-lived thaw. The temperature was thirty degrees higher than it had been for months. The sun shone brightly, old mounds of snow were melting, causing the constant sound of running water. As they left the café hours later, they both instinctively unbuttoned their coats and turned their faces up towards the sun in that kind of rapture that is unique to the inhabitants of the northern Midwest after months of sub-freezing temperatures and overcast days. Lydia couldn't help but smile, despite the weight of her current troubles. She instinctively turned toward the river and beckoned David to follow her.

As they reached the water's edge, Lydia glanced toward her favorite spot. The willow's branches were bare, and through them she could see the bench where she had sat on Reformation Day, the night before that first town meeting. The river was frozen along the banks, but she could hear the rushing sound of the thaw as the frothy, icy waters bubbled through the narrow channel between the two frozen sides.

"If we walk through the cemetery, there's a path along the river we can follow. It's a beautiful day for a walk, don't you think?" Lydia looked back at David, suddenly feeling nervous in his presence. It was more excitement than nerves, she decided . . . More like *butterflies*.

David smiled. His pleasure in the warm weather and company appeared to match her own, and without a word, he followed her toward the path. They walked past the church, picking their way through the cemetery until they reached the opening of the trail leading into the trees.

Lydia practically skipped down the soft, mulched path. The day was so fine, the sun so warm, the river gurgling so perfectly. She could hear David jogging behind her to keep up, but when she turned to look at him, his eyes were bright with enjoyment as well. Suddenly, she found herself falling—she must have tripped on a branch or a root—and before she could hit the ground, a strong hand gripped her arm and pulled her up. He had caught her just in time. She was intensely aware of their proximity. He stood there—his face just inches from hers—for several seconds beyond what was necessary, and his hand lingered on her arm. She could feel the pull between them. It was something entirely different than anything she had ever felt with Zach.

David remembered himself first and stepped back, asking the expected question, "Are you okay?" She nodded, eyes fixed on his face.

Later, when she looked back at this conversation, she would never know where the uncharacteristic boldness had come from. But in that moment, without hesitation, she found herself stepping forward, closing some of the space that he had recreated between them, and asking The Question, "You said last month that if I were single, you would be interested in me. Now that I am, I'm wondering, are you?" She heard herself saying the words and was immediately terrified. *Now he will have to answer,* she thought. *What if it's not what I want to hear?*

He appeared startled for only a moment, then without a pause, he reached for her hand and took it in his. She found it easier to look at their hands joined together than to look into his eyes as she waited for his response. After what felt like an eternity, he spoke only two words, "I am." But there was no hesitation in his voice. It was low, firm, and positive.

She looked up at him but couldn't read his expression. *What happens next?* she wondered with confusion. She pulled her hand away, not because she wanted to, but because the emotions were building too fast, and she needed them to slow down. She turned away from him, and they started to walk again, side by side, but in silence.

Looking back on this moment, Lydia would always wonder what would have been different if she had waited — if she had given him the chance to be the next to speak. But she did not wait. The discomfort she felt at this new honesty and closeness between them seemed to demand a release, and her thoughts were coming far too fast and furious to be held at bay.

"David, I've been thinking. . ." All the ruminations, the possibilities, the fantasies that she had allowed to form in her mind and heart over the past weeks began to pour out.

She heard herself talking but felt disconnected from what was happening, as if she was watching the scene unfold without any control over what happened next, over how much she shared.

Five minutes later, the sound of Lydia's feet pounded in her ears as she hurried back up the path the way they had come, alone. She paused just long enough to catch her breath and moderate her pace to the fastest she could retreat without it being obvious that she was doing just that. *Of course, it's obvious,* she chastised herself. *You made a fool of yourself, and now you're running away.* But her pride would not allow her to run, so she simply walked as fast as she could while trying to appear nonchalant.

She had always considered herself a good judge of character. For as long as she could remember, she had trusted her instincts about people, sure that she could predict their thoughts, reactions, and perceptions. The conversation so abruptly ended had left her shaken. *I have no idea what he is thinking,* Lydia had to admit to herself. She had poured out her heart, admitted her hopes and dreams, had asked *so much* of him.

He had looked at her so calmly. *So indifferently?* No, she was sure he had not been indifferent. A mixture of curious and confused, perhaps. What was it he had said? *"Miss Klein, I am honored by your confidence."* Had he said *confidences* or *confidence*? Oh, what a difference a letter can make! She grimaced as she recalled that painful moment. Perhaps it made no difference. He had not been able to answer her. His face had been unreadable, but if he had felt the same way, surely, he would have said something more!

She was out of the woods, through the cemetery, and back on the road, heading over the bridge toward her house. The sun was still shining, the day still perfect, the breeze cool but not bitter, but she no longer cared. By the time she reached the house she had repented of the entire fantasy, the entire idea. She was hopelessly embarrassed. It took a solid hour of pacing and deep breathing before her heart slowed down, and she could sit and think.

*Did that really happen? Did I really all but propose marriage to David Schaeffer? And do I really have no idea what he is thinking?*

# CHAPTER TWENTY-FIVE

Lydia forgot to eat lunch. She paced in her house, went out on the porch, came back in, and wandered through the backyard, staring absent-mindedly up into the trees. She prayed vague, inarticulate prayers, like *God, help me*, and *please, let him not hate me*. Once she remembered that Danielle would be back in town, and she put on her coat to go to her, but then she took it off again, sinking into the armchair by her front door, not yet ready to tell the story and receive advice.

As she sat there, trying to discern what should happen next, she was startled by a loud, repeated knocking at the door. Her first instinct was to ignore it, but it came again, persistently. She wiped her eyes, stood, smoothed her skirts, and reached for the doorknob. When she saw David standing on her porch, her heart flooded with a dizzying mixture of relief and anxiety. She swung the door wide for him to enter and enter he did. He paced swiftly into her living room and spun to face her. One look at his face told her that the feelings of anxiety were more warranted than those of relief.

"Why would you do that, Lydia?" David's voice dripped with anger and sadness.

She stood there, still holding the door open, and this time she was the one with no words.

"What did you want me to say? How could I possibly have . . . ?" He broke off, turning away again, and Lydia slowly closed the door and took her seat in the armchair again. She could almost feel her heart breaking within her, but she wanted so badly to know what he was thinking and feeling that she dared not interrupt. It was, after all, her own unchecked words that had landed them here.

When he spoke again, his voice was calmer, more controlled. He remained turned away from her, leaning against the mantle. "You must know I've been drawn to you since we first met. You must have known that."

Lydia nodded slowly, forgetting that he could not see her with his back to her.

"You took something from me, Lydia. You took my opportunity to lead. By taking matters into your own hands, you . . . I . . . what if I say yes? What if I agree to marry you and request to be placed in New Augsburg after seminary? What if I use my mother's money to save your press? Would you really be happy with that?" He turned to face her then, his expression earnest, his eyes wet with restrained tears.

Lydia stood instinctively and walked toward him. She heard herself replying, saying that yes, she would be happy. That nothing would make her happier. She heard herself say, "I would never have entertained the idea of marrying someone I didn't love just to save my family's estate." As the words left her lips, she felt the impact of what she had just said—the admission that she loved him—and she realized, to her chagrin, that she had omitted that detail earlier in the woods.

David's expression indicated that he did not miss this either, but instead of replying in kind, his tone turned bitter, and he accused her: "Really, Lydia? You wouldn't marry just for convenience?" She could feel the heat rising to her cheeks as she anticipated what would come next. "I suppose you were also in love with Zach just six weeks ago." Yes, she was starting to understand how he must perceive her.

"I was not," she said stubbornly, lifting her chin defiantly to cover her feelings of shame.

There was a long pause before David spoke again quietly and with finality. "You proposed to me, not one month after breaking off an engagement to another man. You would not have done so if you did not feel you needed my money. If you were not desperate, you would have waited. You would have let our relationship grow naturally. You would have let me lead in it. And if I had accepted your proposal, you would have never known if I really wanted to marry you or if I just felt sorry for you." He looked directly into her eyes, which were filling with tears to match his own. For a moment, she thought he would reach for her, but instead he walked around her to the door, turning before leaving to say, "I'm sorry that I can't give you what you want, Miss Klein. I wish you well."

As the door closed behind him, Lydia sank back into the armchair. What a mess she had made of everything. He had not said anything that was untrue or undeserved, and she knew it. She hadn't the energy to cry, so dropping her head into her arms, she stayed in that chair for a long time.

Lydia must have fallen asleep because she found herself startled awake by the sound of more knocking on her door. She blinked and tried to orient herself. The room was much darker now. The sun must be setting, and the east-facing living room had become quite dim. Wondering how long she had been asleep, she stood and peeked out the front window, hoping to discover the identity of her guest before making the commitment to see them. Two women waited there, and although confused by their presence, Lydia moved readily to the door to answer it.

Danielle and Maybelle stood on her porch, both wearing concerned expressions on their faces, and each holding a basket obviously containing food items. She moved aside to let them enter while asking, "What are you two doing here?"

"We're here for you," Danielle offered, concern in her voice.

"We heard that you might need company this evening, my dear," Maybelle added.

Nodding and holding back tears, she wordlessly lead the way through the little hall to the kitchen table. The setting sun streamed through the bay window in her breakfast nook. Lydia sank into a chair, watching them as they unloaded their baskets of food, turned on the lights, and started bustling about, preparing to warm up the casserole that Danielle had brought and placing a plate of fresh cookies from Maybelle's basket on the table in front of her.

"How did you know? Why are you here?" Lydia asked again.

Maybelle and Danielle exchanged a significant look. Then Maybelle explained, "Elizabeth came and found me at the library. She said that David had asked her to have someone check in on you tonight. She didn't say anything else, but I thought it strange that he didn't check in on you himself if he was concerned, and I said so. Elizabeth said he was busy, and she wouldn't share more. But there was something about her tone . . . I decided to bring Danielle too."

"Even now, even when I've . . . he's taking care of me." Lydia muttered under her breath, staring out the window.

The two women watched her with equal parts compassion and curiosity. She wrestled for a moment with how much she would tell them, but eventually the whole story must come out.

Lydia studied Danielle, whom she had not seen since before her honeymoon. Part of her longed to ask about the trip and to hear all about Danielle's new married life. But she could feel that this moment was going to be about her no matter what, and she didn't want to shortchange her best friend by giving her only a polite inquiry into her nuptial bliss. Instead, she said simply, "Danielle, it's so good to see you," and her friend nodded in a way that acknowledged all that Lydia felt. With a deep breath, she dove in.

"The meeting last night was a disaster. Zach played the role of town savior, suggesting that his plan to buy the press is in everyone's best interest, pretending he is disinterested, generous, and the perfect businessman. I don't know if the council will see past it, and I don't know what I'm going to be able to do about it. I also found out in the meeting that Micah had already spoken with Mr. Barrett and agreed to sell the press to Zach if that's what the council deems best. I was reeling. I'm so angry at Micah. I know I should call him and hear him out, but I can't stand the thought of it. He knew that Zach was blackmailing me . . . I was . . . I am just so confused about Micah right now.

"Anyway, David was so supportive. He was such a gentleman. He walked me home, sat with me—outside, on the steps—and told me he'd come by again in the morning. We went to breakfast together. The day was so beautiful, so spring-like, and his company is so . . . Well, we've been spending a lot of time together, and I rather thought . . ." Maybelle and Danielle were sitting at the table with her now, listening without interruption. "I made a mistake. I proposed . . . It had occurred to me that he and I . . . that is, if we were to get married . . . it could solve all the problems. I know it hadn't occurred to me when we first met. I didn't know he was wealthy then, and I didn't know that Pastor Pedersen was retiring. I was also with Zach at the time." Even saying those words turned her stomach. She looked at her friends, trying to discern if she had said enough to make them understand.

"What did you propose, Lydia?" Danielle asked, placing her hand over her friend's.

"I mean, I don't think I planned it, but I think I *proposed*," Lydia said and watched both Maybelle and Danielle sit back with surprised looks on their faces. She buried her face in her hands, "I'm so embarrassed! How could I do something like that? What was I thinking?"

"Well, how did he respond?" Maybelle said in a voice that was much less stunned than she had anticipated. "I mean, didn't Ruth essentially propose to Boaz under similar circumstances? I don't know that you were so in the wrong, dear."

Lydia stared at her in surprise, "He did not respond the way Boaz did; let's just say that."

Danielle looked at Maybelle with raised eyebrows, "I don't think we'd be having this conversation if he'd said yes, Maybelle!"

Lydia attempted to smile. "No, he said very little. He was almost unphased in the moment, but he came to see me a few hours later and let me know how he really felt. He was angry and hurt. I think our friendship is ruined, and any hope we may have had of . . ."

"Do you love him, Lyd?" Danielle interrupted, characteristically cutting through to the point.

"I think I told him I loved him, yes," she replied slowly. "I really thought I did. But I think he was right. I was selfish. I didn't think about it from his perspective. I wasn't loving."

"Loving someone and behaving in a loving way are not the same things," Maybelle said. "In marriage, people sin against those they love all the time. Marriage is about forgiveness, not loving perfectly."

"I know I hurt him. I see it from his perspective now. I can't imagine what he must think of me!" She lowered her head into her arms on the table, and her friends could barely hear her utter the words. "I do love him, and I've ruined everything."

"There, there, dear," Maybelle said, standing as she spoke to check on the casserole. "David still cares for you, I'm sure. Why else would he have sent us here to be with you?" Lydia could not argue with the sense of this, but her heart still felt the ache of despair.

The conversation moved back to the topic of the town meeting and the press, both of her friends asking follow-up questions. Lydia told them about all the events of the past month: the break-in, the blackmail, the time spent with

David. It was helpful to hear their reactions and to know that she was not crazy. She had not imagined David's interest in her or the depth of their relationship. Both Maybelle and Danielle agreed on that. But Lydia had to acknowledge her own selfishness in it all, and she had to face how her actions during the course of their acquaintance must have appeared to David in the moment.

Talking about it helped. As they ate, Lydia was able to ask Danielle about her first month as a married woman, and the conversation took a more positive turn. Danielle gushed about all the sights they had seen and the experiences they had shared. "But honestly," she said, with a dreamy look in her eyes, "we could have gone to a cabin in the woods and seen nothing, and it still would have been by far the best month of my life." Maybelle smiled, a twinkle in her eye, and Lydia blushed as Danielle laughed. "It makes me love New Augsburg all the more, though. There really is nowhere else quite like this town. I wouldn't mind seeing more of the world someday, but if I never live anywhere else, I think I'll be perfectly happy."

Later, after they had left, Lydia thought back on what Danielle had said. *I wonder if I will ever feel at home here again,* she wondered. *Without the press, without Micah, without David . . . What will keep me here? What will I contribute to this place? What is the point in any of it? Where do I fit into the world?* Sighing, she reached for her Bible and her journal and headed up the stairs to bed.

# CHAPTER TWENTY-SIX

The following morning Lydia wrote a short letter to David. She went to Maybelle's apartment early and asked her to have Elizabeth deliver it after work at the library. She did not want to meet him face to face but felt that he must receive at least this one message from her.

> *Dear David,*
>
> *I want to offer my sincere apologies for yesterday. You were perfectly justified in your admonitions. I was not patient, I failed to trust you, and I failed to trust God's timing and will. I tried to take matters into my own hands, and doing so has cost both of us dearly. I do not presume to suppose that things can be as they*

*were before between us, but I do value your friendship greatly, and I want you to know that I will take all you said to heart.*

*There is only one small point when I think back on our conversation that I wish to address. You accused me of having been engaged to another man a mere month ago, but I wanted to clarify that I was never engaged to Zach. When he proposed, I was unable to give him an answer, and after laboring over the decision for what I now realize was far too long, I informed him that I could not accept his proposal. This may strike you as a mere technicality, but your opinion of me is too important to me to let you go on in a misunderstanding that reflects negatively on me, however minor.*

*I hope this message has not distressed you too much. I wish you the best in your remaining studies and in your future ministry. You will be in my prayers.*

*Lydia Klein*


After delivering the letter, Lydia went to the press and tried to work, but motivation eluded her. The sale would surely go through. She knew she should be fighting it somehow. She should be calling someone, researching funding, looking into the Nova contract, talking to council members. . . . But the past few days had left her so drained and hopeless that she couldn't focus.

She sat at her desk and picked up the phone to call her brother but set it down again. What would she even say to him? She didn't know what he would be thinking, didn't know how to prepare for whatever he would say. It was all too much. She locked up and went home.

The rest of the week passed by slowly. Lydia did not go to the press. Instead, she cleaned her house from top to bottom, filled her freezer with baked goods, finished a sewing project she hadn't thought about in a year and started planning her spring garden.

On Friday morning, when Danielle showed up to check on her friend, she found the house warm and smelling of baked apples. Lydia stood over the stove, pulling jars of homemade apple butter out of the canning pot. Her hair, half-pulled back, stuck to her face from the steam. The counter boasted an apple pie—still warm—a full cookie jar, and several rows of canned apple butter and sauce. Classic romance songs emitted from the speaker on the sideboard, and Lydia looked up as if startled to be interrupted.

Danielle, pretending to be unimpressed by this display of culinary industry, walked straight across the room to the sideboard, turned off the music, and picked up the phone beside it. Selecting Micah's face from the available icons, she held the receiver away from her ear and pressed the speaker button on the handset.

"Lydia . . ." Micah's voice from the other end sounded nervous.

"Hey, Micah, this is Danielle. Lydia is here too."

"Oh." Now he sounded confused. "What's up?" he offered weakly.

"Well, Lydia has been mad at you since she found out during the town council meeting that you were willing to sell the press to Zach. The word she used was 'betrayal,' I believe. When I came over today and discovered she still hadn't called you, and you hadn't called her, I decided that was ridiculous."

"How did you know I hadn't called?" Lydia squeaked out, still startled by her friend's interruption. Danielle gave her a knowing look, gesturing toward the laden countertops.

There was an incoherent verbalization of some kind from the other line before Danielle went on. "Lydia is over here baking like one with no hope. You two are family, and you need to talk. So, I am going to leave the room, but I'm going to be in the next room over, and you're going to have a conversation that is at least twenty minutes long, got it?"

Lydia turned off the stove, wiped her hands on her apron, and sheepishly reached for the receiver. She took Micah off speaker and held it up to her ear. "You're welcome," Danielle mouthed before grabbing three cookies and heading for the living room.

"I'm sorry about that," Lydia began.

"No, I'm sorry, Lydia. I should have called you." Micah's voice was sincere, but Lydia sensed that he was distracted.

"Do you want to talk about the press?" she asked nervously. Her stomach was doing that swirly uncomfortable thing it did when she was dreading a conversation, and she hated that it was happening with her brother.

"Lydia, I simply want what's best for the town. I thought you trusted the council and would respect their decisions. I know you told me Zach blackmailed you, but when I spoke with him, he seemed reasonable and altruistic, and I thought it might all have been a misunderstanding. Like maybe his pride was hurt that you rejected him, so he . . ." Micah sounded tired, like his heart wasn't in the conversation at all. Lydia couldn't help but wonder what was going on with him, but for some reason, she didn't ask.

"I don't know, Micah. Have you looked over the Nova deal? It's pretty bad." She sighed. "Honestly, I'm tired of trying to explain to people what the dangers are here. I thought we all lived in this town and bought into this set of values and vision."

"Lydia . . ." Micah's voice was strained and tired. It didn't sound like him. "There's so much more going on in this world than you can possibly imagine. Our little press is inconsequential in the face of . . ." His voice cracked.

Lydia felt her heart beating faster, her indignance threatening to burst into their conversation, but she tried to stay calm. "What is wrong, Micah? Is something going on with you that I don't know about? Is it Callie?"

"What? No, Callie and I are fine, Lyd. I'm learning some things here . . . things I'm not ready to talk about yet. I'm sorry, I should have talked to you about the press. You have every right to be angry. Forgive me?"

Clearly, he was consumed with his own troubles and was not going to let her in. But he had apologized, and there was nothing else to do, so she assured him that he was forgiven. After an awkward pause, she asked, "But what about the press? You're really going to sell it? Could I ask you not to?"

There was silence for an uncomfortable moment. "I think we may have to sell it, Lydia. Even if we manage this set of repairs, what about the next? I just don't know if it's viable for the long-term in this political climate."

"Well," Lydia spoke resolutely, "I can't fight this battle on my own. I don't have Zach, I don't have you, and I don't have David. Mom and Dad are gone. If the council isn't on my side, then I think I will have to give in." She heard herself saying the words and felt a small sense of relief. She knew the weight of the loss would hit eventually, but the panic, the loneliness, the struggle could be over. She could just give up.

"What do you mean, 'You don't have David'?" Micah asked, and she realized that he didn't know.

"Oh . . . I accidentally proposed marriage to David and asked him to use all his influence to get a call to our church here and spend his mother's inheritance on buying the press so that Zach couldn't get it. Then he accused me of being mercenary, calculating, and coldhearted. So, he hates me now."

Micah whistled in appreciation. "Wow, Sis," he replied in a voice that matched her sarcasm. "I can't believe he turned you down. You sound like quite the catch."

"For sure. If you find any rich, eligible men with a savior complex and no pride, send them my way."

Her brother caught the hurt in her voice, as she knew that he would, but he said simply, "Well, I'm sorry, Lydia. I know you're not calculating or coldhearted . . . Well . . . not coldhearted anyway." They shared a forced laugh.

"I'll let you go, Micah, but please call me soon and tell me what's going on with you. As soon as you're ready to share."

"Will do, Lyd. I'm sorry about everything. Let me know if there's anything you need."

She ended the call and went to the living room, where Danielle was perched innocently in a chair, eating her last cookie and pretending to read a copy of *Little Women* that she'd taken down from the mantle.

"Thank you," Lydia said, sinking onto the couch. "I don't know why I put that off so long."

"Lydia," Danielle's voice was full of compassion. "You've been through so much in the past month—or, let's just say, in the past *two years*. There is no expectation that you should be okay and fully functional on your own right now. I'm *not* sorry that I was gone this past month," her eyes twinkled at the reference to her honeymoon, "but I am sorry that I wasn't here for you. I want you to know that even though I'm a newlywed, you are welcome to drop by anytime you need me. I want to know if you're having a hard time."

"Thanks, Danielle, but I promise not to drop by unannounced."

"I guess you should at least knock," Danielle said with a wink, and they both laughed.

On Sunday, Lydia entered the church nervously. She dreaded seeing David and had considered staying home but ultimately could not do it. She had never missed a Sunday service except for illness, and the strength of the habit carried her through the church doors and into her usual pew, despite the whisperings of the flesh tempting her to make an exception. Subtly, she scanned the sanctuary over the top of her open hymnal but did not see him. She felt a confusing mixture of surprise, relief, and disappointment at his absence that was impossible for her to interpret. She did her best to focus on the liturgy and the Word, but it was difficult. There was something about being in church that made every emotion of the past week surface, and she found herself using all of her energy to keep the tears at bay.

After the closing hymn, Pastor Pedersen informed the congregation that the board of elders had been in communication with Bishop Hart and would be pursuing the calling of a candidate from the seminary that spring. "My last day with you will be Easter Sunday. God willing, you will have a new pastor by the end of the summer. Bishop Hart and the elders are working on plans to cover preaching during the vacancy, but please keep this process in your prayers as we seek God's will for the future of our congregation." Lydia could not hear this announcement without gut-wrenching guilt. Had she prayed for God's will before suggesting that David circumvent the entire call process just for her? She knew she had not.

After the service, she started to make her way toward Danielle and John, who stood near the back of the sanctuary, but Elizabeth reached her first.

"Lydia, how are you, dear?" Elizabeth smiled at her warmly, reaching out to take her arm.

Lydia pulled back with surprise. Did Elizabeth know what had happened between her and David? Would they still be friends? Unsure of what to say, she returned the smile while her mind raced in search of safe words. Luckily for her, Elizabeth was always able to carry the conversation.

"I wanted to invite you and Danielle over for tea tomorrow afternoon. I can't believe we haven't had another one of our teas since December! Well . . . I suppose it might be because Danielle was out of town, but no matter. You'll come, won't you?" Before Lydia could respond, Elizabeth added in a quieter voice, "Also, I wanted to let you know that David is gone. He left yesterday for St. Louis."

"Oh, he did?" Lydia felt lightheaded as she and Elizabeth walked toward the doors, arm in arm.

"Yes." Elizabeth leaned in and whispered, "I know what happened, Lydia. David told me. But I want you to know that I don't fault you at all, and I want us to still be friends." Lydia couldn't conceal her surprise at this, and Elizabeth went on, "I think that any sane woman would want to marry my brother, and I told him so. You should give him some time to come around. But in the meantime, come to tea tomorrow, and I promise we don't have to talk about him at all if you don't want to. No matter what happens, we're going to be friends." Elizabeth patted her arm with finality as they reached Danielle, where the invitation was repeated and accepted by both parties.

# CHAPTER TWENTY-SEVEN



A week after his sudden departure from New Augsburg, David woke to the sound of babies crying. This was becoming his new normal. He groaned and rolled over in an attempt to recover sleep but knew it was pointless. After a few hopeless minutes of trying to deny reality, he resigned himself to his fate and rose from the futon that had become his new bed. He pulled the folding chair out from the card table that was now his desk and opened up the exegetical assignment he'd been working on until midnight, six short hours ago.

His friends, Chase and Miriam, had been kind enough to lend him the third bedroom of their seminary apartment. Finding an apartment for only a few months would have been difficult, and due to the budgetary cuts, the dormitories had been closed. The only facilities on the campus still in operation or occupied were the library, the chapel once a week, and the married student housing. Their three-month-old twins took up every inch of Miriam's time and attention, and when Chase wasn't studying, he was relieving his wife so she could catch some much-needed sleep. They had been happy to give David a place to stay, but he did his best to be as unobtrusive as possible.

Even now, he waited until he could hear they were both done with the bathroom before gathering his clothes from the suitcase on the floor and making his way past the two bleary-eyed parents, each holding a newborn on the second-hand sofa in the living room.

Within an hour, he was walking across campus toward the library, convincing himself that he was serving the Kingdom in some vital way by assisting with administrative tasks and maintaining the seminary's vast book collection rather than running away from the woman he loved for reasons he could not fully rationalize.

That fateful day in New Augsburg, after confronting Lydia in her home and accusing her of being mercenary and unfeeling—things he knew he did not truly believe—he'd received a message from his favorite professor asking him if he was in the area and if he'd be able to come into the library and assist with some administrative duties, even though the seminary could not officially pay him. He'd taken it as a sign, an opportunity to walk away from a confusing situation and feel that he was doing something noble and needed. But he'd wondered every minute of every day since then if he was simply choosing the coward's way out.

By the time Elizabeth had delivered Lydia's apology note, explaining the misunderstanding of her relationship status with Zach, he had already determined to leave town. His suitcase had been packed, and his mind made up. He'd read it quickly and dropped it in the waste basket. A moment later, he pulled it out and set it on the dresser but did not look at it again. He couldn't allow himself to go there. He had fallen for Lydia so hard, so quickly. He'd put himself out there, and yet . . . He had thought she had feelings for him too. But all the time they'd spent together had been overshadowed by her fears of losing the press and her fears of Zach and what he might do. David had never been able to tell for sure if Lydia truly cared for *him* or if he just made her feel safe, less alone.

David looked up from behind the front desk where he was working, preparing the reports that the Council of Bishops would need for the upcoming meeting where they'd assign the graduating new pastors to their first congregations. Chase stood before him, a raisin bagel in his outstretched hand.

"You left without breakfast this morning," he offered as explanation.

"Thanks, man. You didn't have to . . ." David said as he took the bagel and bit into it eagerly.

"I know. Sorry about the twins. They just will not sleep

past six. And Miriam refuses to feed them at the same time, so someone is always crying . . ."

"Hey, I'm not judging," David shook his head with a smile. "I'm sure I get more sleep than the two of you."

Chase laughed good-naturedly. "Mail came for you yesterday, but I didn't check it until this morning." He placed an envelope on the counter between them, and David recognized Elizabeth's sprawling handwriting. Then, glancing around to assure himself there was no one else within earshot, Chase leaned in, "Why'd you really come back, David?"

David smiled at the show of confidentiality. No one else had entered the library yet that morning. They were completely alone. "I told you. Dr. Finch asked me if I was available . . ."

"But were you available? What happened? Last time you messaged me, you said you'd met someone, but now you're back here, and I can't see why. I've been waiting for you to crack, but since you haven't, I guess curiosity is getting the better of me."

David looked at his friend thoughtfully, weighing his need to unburden himself with the desire to keep Lydia's memory with all his confusing emotions about it private. "Lydia Klein . . ." he began shyly.

"Klein, like . . ."

"Yep, like Klein Press." David tore a piece off the bagel and fidgeted with it.

"Well? And . . ."

"I don't know. I thought I was in love with her. I thought she might like me too. But she was going through some things, and she was with someone else at first . . . and then . . . She wasn't interested in me until she found out about my money. I suppose I couldn't tell if she really liked me anymore or if she just wanted to feel safe."

Chase frowned. "You still haven't told me what happened."

David sighed, meeting his friend's eyes. "No, I guess I haven't."

Chase waited silently, eyebrows raised.

"When I make sense of it all, I'll tell you what happened."

"Do you still love her?"

"I mean, I met her in November. How can I . . ."

"Just answer the question. I knew with Miriam within a week."

"Yes, I still love her."

"Did she do something unforgivable? Or do you know for sure she doesn't love you?"

"No, not unforgivable. What she did . . . I'm not even sure it requires forgiveness, now that I think about it, but even if it does, I've already forgiven her."

"So, what's the problem?"

"I'm going to be a pastor in a couple of months. That's a serious thing. I just don't know if I can sort through it all at once."

"I don't understand. I'm going to be a pastor in two months, too, and I'm caring for newborn twins. I'm sure I'll be a bit distracted. Having other things going on doesn't disqualify you from ministry."

"I know, but it's so hard to follow God willingly wherever He leads when I've already decided where I want Him to lead. It's too confusing. How can I . . . ?" David trailed off. He didn't know where his thoughts were taking him, but he was having a hard time remembering why he'd been so mad at Lydia.

"Marriage is a godly vocation too. Perhaps God sent you to New Augsburg for a reason, just as He'll send you wherever you go on Call Day for a reason." Chase watched David closely for a moment as he continued pretending to work. "Couldn't hurt to tell the placement director where you're hoping to go. God is still the one in control."

David's head snapped up. "Tell the . . ."

"Lots of guys have family commitments or preferences that get taken into account." Chase shrugged.

"Yes, I suppose they do."

After Chase left, David turned his attention to the letter from his sister. He opened the envelope and found the letter that Lydia had sent him the morning after their fight, along with a note from his sister:

> *David,*
> *Found this on your dresser. Thought you might*
> *want it. Pardon me for snooping, but I think you*
> *should come back and fix all of this. I like Lydia.*
> *Your sister, E*

He reread the contents of Lydia's letter. Removed from the heat of the moment, he could not help but feel ashamed for the assumptions he'd made and the haste in which he'd left. Her tone was calm and distant, but she took full responsibility, and her apology seemed sincere. He groaned, folding both notes carefully and pushing them into his pocket as he paced the campus courtyard, trying to sort out his thoughts.

Elizabeth was right. He prayed a silent prayer of thanks for a sister who wasn't afraid to be a bit nosey. She pushed him, but in the right direction. In that moment, David knew if he could, he'd fix it. But one thing still bothered him. Try as he might, he could not reassure himself of Lydia's feelings for him.

Over the next two months, David worked hard, finishing classes, making phone calls, praying, and waiting. He replayed his memories of Lydia, tracing each of their exchanges with his thoughts, trying to satisfy himself with the answer to that all-important question: *Did she love him or not?*

# CHAPTER TWENTY-EIGHT

Lydia exited the church, fingering her palm branch as she walked down Second Street toward the press office. She had an hour to spare before the annual Palm Sunday brunch at the community center, and rather than go home or attempt to pass the time in small talk, she thought she'd get some work done. This Holy Week promised to be especially busy. Micah would be home on Maundy Thursday and stay until the following Monday morning. She was not sure yet if Callie would be with him, but she had plenty of housework to do to prepare for Easter. The sale of the press to Zachary Barrett was set to be finalized at the end of the month, and Micah's trip was due in part to the necessity of signing paperwork. Meanwhile, Lydia had spent the past few months trying to separate her family's intellectual property from what would be included in the transaction.

She entered the office, lifted a box from the pile of flat moving boxes balanced in the corner and grabbed the packing tape to assemble it. Setting it on her desk, she began sorting and packing the books from the wall of shelves that her grandfather had built with his own hands. It was slow going. Every inch of this office had memories attached. Not just her own memories of growing up here and watching her father work, but also the feeling that her grandparents and great-grandparents had been here, had worked at this same desk and sat in this same spot, looking up from their work to see the same view from the window.

Those memories now mixed with ones of the break-in. She avoided standing in the spot where Zach had cornered her, ripping her family's personal files from her hands, his presence threatening. She couldn't believe that one day he was threatening her and stealing from her, and then mere months later, the two of them had sat down in this very office with a representative from the town council, an attorney, and Micah on speakerphone and negotiated the terms of the sale. The sale that he would never have been able to broker without theft of personal information and property.

At least she had been able to negotiate for her house. They were to keep their residence in Micah's name, and she had also convinced Zach to let her keep the books already in print and some digital files. Nothing from the warehouse, but anything that was in the offices, she was allowed to take with her. She planned to take the books over to the house and turn the extra upstairs bedroom into a library, at least until she could get a sense of what to do next with her life. She had also been moving digital files over to a separate hard drive for safekeeping—any projects that she had been working on that were in progress, and the rare books and translations she had yet to bring to print were hers to keep.

By brunch time, Lydia had managed to pack up two boxes, labeling them carefully and taping them shut. As she locked up the office, she thought of David. She was always thinking about David. Descending the front steps, she pictured him pacing in this very street, waiting for her after they had realized which documents had been stolen. She remembered the look on his face after he had argued with Zach later that evening.

Sometimes she couldn't wrap her mind around his absence. He had seemed so invested, so protective. She had truly thought he cared about her. Sighing, she wondered for the thousandth time how much of his affection she had made up in her head.

Entering the community center, Lydia wove her way between the tables, elegantly set and decorated with daffodils, to Danielle's side.

"Still packing up at the press?" her friend greeted her.

Lydia nodded. "Please pass on my thanks to John for all his work. The warehouse and print rooms have probably never been so organized or clean."

"He's happy to do it, Lyd. He loves that press as much as you do."

"I won't be offended if he comes back and works with Zach," Lydia said, even as Zach's name brought a lump to her throat.

"Over my dead—" Danielle began to protest, but Lydia interrupted.

"No, honestly, I think it would be comforting in a way. To know he was still there, watching over things. I don't think I can, though, so I would understand if . . ."

Danielle shook her head firmly. "He's enjoying working with Mr. Strauss over on the farm. With young Eli gone, Mr. Strauss can use the help."

Lydia nodded. "But if he ever wants to go back, be sure he knows I won't be hurt by it."

"I'll keep it in mind, but come, let's be cheerful!" Danielle linked arms with Lydia, steering her towards Elizabeth, who was helping out at the beverage table. As they prepped their coffees, Danielle casually inquired, with a side-glance toward Lydia, "Will David be home for Easter?"

Elizabeth shook her head, pouring cups of orange juice. "No, he told us that he has too much studying to do to make the trip."

Lydia was surprised to feel the disappointment wash over her. To be sad to not see him after all that had passed, *did it mean she still held out hope?* "That's too bad. Do you think he will be back for a visit after graduation before he moves to his new church?"

"Oh, I should hope so!" Elizabeth nodded adamantly. "I can't imagine Mother and Papa would be okay with him not coming for at least a week or two this summer. But I suppose he won't know for sure until after Call Day."

"I can't believe it's only a few weeks away!" Danielle joined in. "I think they're planning a watch party here, in part for David, but more because everybody is on the edge of their seats to know if New Augsburg will be getting a new pastor. I wonder how many people here can even remember a time before Pastor Pedersen!"

Lydia shook her head in agreement, wondering what it would be like for a young pastor straight out of seminary to try to fill the shoes of someone like their beloved Pastor Pedersen, who had been a pillar of their unique community for so many decades. She felt the enormity of what she had casually asked David to do months ago, and the familiar feelings of guilt and shame were back in an instant.

*If he were here now,* she thought to herself, *I'd tell him that the press doesn't matter. I'd tell him that there are countless ways to live a life that honors our parents' legacies. I'd tell him that I would live anywhere in the world if I could live with him.* Startled, she corrected herself. *I probably wouldn't have the courage to tell him any of that. I'd just sit here, avoiding eye contact, hating myself, and regretting everything.*

"Lydia?" She had completely missed whatever Danielle had been saying. Putting her thoughts aside, Lydia followed her friend to find a seat and enjoy the festivities.

# CHAPTER TWENTY-NINE

Micah and Lydia sat together at the kitchen table on Good Friday, sipping their morning coffees and eating the oatmeal muffins that Lydia had just pulled from the oven. Lydia could tell from her brother's posture and general broodiness that something was on his mind. He seemed to be gearing up for a serious conversation. She sat quietly, waiting for him to begin, spreading another scoop of apple butter on her second muffin.

"You know, don't you?" he finally led in.

"That you have something big on your mind, and you don't know where to start?" Lydia prompted.

Micah smiled, "Yep, that." She waited. He finished his muffin and then leaned back in his seat, staring out the window at their backyard. There were still no visible signs of spring, despite it being April. Sometimes when the winter was long, it took a few more weeks to see the flowers and green this far north. "Okay," he began. "Here it is. Callie is running for office in November for a seat in the Ohio state legislature. I proposed to her right after Christmas, early in January." He gave his sister a sidelong glance.

"Wait, you proposed to Callie, and you didn't tell me?!" Lydia's tone was understandably high-pitched.

"I was going to, but other things started happening, and I just . . . you need to keep listening."

Lydia nodded, drinking her coffee and trying to be patient.

"Anyway, she said yes, that she wanted to marry me, but she was worried about her plan to run for office. She wondered if it might make things complicated for us. I wasn't sure what she meant, but I have to marry her, so I told her nothing else mattered and that we were meant to be together." He stated this in such a matter-of-fact way that Lydia found the disconnect amusing. She wondered how this declaration had sounded when he made it to Callie. Hopefully, more impassioned.

"Anyway," Micah went on, "when she filed the paperwork to run for office, she listed me as family, and I ended up needing a background check. I didn't realize how deep it would go . . . I thought it was just my criminal record they'd be checking. But something came up . . . about Dad."

"About Dad?" Lydia echoed. They hadn't heard anything from their father in the decade since his disappearance. It wasn't something that they talked about, but Lydia had always assumed that he was dead. Why else would he have never come back?

"He has a felony conviction," Micah said. "The year on the file was 2110."

"That's when he left," Lydia said softly.

"Yes."

"What was it for?" Lydia asked the obvious question.

"That's the strangest part about it; the file was classified. I tried to find out, but the government agencies I spoke to all told me the record was sealed and that there was nothing else they knew."

"Do you think he's alive somewhere? In prison . . . or on the run?" The possibilities started running through Lydia's mind faster than she was prepared to face them.

"I don't know. I had just found this out when I spoke with you on the phone in February, and I was hoping I could have more answers when I told you." Micah stood up and began to pace. "I'm going to find out, though. I'll get to the bottom of it. If our dad is out there somewhere, we're going to know about it. Even if he's gone, we deserve to know what happened."

"I should have asked Mom more questions before she died," Lydia said. "I can't believe that she would leave us without telling us whatever she knew. She let me believe he was dead. If she didn't say so outright, she never corrected me when I said it." She tapped her cup thoughtfully. "I should go through everything, all of her stuff, see if there are any clues."

Micah nodded agreement. "I've been sitting with this information for a little while, but I suppose it doesn't really change much. We didn't know what happened to Dad before, and we still don't. He could have done something horrible, or he could have been wrongly accused."

"Or he could have stood up for something he believed in and paid the price," Lydia added.

"Yes, or that." There was a long silence as Lydia grappled with what she'd just learned, and Micah felt no need to fill it.

Sighing, Lydia stood up and started clearing away the breakfast dishes. "You're right," she said at last. "It feels like a big discovery, but it doesn't really change anything."

When Micah left later in the morning to meet with the attorney and sign the sale papers, Lydia went upstairs and opened the door to her mother's room. She hadn't entered this room since the week of the funeral when she'd selected an outfit for her mother to be buried in. Someone else must have come in and cleaned that week. The bed was made, and everything was in place, just the way Mother had left it, now coated with almost a year's worth of dust. Lydia sighed, went downstairs to find her dust cloth, and then came back up. Mother hated to have things visibly dusty.

She started along one wall and worked her way around, dusting the vanity, the dresser, the bookshelf, the end table by the bed, and the headboard itself. She finished up with the windowsills and then perched on the end of the bed, surveying the room and letting the memories wash over her.

Their father's disappearance had been the great mystery of her childhood. When he left, Mother said he was going away for a while to do something important that he needed to do for the family. When he still hadn't returned after a year or more, Micah and Lydia asked where he was, and she replied simply that she didn't know. Lydia thought she remembered asking once if he was dead. She couldn't remember her mother's response, but after that conversation, she had always known he was gone. *How could you have left us without telling us what happened to Dad?*

She had wanted to ask her. Many times during that last year they'd had together, she had thought about asking, but it had never seemed like the right time. And now she might never know. Maybe it was better not to know. Maybe she should trust that her mother would have told her if it had been something she should have heard.

She stood and moved to the closet, opening the door and staring inside at the clothes still hanging on their hangers. On the shelf above them she could see several boxes. Perhaps one of them contained answers. But suddenly, it was all too much. She closed the closet, picked up her dust cloth, and quickly left the room, shutting the door behind her. *It will all still be there later*, she told herself. *There is enough going on right now. I don't need to add to the pile.*

Micah was in their pew when Lydia arrived for church that afternoon. "It's done," he said to her as she took her seat.

Lydia nodded without taking her eyes off the cross positioned in front of the bare altar. It was draped in a single piece of black fabric. *We can do nothing,* she told herself. *Jesus does it all.* She had known that her brother signing the sale papers would be a difficult day, but she was glad it was today. *The ways of God are not the ways of man. The cross looks evil. The death of Jesus appears to us as a tragedy. But it is all part of God's plan. His plan is greater than our plans. His ways are higher than our ways. I may not know what the future holds for me, for my family, or for this town, but our destinies have been baptized into this cross. My future is tied up with Jesus. And Jesus reigns permanently over all things, even when we cannot see it.* Feeling a deep sense of peace, even amidst her grief, Lydia stood with the congregation to sing the opening hymn.

# CHAPTER THIRTY

"Are you going to the Call Day watch party tonight?" Danielle asked as they worked together in Mrs. Thomas' shop on a Tuesday afternoon.

Lydia kept her eyes fixed on the mountain of fabric at her feet and pretended to consider her response. "I don't think so," she replied at last.

"Why not? I think it will be well attended. My mom is bringing snacks."

Lydia looked at her friend, eyebrows raised.

"Oh, because of David?"

"That sounds pretty silly, doesn't it?" she admitted, working to untangle a large wad of cotton sheets that had come out of the bag tightly intertwined.

"No, I get it. But he will only be on the screen for a few

seconds, I'm sure, and you need to get out more. Plus, don't you want to catch that first glimpse of our new pastor?"

"If we get one." Lydia had to stand up to unfurl the mess of sheets. "We may not. There are more churches calling than there are candidates, remember?"

"True." Danielle waited a moment before coming out with *the* question. "Are you still in love with David, Lydia? Do you think you're ready to move on, or is there still something there?"

"I don't know what he thinks of me," Lydia said as she ran her hands over the sheet she had finally freed, searching for tears or thin spots.

"I asked what *you* thought of *him.*"

Lydia smiled, "Well, 'He may live in my memory as the most amiable man of my acquaintance, but that is all.' "

"Ahh, I see 'My dear, sweet Jane,' " Danielle laughed at her friend's *Pride and Prejudice* reference. "Are you 'perfectly content' then?"

Lydia blushed and laughed, still unwilling to look up from her work.

"So, you're hopelessly in love, and hearing his name spoken aloud during the Call Day service is far too much for the world to ask of you," Danielle summarized.

"Something like that." Lydia had always admired the way Danielle could keep a conversation light and yet still uncover all she desired to know.

"Well, should I come by after the service and tell you what happened, or would you like to find out tomorrow?"

"It will be late," Lydia said, feigning as much indifference as possible. "I'm sure I'll find out at some point." Danielle nodded, but did not look at all satisfied, and Lydia managed to steer the conversation in a different direction.

Lydia tried to go to bed early that night but could not sleep. Her thoughts were with David, wondering what his evening had been like. She could not imagine the thrill of one moment having no idea where one might go, where one might live and serve God's people, and then the next minute having a congregation's name read off . . . a church, a city, a state, and just like that, your possibilities go from infinite to one. She would have been a nervous wreck if she had been there with him—she just knew it. *Why would I picture that?* she berated herself. *There was never a possibility of me being with him.* She had never wanted to leave her town. She had imagined raising her children right here in New Augsburg. And now she lay in bed awake, aching for the possibility of being somewhere else . . . *anywhere else* . . . if she could be with him.

The next morning, Lydia stayed home. She was organizing and moving furniture around in the vacant upstairs bedroom, preparing a place for all the books to be moved out of the press office. Part of her wondered if Danielle would come by and tell her the news. She caught herself listening for the front door, even while packing up linens and household goods from the room to be moved to the basement. Mother's room would have been perfect for the library. It was bigger, already contained shelves, and had more windows. But she could not bring herself to move anything in that room. Not just yet. *Perhaps a compromise,* she thought. *I will just bring that bookshelf in here, and when I bring in the one from Micah's room as well, we will have a good start, at least, toward finding a home for the collection.*

By noon, however, her curiosity could not be tamed. She realized that she had an urgent need to go to the library for a coffee. *Maybelle or Elizabeth will be there, and either way, I'll find out what happened last night.* Very likely, she would not even need to ask.

Twenty minutes later, Lydia stood at the coffee counter as Elizabeth prepared her usual latte. Casually, she asked, "How was the call service last night?"

From the general bounciness in Elizabeth's current demeanor, Lydia thought that it must have gone well for David. Perhaps his church would be within a day's travel. "Of course, it was simply wonderful! Such a welcome surprise!" she gushed. Looking up at Lydia, she paused, the excitement on her face growing even more pronounced. "Wait, you don't know?"

"Know what?" Lydia's hands began to shake, and she placed them on the counter to steady herself. For some reason, she felt dizzy. "Is there something I should know? I wasn't there last night at the community center."

"But I thought for sure he would have . . ." Elizabeth eyed her quizzically. "Have you spoken with David recently?"

"No." She focused every ounce of spare energy on appearing calm. "Not since he left."

Now it was Elizabeth's turn to look uncomfortable. "I'm sorry, Lydia. I figured you must have been in on it. David got the call here, to New Augsburg."

The room began to spin around her as Lydia tightened her grip on the edge of the counter. "What? He's coming . . . he's going to be here?"

Elizabeth nodded, pushing Lydia's finished coffee towards her before sticking her hands in her pockets. Lydia could feel her curious gaze and attempted to gather herself. "Well, that's . . . Your parents must be so pleased."

"Yes, we are all so excited about it! To have him so close, it's a dream come true."

"A dream come true . . . of course it is." Lydia felt her stomach churn at the expression. *What does it all mean? Is this luck of the draw? Not luck, no. Is this his doing? Did he . . . No, surely not, with how things ended between us. Is this the Holy Spirit? Is He giving us a second chance? What does it mean?* Attempting to smile at Elizabeth, she managed to continue the conversation. "Did he know ahead of time? Did he say anything to your family?"

"No," Elizabeth shook her head. "He didn't. Mother spoke to him on the phone this morning, and he said he had known it was a possibility but didn't want to tell us in case it didn't happen."

"Is he excited?" She couldn't help but ask. "How did he sound?"

Elizabeth gave her a curious expression. "I didn't talk to him, so I don't know how he sounded, but I'm sure he was excited. You really haven't spoken to him at all since February?"

"No." Lydia picked up her coffee, sipping it and staring into the foam avoidantly.

"Graduation is May twenty-first, so I expect he will arrive shortly after that," Elizabeth offered. "Do you have his contact code? You should call him. I'm sure he'd love to hear from you!"

"He knows how to reach me if he wants to talk to me," Lydia snapped abruptly, then attempted to soften her tone. "I'm sorry. I'm so happy for you and your family. And thank you for the coffee." She walked quickly to a table far away from the counter, hidden behind a bookshelf, and took a seat. For a long while, she sat motionless, staring at the swirly brown heart Elizabeth had made in the top of her latte, her feelings a jumble of hope, anxiety, anger, and self-loathing that would not settle down long enough for her to identify which one might predominate.

An hour later, Lydia walked out of the library and down the street toward home. She didn't have a plan for the rest of the day, but her empty coffee cup had told her it was time to go. As she passed Danielle's apartment, she saw movement at the window, and the next thing she knew, Danielle came running out the front door, accosting Lydia and grabbing her by the arm. "You've heard the news?"

"David got it," Lydia said numbly, watching the excitement on her friend's face as if in a daze. Danielle at once steered her friend back around and into the quaint studio apartment, planting Lydia in a kitchen chair and sitting down across the table.

"How do you feel, Lydia? Did you know? Has he talked to you? Is he coming back *for you*?" Danielle's eyes were as wide as they could go, and she leaned forward eagerly in her chair, yet she spoke with more compassion than curiosity.

"I don't know, no, no, and I don't think so," Lydia replied, answering each question in succession.

Danielle took a moment to sort it out, then nodded. "Do you want to talk about it?"

"I just found out an hour ago from Elizabeth at the library. Honestly, I think I feel embarrassed. He's going to come back here, and this is exactly what I wanted him to do. I don't think he did it for me. We haven't spoken at all. It's such a strange coincidence, and I don't know what it means. Is it *God's Plan*? If it is, what does that mean? And what if he didn't ask for this, and it just happened? How will he feel about coming back here after . . . after what I said and what happened between us? What if he wants nothing to do with me, and now he's stuck being my pastor in this inescapably small town? Perhaps this is a nightmare for him."

Danielle said nothing but reached for Lydia's hand.

"Maybe I should move away before he gets back and save us both from any awkward conversations."

"Yes," Danielle said with mock solemnity. "You should move away from everything you've ever known at a moment's notice because surely there is nothing worse in life than awkward conversations."

Lydia laughed. "Well, if I'm not to run for the hills, then I suppose the other option is to wait and see."

"Oh, no!" Danielle was joking again. "That sounds immensely impractical! Wait, and see? Come on!" They both laughed. "Stay for dinner," Danielle offered. "You can help me with some sewing, and then we'll make it together before John comes home." Grateful for the distraction, Lydia agreed.

# CHAPTER THIRTY-ONE

May twentieth. The day Lydia had been dreading for almost a year had arrived. It was a perfect spring day. The daffodils and tulips were in full bloom, and while the breeze was cool, the sun was warm. Despite the weather and general cheerfulness spring stirred throughout the town, Lydia felt grey inside. Of course, Micah wasn't here. She hadn't even asked him to come, so sure was she that he would make excuses, and it would only exacerbate her sadness. *How does my brother even exist? How does he go about his days without any visible appearance of grief?* She was both envious and angry at the thought, but she knew that she'd rather feel the sadness than not feel it.

Originally, she had made plans to distract herself on this day, but yesterday, she determined to scrap them all.

Instead, she stayed in bed as long as possible. Now at nearly noon, she packed a picnic basket with dried fruit, nuts, a bottle of water, and some cheese—nothing fancy, just what she could find quickly—and reached for her wrap to head to the cemetery.

Picking her way through the narrow rows between the tombstones, she read each name she passed until she found the one. There, she sank to her knees. Taking a deep breath, she ran her finger through the letters of her mother's name.

*Elliana Marie Klein*
*July 5, 2060 – May 20, 2117*
*Job 19:25-26*

Pulling out the picnic blanket, she positioned it, still folded like a pillow, on the ground by the headstone. She laid down with her head on it and closed her eyes.

She didn't sleep, but neither did she know exactly how long she had been there. After a while, she sat up, rubbing her lower back. The discomfort had necessitated a change of position. As she looked around, she saw someone walking toward her from the church. She recognized him immediately by his walk, even before his features were distinguishable, and she panicked. Here she was, lying in the grass, wearing an old sweatshirt of her mother's and oversized sweatpants that she had stolen from Micah's room because their softness soothed her. She could feel the tangles in her hair that she'd forgotten to brush that morning, and her embarrassment was beyond words. She thought she should stand up and go to meet him, try to appear unphased, but that might highlight how disheveled she was. Before her indecision passed, he had crossed the cemetery until he stood only a few headstones away from her.

"David," she managed, sitting up as straight as she could and resisting the urge to touch her hair to ascertain how bad it might look.

He looked from her to the headstone she sat beside and said with gentleness, "I'm sorry to startle you. I didn't realize it was today."

"I thought graduation was tomorrow," Lydia said.

"Yes, it was. But the seminary isn't holding a ceremony due to the financial situation. I finished classes already, so I came back early."

"Oh. Yes, of course."

The silence between them stretched on. Lydia didn't trust herself to speak.

"Would you like me to go and leave you alone? Or may I sit with you?"

Lydia swallowed. As he stood with the sun nearly behind him, she couldn't make out his expression exactly, but he was the opposite of disheveled. He was wearing khaki pants, a dress shirt, and that grey sweater vest with the knit cables that she thought so becoming on him. His sleeves were rolled up to just below the elbow, and his hands were in his pockets. She felt completely unequal to his company and yet could not bring herself to send him away. "You can sit," she said at last. Moving quickly, before he might ruin his nice clothes in the damp grass, she unfolded the picnic blanket and laid it out before her.

"Thanks," he said with a smile and sat down beside her. He looked at the tombstone, but before he could say something kind and thoughtful about her mother, she decided to dive in.

"David, I'm so sorry about what happened this spring. I'm sorry that I chased you away with my . . ." she searched for the words, "selfishness and impulsiveness. I wish I—"

But he interrupted her before she could go on. "No, Lydia, *I'm sorry.*"

She was shocked. What could he be sorry for?

"I should not have left like that, especially without responding to your letter. I bailed on you. One day I was promising to do whatever I could do to help you, and the next, my pride was hurt, and I was gone when you. . . ." She thought he was going to say when she needed him, but he didn't.

"You were right, though," Lydia said. "I was frantic. I was thinking only of myself, and I was not trusting God or trusting you. I thought if I could come up with some perfect arrangement, some perfect system or plan, that I could take care of everything on my own." She paused, looking down in her lap as she thought about her next words. "I realize now that I was trying to do Jesus' job for Him. We don't build the Church, we don't preserve the Church, and we can't save the Church. There was a time before New Augsburg, and the Church was fine. And there will likely be a time after New Augsburg, and the Church will still be fine. It's not up to us."

She looked up, and David's eyes were staring at her intently as they had so many times before, in that way that she found both disconcerting and irresistible. He opened his mouth to speak, but Lydia jumped in again. *Why am I nervous to hear what he has to say?* she wondered to herself as she said aloud, "I hope this won't be awkward for you, being here, considering . . ."

David moved, and for a moment, Lydia thought he was going to take her hand, but then he looked past her and stood up. Pastor Pedersen was coming down the path from the parsonage toward the church. "Good afternoon, Pastor," David greeted him.

"Good afternoon!" he replied. Lydia stood as well, attempting to put a smile on her face for her pastor, but he walked right up to her and placed a hand on her shoulder. "My dear child," he said soothingly, "I'm glad to see you here. I know this day is a hard one."

"Thank you, Pastor," Lydia replied meekly.

Turning to David, Pastor Pedersen said, "You and I have a meeting right now, do we not, Son?"

"Yes," David said, "I believe we do."

"Take your time. I'll be in my office." And Pastor Pedersen continued on his way toward the church building, leaning heavily on his cane with each step.

David and Lydia watched him walk away for a moment. "I think I shall go home now," Lydia offered. "Don't let me keep you from your meeting." He looked as if he wanted to say more, but Lydia was reaching for her basket and bunching up the blanket, hastily stuffing it into the top.

"It was good to see you today, Miss Klein," he said. "I'm sorry if I interrupted a personal moment."

"No, it was good to see you, too, and you didn't interrupt." Even as she said it, she looked down at her outfit with what was obviously discomfort.

"I'll be gone this Sunday," he said as he took a few steps toward the church. "A friend is being ordained in the Twin Cities. But I'll be back later in the week." She nodded, remembering from the announcements in church on Sunday that his ordination was scheduled for the following Sunday. "I'll see you then?" It was almost a question.

"Yes," she managed, nodding again. He smiled at her before turning to leave, and she realized she had been holding her breath. *What was going on between them? Now that he was back, and clearly no longer at odds with her, what did that mean?*

Lydia lifted her basket to her arm and headed back toward the river and home, replaying their brief conversation over and over again in her mind. One question she kept returning to: *What would have happened if they had not been interrupted?* In that brief moment before Pastor Pedersen appeared, she had thought . . . but perhaps she was imagining things. She would not make the mistake she made last time. She would not go first. She would not be the one to tell him how much she cared. If he wanted to be with her, he would have to say so.

Reentering her house, she was surprised to see suitcases in the entryway. Micah appeared in the doorway to the kitchen—a welcome and unexpected surprise.

"Micah! You're here . . ."

"Hey, Lyd." In an uncharacteristic manner he crossed the distance between them and gathered her into a hug. Pulling away, he took in her appearance and the basket in her hand. "You've been to the cemetery already."

She nodded wearily. "How long are you here for?"

"Maybe a month or more," Micah watched her as if to gauge her reaction and his welcome. "I have a job offer, but it doesn't start until July or August."

"It will be wonderful to have you. But . . ." Lydia frowned at him, "you should have told me you were coming. Your room is now a library."

"What?" Micah picked up his suitcases and started up the stairs, Lydia trailing behind. He opened the door to his old room, and sure enough, the walls were lined with books, stacks of boxes, and even the grand old desk that had sat in the press office, a family heirloom that Lydia had refused to part with and had entreated John to help in moving to this location.

"I'm sorry," she said, but her voice was unrepentant. "The guest room was simply too small once I got going."

"There isn't even a bed . . ." Their eyes locked, and without words, they both looked across the hall to the doorway to their mother's room. "I don't think I can . . ." Micah shook his head.

Lydia thought for a moment that he was going to open up to her, that they were going to address the unspoken heaviness in the air that was their shared grief, but Micah shook it off as he always did and turned back to his old room turned library.

"Honestly, I'm surprised you ended up moving all this stuff, Lydia. I know Zach is owner of the press now, but I thought you would have stayed, now that the Nova deal is out of the picture, and . . ." He stopped when he saw her face. "You . . . you didn't know, did you?"

"Know what?" Lydia asked, her discomfort and surprise obvious.

"I thought for sure that you knew."

"Micah, knew what?" Lydia asked again with an edge to her voice.

"Days before the sale was to be finalized, I got a call from old Mr. Barrett, saying that there was someone else interested in investing the down payment for the press, and the Nova contract was no longer a necessity. He asked me if he could send new documents to review and if I could get them signed, notarized, and overnighted back to town. It was all such a rush that I didn't have time to talk to you about it, but I knew you'd be in favor. Honestly, I thought you'd orchestrated the whole thing after our last conversation on the subject."

Lydia felt a bit dizzy and reached out to grip the doorframe of their new library. "I didn't know any of this," she said, her thoughts a jumble. "Where did the down payment come from then?"

Micah looked at her incredulously. "You really don't know?" She shook her head. "David."

With those two syllables Lydia felt her legs threatening to give way. She sank to the floor, sitting with her back against the doorframe and her knees drawn up to her chest, trying to make sense of it all. Micah looked at her with concern and curiosity. "So, you and David . . . ?"

Lydia shook her head. "I ran into him today at the cemetery, and he didn't say anything about it. It was the first time I'd seen him since. . . ." she trailed off.

Micah's eyebrows rose, and he sat down next to her. "So, I guess the question is did he do this for you or for the town?"

Lydia shook her head; a new thought had entered her mind. "Zach!" She spoke the name with venom. "I met him to exchange keys the day the sale was finalized. He didn't say anything to me. I wouldn't work for him anyway, even if he'd asked me to."

"Am I missing something here, Lyd?" Micah looked confused.

"I've already told you!" Lydia tossed back. "He threatened me! He stole from our family. He . . ." When she thought back on their encounters, none of them rose to the level of physical violence. Was she imagining it? Was Zach really not that bad? *He intimidated me,* she reminded herself. *He broke into my office and cornered me there.* She shook her head. Zach and Micah had known each other since childhood. It wasn't worth it to try to make him understand. "I think I'll go lie down," she said finally, gingerly rising from the floor and making her way down the hall to her own room. Micah looked after her with concern, so she turned back with a forced smile. "Don't worry. I'll make you dinner tonight."

"You better," he said teasingly, and her smile turned genuine for a second before she closed her door.

She went to her bed, lay down, and stared at the ceiling. *What is going on? Does David love me? Did he do all this for me?* At the thought she was surprised to find herself overcome with fear. He had been right after all. She had had no right to ask him to do anything for her. After what he had said, the way he had resented her, if he had done it anyway . . . what would that mean for them? For their future? *No,* she told herself. *Micah said a few days before the sale was finalized. That would have meant after Call Day. He didn't reach out until he knew he was coming here.* Her heart sank. *It's not for me. It's just for New Augsburg. Now that this is his town, it's his way of stewarding his mother's inheritance in a way that serves his people. Perhaps I gave him the idea, but it's not for me.* Although not exactly comforting, this reflection helped her regain her bearings. *Nothing is really different. No Nova contract is a good thing, but it's not personal.* Overcome with the emotional toil of the day, she turned to her side and fell asleep.

# CHAPTER THIRTY-TWO

The morning of David's ordination dawned sunny but cool. The apple tree outside Lydia's bedroom window was finally in bloom. It happened to also be Pentecost, *the perfect day for an ordination,* Lydia thought to herself as she flipped through her closet. She selected the red skirt with the embroidered flowers, pushing away the memories of the last time she had worn it—the Barrett family Christmas party. Worn in December, it clearly communicated holiday cheer, but it was also the perfect shade of liturgical red, and this far north, late May was not particularly warm. Paired with a lightweight, white chiffon top, it felt close enough to seasonally correct. She had not seen David since the cemetery and was working hard to keep her thoughts of him neutral and appropriate, but her choice of skirt worked against her. It swooshed around her legs as she descended the stairs, and the movement transported her to the dance she had shared with David in December. *"If you were single right now, I would be asking you out on a date."*

She tried to shake off the memories. She had been single now for months, and it felt like he had been playing with her the whole time. *No, that's not David,* she corrected herself. *It has been a complicated season—for both of us.* But as her thoughts lingered on that night in December, she couldn't help but wonder why she had allowed herself to take all of the fall for their relationship in her own mind. He had made the first move. That much was crystal clear. Sure, she had gone a bit crazy on him, but she had also been in a very difficult position. She sighed, pulling toast from the toaster and reaching for the coffee that Micah had already made.

*If only Micah was down here,* Lydia thought to herself. *I could make him listen to the whole story and explain to me how men think.* She shook her head, laughing to herself at the idea of her brother having a long, drawn-out conversation about her emotional struggles. It didn't sound like anything that had ever happened before.

Micah materialized at the front door at the exact moment they needed to leave to avoid being late, and they walked to the church together in something close to comfortable silence. *It certainly appears to be comfortable silence for him,* Lydia thought to herself.

The organ was already playing the prelude as they entered and took their seats. The Divine Service proceeded in its usual order until after the sermon, when Pastor Pedersen, Bishop Hart, David, and two other pastors gathered at the kneeler in front for the ordination and installation rites. She felt Micah shifting beside her as the service went on and on. His leg started shaking, and she put her hand on it to steady him. He gave her a sidelong look that told her what he thought of the lengthier-than-usual Sunday morning so far.

Lydia couldn't take her eyes off David. What was happening today, what David had committed himself to. . . . As she listened to the scripture verses, prayers, and vows, it all struck her as something so grounding and beautiful. She saw that to have the opportunity to serve God's people in this way would be a blessing for him, even when it would be a challenge. It gave her comfort, witnessing this solemn occasion and picturing all the ordinations that had come in the centuries since the Holy Spirit descended on the apostles that first Pentecost. *It doesn't matter,* she thought. *I could live anywhere. I could do anything. My life could go well, or it could go poorly. Our town could survive one more generation or one hundred more, but Jesus will be back, and His Church will be here waiting for Him, just as He promised.*

"Do you confess the Unaltered Augsburg Confession to be a true exposition of Holy Scripture and a correct exhibition of the doctrine of the Evangelical Lutheran Church? And do you confess that the Apology of the Augsburg Confession . . ." As Lydia listened to the rite of ordination, she looked from David to his parents, sitting in the front row together with the rest of their children. His mom was wiping tears from her eyes, and his father was sitting up so tall. *He's proud,* she thought to herself.

"Yes, I make these Confessions my own because they are in accord with the Word of God." David's voice was clear and unwavering.

Next thing she knew, she was picturing herself seated there, beside his parents, right on the aisle, and she was flooded with an overwhelming sense of loss. It was all she wanted, to be with him, to be part of his life. The strength of the sensation was torturous, her insides feeling like they would be wrenched from her. She stared down into her lap, attempting to regain her composure. Micah put his arm around her for the briefest moment and gave her a squeeze. "I've been there," he whispered to her as the rite concluded and the congregation rose for the service of the Eucharist.

Lydia did not trust her emotions to get her through the receiving line. She hated herself for it, but she pretended she needed to use the bathroom one verse into the closing hymn and slipped out the side aisle. As she exited the ladies' room a few minutes later, people were already coming out of the sanctuary and greeting Pastor David Schaeffer on the front steps of the church building. She slipped out the side door and headed for her spot between the willow and the river.

Lydia stared into the water, trying to calm the perpetual swirl of thoughts and feelings by focusing instead on the movement of the current. She was not sure how much time had passed when she heard the sound of footsteps and turned to find *him* standing behind her on the path, no longer in his vestments, hands in his pockets. He hadn't looked nervous all day. He had seemed to have a sense of purpose, of peace, of certainty. But now, standing before her, she sensed something else. Here he was just a man, and she could tell by the way he stood that he was nervous to be with *her*.

"Hey," she said, no louder than a whisper.

"Hey." He took a few steps toward her, looking with indecision toward the seat beside her on the stone bench.

"Congratulations. It was a beautiful service."

"Thanks. They let me choose the hymns."

There was an awkward pause. Lydia scooted over a few inches on the bench, patting the spot beside her in silent invitation. David sat down, and they stared at the water together. *What is he waiting for?* she wondered. *Why is he here?*

Lydia could not bear the silence much longer and reached for her standby strategy — humor. "So, I should call you Pastor Schaeffer now, I imagine?" But while her tone was lighthearted and teasing, as it came out, she knew it wasn't a joke. That was the reality of their relationship now. He was her pastor. She was going to have to get her feelings for him under control.

There was a pause, then he said quietly, almost in a whisper, "That's not the relationship I want to have with you."

He had spoken calmly and with certainty, but she wasn't sure she had heard him right. *What is he saying?* Lydia didn't know where to look. The ground, her hands, his shiny black church shoes. But he was looking straight at her, and there was a question in his eyes. If only she knew what it was. She gestured behind them to the church building peeking out through the trees. "Did you do this?"

His eyes never left hers. "What part? My ordination? The call to New Augsburg? But you know as well as I do that to either of those, the answer is no. The Holy Spirit builds the Church."

"I know, but . . ." She understood his point, but her question was meant to be entirely practical. "I mean, I hope you didn't do this for me."

His brow furrowed. "Why?"

"Because it was wrong of me to pressure you, to try to take things into my own hands. I don't want you just to do things to make me . . . or anyone . . . happy. I care about you." Her voice broke as she admitted, "I want you to have everything you want."

He looked away into the distance across the river. The pause before he spoke felt like an eternity to Lydia, but it was only a moment before he replied. "I did it for me."

"What? Why? It's not what you wanted."

He turned again to face her, and their eyes locked. "I want you."

Her breath caught in her throat, and she felt the world fall away around her. It was just the two of them. Nothing else existed. David took her hand in his, his thumb tracing circles on the back of her hand as he spoke.

"You are New Augsburg to me. This is what I want."

"I don't have to be New Augsburg, though. I could be anything . . . or anywhere . . . you wanted me to be."

He smiled down at her, running his finger along her cheek. "Well, now I'm here. So, if you want me, you'll have to keep on being New Augsburg."

David leaned closer until their foreheads touched, and they sat there, hand in hand, still in the shared knowledge that all would now be right in the world because they would face it together. After a few moments David stood up, pulling Lydia to her feet beside him.

"There is so much more I want to say to you," he said, his voice betraying the depth of his feelings, "but my family is throwing a party at their farm, and I don't think I should be late. Will you come with me?" Lydia nodded and allowed him to lead her back up the path to the street.

David instinctively turned to take a less-traveled route, avoiding Main Street and the inevitable migration of people they would find on the most direct path from the church to his parents' home. They walked the entire distance to the Schaeffer family farm in comfortable silence, hand in hand. Lydia found herself so preoccupied with the new feeling of his hand wrapped around hers that there was room for no other thoughts. When they came in sight of the farmhouse, and she saw the tables set out on the lawn and the bustle of guests milling about under the party canopy, she instinctively withdrew her hand and glanced at David shyly.

During their exchange at the riverbank and the all-too-short walk, she had almost forgotten his new position. Now she discovered that she was not willing to arrive to a party full of townspeople inexplicably holding their new pastor's hand. No one would talk of anything else for weeks. David glanced at her with a smile of sympathy and widened the space between them. His eyes were merry as he discreetly said, "Allow me to call on you tomorrow morning, Miss Klein? And make sure your brother is home." Then she watched as he started making his way through the crowd, greeting each person with a smile, a handshake, a thank you for coming. He looked so natural in his clerical black, showing interest and care to each and every person who wanted to speak to him. She found herself overwhelmed by the strength of her feelings for him and only realized that she was standing at the gate staring quite conspicuously when Danielle came out of the crowd to take her arm and steer her toward the food tables.

The open house at the Schaeffer farm lasted well into the evening, but Lydia surprised herself by being reluctant to leave after the first few hours. After everyone had eaten but before a lull could occur, the younger Schaeffer boys dragged a large roll out of the barn, and a dance floor appeared under the tall oak trees. They retreated into the house and reappeared with string instruments, and just like that, the gathering was transformed into an impromptu dance. Lydia smiled as she saw Micah making his way toward her. He took the seat beside her and stared at the dance floor. "Too bad Callie isn't here," she said, giving him a playful nudge with her elbow.

"Yep, too bad indeed," he replied. "What's your excuse? Didn't you make up with David yet?"

Lydia focused her eyes on the dance floor, smiling with a mixture of pleasure and embarrassment. "Let's just say I need you to stay home tomorrow. I'm expecting a caller, and it will be much more appropriate with you present."

Micah replied with teasing seriousness, "Fine, I will help you and Pastor Schaeffer maintain propriety, but just this once."

"In exchange for this service, I will dance with you, but just this once."

Micah rolled his eyes but obliged his sister's teasing pull to the dance floor. As they took their places in the lines forming for the reel, Lydia asked, "Are things good with you and Callie? I can't help but notice she's not here with you, and you never officially told me how your proposal was received."

"We are engaged," Micah admitted.

"I would have expected a bit more enthusiasm with a statement like that," Lydia pressed gently.

"It's complicated. She's running this campaign now, and her campaign manager thinks I'm a liability."

"Oh . . ."

"I don't really want to talk about it. I think we will set a date for after election day. Maybe Christmas?"

"But are you two okay? Your relationship is . . . she's not embarrassed of you, is she?" Lydia's protective sister streak threatened to come out.

"No, she's great. She told me that she'd defy her campaign manager for me if I wanted, but I didn't want to put her through something like that. I figured, I'd come back here for a few months and then start my new job in the city. We'd see each other often, and we'd just be subtle about it during the campaign. Plus, I still want to do some investigating this summer. See what I can find out about Dad."

"Well, as long as it's what you want . . ."

Micah repeatedly assured Lydia that all was well and that she should have no concerns. Lydia took him at his word and dropped the subject, saying merely that she hoped Callie would come visit at some point during his summer stay in New Augsburg.

As Lydia and Micah exited the dance floor, Mr. Barrett approached them. "Miss Klein, Mr. Klein, I was hoping to catch you for a moment."

Lydia nodded coolly as Micah exchanged pleasantries. She could no longer bring herself to think well of Mr. Barrett, but she tried to control her expression.

Mr. Barrett turned to her and surprised her with a question: "Miss Klein, I was hoping I might prevail upon you to resume management of the press. Although

I recognize that the sale has been finalized, my son has expressed that he now has no interest in managing the day-to-day operations."

"I'm surprised to hear that. He was so set on the press just a few months ago," Lydia replied. How could he have the audacity to ask this of her after how little support the council had given her over Zach's stealing and blackmail?

"You see, we didn't realize how attached he was to the Nova contract." Mr. Barrett did not appear to sense her frustration. "Without it, he says he can scarcely keep the press afloat, even with the down payment received from . . ." Here delicacy kept him from finishing his sentence. "Anyway," he concluded. "You always handled everything so well, and we were hoping you could continue to operate under the current business model after the repairs are made."

"I don't know." Lydia realized with surprise that she honestly didn't know if she wanted to work at the press or not. "I will have to think it over. But I'm not sure that Zachary and I will ever work well together. And honestly, I'm not sure I feel supported by the council. I was quite surprised that there was no further action taken against your son." She turned a deep red as she spoke these last words. Where was she finding the courage to speak so boldly? Pulling back her offensive, she concluded with a meek, "I hope you understand."

Micah shifted beside her, and she sensed his discomfort. Mr. Barrett lifted his nose and peered at her over his glasses for a moment. "Of course, I understand completely. The investigation into Zachary's wrongdoing is still ongoing, and when the council determines what is best to be done, I shall be sure you are duly informed."

"It seems a little late for that, sir. He has my press."

"Probation. Most likely, Zachary will be found guilty and will need to make reparations to your family, and he will lose his seat on the council, at least for a time, as a probationary measure until he can demonstrate his trustworthiness again in the community."

"But Zachary does not yet have a seat on the council. It doesn't seem like it fits the crime." Lydia longed to be out of the conversation, but having come this far, she felt obligated to continue pushing. There was no knowing when she'd find the courage to bring the matter up again.

"I understand your feelings, ma'am, and the council will take them under advisement." Mr. Barrett looked past her as he spoke these last words and then walked swiftly away. Micah looked at her with raised eyebrows. She shrugged.

Catching sight of Elizabeth standing alone by the refreshment table, Lydia started towards her. She had not spoken to Elizabeth all day and thought the growing depth of their friendship and the hope of their future relationship required an exchange on such an occasion. But before she could reach her, Elizabeth turned and, catching sight of Zach Barrett, set down her punch glass and walk purposefully across the lawn to ask him for a dance. Lydia could not hear their conversation, but she could tell by Elizabeth's posture that some level of innocent flirtation was underway. Zach gallantly took the offered hand and led her to the dance floor, passing intentionally close to Lydia and raising his eyebrows in a knowing expression that could hardly be misinterpreted. Lydia sighed and turned away. She would have to warn Elizabeth about Zach's true character at some point. *Why had she not yet shared more openly with her friend?* She pondered the question as she watched them dance. Zach seemed to be showing off just for her. What nerve he had to show up here now, after everything!

She and David did not speak directly for the entirety of the gathering, but she often caught him looking in her direction, or perhaps he was the one catching her. She enjoyed their secret exchange of smiles, the understanding between them that was theirs alone.

Late in the afternoon, the Klein siblings made their way to the gate, where David was exchanging goodbyes with those who were leaving. He hid it well, but Lydia could detect the weariness behind his smile as he shook hands with the departing guests. *It's been an incredibly long day for him,* she mused. The thought of joining him in the small talk requirements of ministry life simultaneously thrilled her and filled her with dread.

"You must be tired," she said as he took her hand.

"I won't be too tired to stop by tomorrow morning," he replied.

Her heart skipped a beat. As they walked, Lydia couldn't help but wonder at the difference a single day could make to a person. She felt light, happy . . . carefree. It was a foreign feeling to her, and she relished it. Micah struggled to keep up with her pace as she practically flew along the road toward home.

# CHAPTER THIRTY-THREE

When David made his way up the lane to the Klein house the next morning, Lydia was sitting on the front steps, pretending to read a book. Somehow, she had known he would not make her wait, and she was not disappointed. It was scarcely eight-thirty. By any polite standard, he was scandalously early.

"Hey," she said, setting her book down.

"Hey." His eyes were warm as he smiled down at her.

"You wanted to see me?"

"Always. Would you mind walking with me for a few minutes?"

"That's probably wise. You're so early that Micah might not be dressed yet."

He smiled, and they started north up the road. "I have a question for you, Lydia, which I think you must be expecting," he began haltingly. She held her breath. "But before we get to that, I wanted to apologize to you for the way I handled everything this spring." She began to protest, but he interrupted. "No, please hear me out." And she submitted to listen.

"You were right. Your suggestion of me buying you the press . . . that was a good idea. I know my pride was hurt by the mode of delivery, but my hurt was based on misconceptions. I accused you of being unfeeling, of lying to me about your feelings, of . . ." He shook his head, unable to meet her eyes. "I didn't know that you had never been engaged to Zach. I should not have assumed. If I had stayed and talked to you, you would have helped me understand. I see that now."

Lydia had not expected this apology, but as he spoke, she felt an invisible weight she had not realized she was carrying being lifted. "I . . . I'm sorry, too, though. I was not honest with you. I know at the moment, I was overwhelmed and perhaps could have communicated more clearly, but back in December when you asked me about Zach, I let you think that we were engaged simply to spare myself embarrassment and awkwardness. That cowardice ended up hurting us both, and I should apologize for it."

"But you did apologize," he said earnestly. "Which brings me to another thing. I am sorry that I never responded to your letter. I was immediately ashamed when I read it and realized my error, and I didn't know what I wanted to say or do at that point. I should have reached out to you this spring."

"Why didn't you?"

"I've asked myself that lots of times," he admitted. "The first time I read your letter, I glanced at it in haste, and I left it in my room at my parent's house. Elizabeth found it and sent it to me, and when I reread it, I realized . . . Well, I was no longer mad at you. I could see my own actions for what they were, and I wanted to fix everything so we could be together."

"That still doesn't tell me why you didn't reach out."

"I guess I didn't know if it would work. Until Call Day, I didn't know if I'd be able to come back. And although I hoped that you loved me, I truly didn't know. I could write the story either way in my mind."

"I did think that you had abandoned me," Lydia admitted thoughtfully, "but I see now that it was only my perception. You were working on all of this the whole time, weren't you? Even though I couldn't see it, you were trying to take care of me, even from afar. And all of that when you weren't even sure if I cared for you? What would you have done if you'd returned, and I wasn't. . . . " She stared at him wide-eyed, and he laughed.

"It was a risk, but the best one I've ever taken, and I would do it again."

They had reached the end of the road, and rather than cross the river, they turned around to start back. David reached for her hand, lacing his fingers through hers as they walked. "I didn't buy the press, though." Lydia nodded, waiting for his reason for what he had done in just buying out Nova's shares and leaving Zach as the owner of the press. "Even though I did receive the call to New Augsburg . . . And don't worry—I talked to Pastor Pedersen and the placement director, explaining the situation and leaving it in their hands and God's—they both assured me that I didn't do anything inappropriate . . . But I'm still a pastor. I may someday receive a call somewhere else. I didn't feel that it would be right to buy the entire estate. But when you're my wife, I will want your input on those kinds of things, and I promise to let you influence all our decisions."

Lydia stopped walking, pulling on his hand and feigning shock, "When I'm your *what?*"

"Oh," David smiled. "I think I forgot something important." Kneeling down in the street, he pulled a small box out of his pocket and opened it. "Lydia Jean Klein," he began, "on February first, you told me that you loved me. The most foolish thing I have ever done was failing to tell you the truth then. The truth is, I love you too. I want the opportunity to love you every day for the rest of my life. So, to that end, I have a simple question: Will you marry me?"

When they entered the house fifteen minutes later, Micah greeted them at the door with a lighthearted, "Hey, aren't I supposed to be chaperoning you two?"

Lydia brushed past him and, waving her ring in his face

and saying something about coffee, disappeared into the kitchen. She smiled as she overheard the cheerful voices and slaps on the back that signified her brother congratulating her new fiancé. She felt the fullness of the coffeepot with satisfaction and pulled three mugs from the cupboard.

"Wait a second," Micah said as the men followed her into the kitchen and reached for the coffee she offered. "Have you two even dated? Didn't you skip an important step or something?"

Lydia looked at David, eyebrows raised, waiting for him to respond.

"Well. . . ." he said with mock thoughtfulness, "it's much less complicated to be engaged to the pastor than to be dating him." Lydia hid her smile behind her coffee mug, and Micah laughed.

The best day of Lydia's life to date ended right where it had begun, sitting with David on her front porch as the sun set behind them and the pink light danced through the trees. "Your parents were so welcoming today," she said, laying her head on his shoulder and nestling into his arm wrapped around her.

"Well, why wouldn't they be? You're perfect."

"Oh, come, David, don't start lying to me now. I think you said earlier today that the most foolish thing you'd ever done was not telling me the truth."

"You have a good memory," he said, lifting her left hand to admire his mother's ring on her finger. He moved his thumb over the smoothness of the center stone as he spoke. "I know my mother's legacy is not without blemish. I know that most of what she did and accomplished in life did not bring glory to God. But I still love her, even though I've never known her and can hardly remember her. She's where I came from. And I know that even though she may have failed, she did her best. She loved me and wanted me to grow up in the truth of that love."

"I'm proud to wear her ring," Lydia said softly. "None of us are perfect. None of us are even all that good. But Jesus covers all that, doesn't He? He takes our sin upon Himself."

"Not only that," David said thoughtfully, "but He actually makes us perfect—'presenting the Church to Himself without spot or wrinkle or any such thing.' " After a pause, he added sheepishly, "I suppose that's what you get when you marry a pastor. Bible verses generously littered throughout everyday conversation."

Lydia shook her head, "No, that's what every woman should get." She examined the ring thoughtfully. "You love your mother not because of what she did in her life but just because she's your mother. When I look at this ring, it will remind me that I'm loved not because of what I do but because of who He says that I am."

"I'm glad that who you are is going to be all mine," David said, pulling her close. She looked up into his eyes, reveling in the feeling of his arm around her waist. Slowly, he turned to face her, running his hand gently through her hair before pulling her in for the perfect kiss.

# ACKNOWLEDGEMENTS

Every book comes with a list of people who must be thanked. I could never have brought this story from its first draft to your hands without help and encouragement from many friends, family, and colleagues. There are too many people to name, but here is a modest beginning. Thank you. . .

To my dear friends, Sarah and Deanna, who first encouraged me with their enthusiasm for this story.

To Jennie, Elaine, and Uncle Phil, for their thoughtful suggestions and praise for my early drafts.

To fellow authors Rachel Kovaciny, Jennifer Q. Hunt, and Candice Yamnitz for their feedback on various parts of this story and expertise on all things writing and publishing.

To Britt Howard of Pro Book Edits, whose copyediting skills made this book clean and whose encouragement made me confident.

To Rebekah Young, my favorite developmental editor.

To my children, whose patience and love I often do not deserve.

To my husband, Jonathan, without whom I would never have written this book (or quite possibly any book).

Finally, and most significantly, to my Lord and Savior, Jesus Christ, whose love for His bride, the Church, is the ultimate and most foundational romance.

# NONFICTION
## By Christa Petzold

### Gathered by Christ: The Overlooked Gift of Church

"I like Jesus, but I don't know about church."

How do you respond when you hear such words? Have you, or someone you care about, ever felt this way? When someone has experienced the dark side of religion—the hypocrisy, the division, the pain—it can be hard to see the Church in any other way.

But how does Jesus see the Church?

*Gathered by Christ: The Overlooked Gift of Church* will help you see the Church through the eyes of Christ, her Creator, Redeemer, and Sustainer. Each chapter features Scripture and writings from believers throughout history to illuminate the gift of Church and explain what the Church is and what the Church does according to Jesus.

*Gathered by Christ* offers a reassuring glimpse of the Church as Jesus sees her, helping you to find comfort, forgiveness, and assurance through His gift of Church.

### Male & Female: Embracing Your Role in God's Design
*Co-authored with Rev. Jonathan Petzold*

Our culture is consumed by the question of male and female. Incorrect views on the two sexes result in confusion, hurt, and even abuse. There is no lack of books on how to view gender. What is often lacking, even in Christian books on the issue, is the perspective of Scripture. God's Word teaches us that marriage is a picture of Christ and the Church. The same God who sent His Son to save us created us male and female. Explore how men and women together bear God's image and how one's sex is an inescapable part of understanding one's identity in Christ.

AVAILABLE FROM CONCORDIA PUBLISHING HOUSE
FIND AT CPH.ORG AND ON AMAZON